YOUR RULE TO BREAK

YOUR RULE TO BREAK

RACHEL LABERGE

Please Take Me Home | Blink-182

I Only Want To Talk To You | The Maine

San Dimas High School Football Rules | The Ataris

Pull My Hair | Bright Eyes

All I Need To Hear (live) | The 1975

Secrets | State Champs

I Think There's Something You Should Know | The 1975

Hands to Myself | Selena Gomez

How Much Do You Love Me | Kelsea Ballerini

Everything Has Changed (Taylor's Version) | Taylor Swift

Packing It Up | Gracie Abrams

Girlfriend | Brighten

The One | Taking Back Sunday

Act Like That | State Champs

Bigger Person | Lauren Spencer Smith

Everything Is Alright | Motion City Soundtrack

Serotonin | girl in red

This Love | Taylor Swift

For anyone who battles their brain on a daily basis...
I see you.

Letter from the author

YOUR RULE TO BREAK is book two in The Play Caller Series and can be read as a standalone. If you want to start with Willow and Tripp's story, pick up YOUR PLAY TO CALL.

If you're someone who doesn't like to read about content warnings or triggers, this is your chance to skip. Content warnings are about to start... triggers incoming... if those aren't your vibe, MOVE ALONG. QUICK. DON'T LOOK ANY FURTHER.

SERIOUSLY.

YOUR RULE TO BREAK features topics readers may find distressing such as on-page anxiety, panic attacks, obsessive compulsive disorder struggles, heavy intrusive thoughts, tumultuous familial relationships, and gaslighting. I always aim to be as transparent and authentic as possible when it comes to including mental health content in my books—these topics all come from my own lived in experience. While they may look different for everyone, these are real ways I've encountered these topics.

YOUR RULE TO BREAK also includes explicit language and sexual content.

Take care of yourself.

xoxo- Rach

Character art by Juni Given, @junidraws_

Chapter 1
Emilie

DID I THINK MY younger sister would end up dating my ex-boyfriend? No.

Did I think she would agree to marry said ex-boyfriend? Fuck no.

I watch Eliza and Mitch walk hand in hand into the event. *My* event. Well, it's really Tripp's fundraiser, but I planned it. And I did a damn good job.

That's the thing about the two of them—they've always been good at taking things that weren't theirs.

The worst part of this whole thing? One of my biggest regrets is going to become family. I almost gag at the thought. Instead, I take a sip of champagne, the bubbles bright and promising on my tongue.

People mingle and chat before finding their seats in a comfortable kind of lull. Tonight we're raising money for a non-profit, *When We Play*; a passion project for Tripp Owens focused on supporting single-parent families and the cost of playing sports. Tripp is the star wide receiver for the Upstate Cosmos—the first expansion team to win a Super Bowl. I think, or have a very strong hunch, that this is his exit strategy from the NFL.

"Em, this place is packed!" Willow says, eyes sparkling with what this means for the non-profit. "You really outdid yourself." She smiles while taking in the ballroom, every table full, and as the most popular recording artist of the century, she knows about filling a space.

Bumping my shoulder with hers, I joke, "Don't sound so surprised. When have I ever let you down?" I look around, reveling in the success.

Willow says hiring me is one of the best things that's happened to her; but really, it's one of the best things that happened to me. It's ironic considering I had no business applying for that job—she was looking for a seasoned assistant—but I took a chance, and it paid off for both of us. Now, I'm more involved than that—she promoted me last year when she went out on her own to start her own label: True Blue Records.

When I'm not working with Willow, I'm helping Tripp get his non-profit up and running. Typically, I help plan and coordinate events while sometimes assisting with social media. Some days are longer than others, but my paychecks reflect that.

With the two, I learn something new every single day, and it's rewarding. Plus, I'm spoiled, like how Willow lets me rent her SoHo apartment.

"I can't believe they really came. " Willow takes a sip of her champagne, lips pressed tight. She looks over at Eliza and Mitch, who are sitting with couples I don't know at the table Mitch paid for.

I can't roll my eyes hard enough. The last time I saw them was enough to last me the rest of the year, and it was only last week.

"What's new with you, Emilie? Still managing Willow's appointments and things?" my mom asks from her end of the table, her voice bookended with condescension.

Appointments. A hot wave runs over my skin. My silverware clinks on the edge of my almost-full plate. No matter how many times I remind my parents I don't like salmon, they still seem to make it for every family dinner.

I'm the Artist Relations Manager for True Blue Records, which means I'm first up when it comes to managing artists and their relationship with the label. I get to support artists while making sure the label also benefits.

I fold my hands in my lap, digging my nails into my palms.

"She's some sort of manager, Mom. Not an assistant," Eliza explains but her eyes don't lift from her plate.

At this point, I'll take even the lukewarm support from my sister.

"I'm also planning the kick-off fundraiser for Tripp Owens' new non-profit. It's a black tie dinner and we've already exceeded the projected tables." I can feel the pride in my voice.

"Tripp Owens. Hell of an athlete," my dad responds, pulling out the only piece of information he deems valuable.

It would sting if I didn't expect it.

"When are you getting me tickets to see Willow?" Eliza asks, jumping to what serves her. She's talking about Willow's current tour, which is being held at small venues for a more intimate feel. It's exactly what Willow wanted for this new album, and it's been an insane success.

"I'm not asking my boss for tickets. Buy them if you want to go." I slowly turn to face my sister. Perfect Eliza, with her hair hanging in loose curls, looking like the result of every Internet tutorial we've tried that never seems to work.

She was always too pretty for her age. Flawless porcelain skin, green eyes, and rich strawberry blonde colored hair which made her look sophisticated—or at least older than she was.

"Oh, Emilie. I'm sure Willow wouldn't mind." My mom teams up with Eliza, like she always does.

"I mind," I emphasize with a hand on my chest.

"Do you have any extra tickets for the boring fundraiser?" Eliza asks, rolling her eyes.

"It's a fundraiser, meaning the whole point is to raise money. There are no free tickets," I reply.

"Don't worry, El. I just bought a table," Mitch announces, while showing the entire family the confirmation message. "Maybe Emilie can introduce *you to Willow then?" He knows this is the last thing I'd ever want to do, which is why he brings it up.*

I fall back in my chair, slouching, even though my mother will scold me any second. What did I do in a previous life to deserve this?

Every time he uses that nickname, I wonder how many times he's slipped up and said Em instead of El.

"Isn't that nice, Emilie? Mitch, you're really a keeper." My mother takes the knife and twists it—her favorite pastime.

Mitch makes sure to lock his eyes on mine before pulling up one corner of his mouth in a grin. The rage bursts from my racing heart to the top of my skin as a flush runs up my neck. I hate how well he still knows me.

"Emilie, don't sit like that." My mother's voice is sharp. I respond by sitting up straight like it's programmed into my being.

My head shakes with a touch of annoyance and the rage that is always sitting right under my skin. If I'm not careful, it could swallow me whole.

Not tonight.

I sit up straight, shoulders back, very aware of my open back dress. My dark red curls are pulled back, tamed in a low bun.

Willow covers one of my hands, which rests on the table, with hers. Her golden eyes, full of gratitude, catch mine. As I swallow back the lump in my throat, I reach for the glass of champagne, finish it, and smile at Willow. We're able to say so much without saying anything at all.

Good thing, too—because if I open my mouth now, I'm not quite sure what obscenities I'd scream across the room.

Chapter 2
Zack

It turns out I *did* invite Selena to this thing, which is unfortunate because I also invited Grace. Both women, possibly both models — I can't quite remember —stand in front of me, and I'm afraid to speak.

"You're joking, right?" Selena is the first to break the silence. "Who forgets they already had a date to something like this? Something with a dress code?" She gestures down to her dress.

Fuck me. There's no way to come back from this.

"To be fair, I'd had quite a few drinks and—"

"You forgot," Grace finishes my sentence, tilting her head and looking at me through squinted eyes. People walking into the event snicker and glare as they walk by, judging my personal life from the two seconds they overhear.

I wipe my hands on the front of my Tom Ford pants, black enough to not show the sweat marks. I try to swallow but my mouth feels like it's full of sand.

"Listen, we can choose to dwell on this idiotic thing I did, or we can make the best of it." I clap my hands together, looking back and forth from Grace to Selena.

"Fuck off, Zack," Grace says just as Selena chimes in with a "Lose my number."

Both women turn and walk away—I put my head in my hands, the clamminess still there. The embarrassment reddens my cheeks, my skin hot to the touch.

"Good thing I've never needed your advice about women because that was truly pathetic," a voice interrupts the smallest pity party ever thrown.

Tripp Owens, in all of his Chanel glory, shakes his head and rests his hands on his hips.

"I love that suit. I'm bummed you got to it before I did." I walk up and dust an imaginary piece of fuzz off his shoulder.

"Less about the suit and more about whatever that was." Tripp points to the exit. "Did you accidentally invite two different women to be your date?" His voice comes out almost like a disappointed dad, but it's much too tame to be mine. If my dad knew about this, he'd use the tone that would make me crawl inside myself—the one that was still supportive and loving but dripped with the dreaded "you're better than that."

He might be right, but lately it's been hard to convince myself of that. It sounds stupid, but I've sort of leaned all the way into the careless jock mentality after seeing a little success, and it's hard finding your way back. Especially when people look at my behavior and comment on it like it's acceptable, for someone like me.

"It was an honest mistake." I mean it. I may like to dabble from week to week, but I didn't intentionally set myself up for that disaster. "I paid for the plus one, so consider my mishap a donation."

I look around the room, surprised at the number of full tables and beautiful people. The event is a hit; not that I'd expect anything less from Tripp, or Emilie for that matter.

"Your better half around?" I ask about Willow. As much as I love Tripp, I see him at practice all the time. Willow is too busy changing the music world—whether it's a record-breaking tour, starting her own label, or being the surprise Super Bowl halftime performer.

Tripp points over to a table, a smile pulls at one corner of his mouth. "She's with Emilie." Smitten bastard. How Tripp went from never dating to falling in love with Willow blows my mind. But it feels perfectly right at the same time.

"Do you need help with anything?" I ask Tripp, even though the event seems to be just fine.

"Nope." He claps his hands and rubs them together. "Emilie took care of pretty much everything and left detailed notes for anything else. She's so good at this."

I figured he'd say that. That's the version of Emilie I've seen—meticulous and prepared. It's not that we spend time together alone, but we usually find ourselves hanging out in a group. When it comes to hang outs and events, the four of us tend to end up together.

I glance over at the table and see the two of them sipping champagne. Emilie's hair is sleek and pulled back, showing the curve of her neck. Her dress, with tiny black satin straps on her shoulders, plummets to an open back—her creamy skin on display.

My legs ache as I walk toward the table, evidence of the football season that's about to start. Training camp has been kicking my ass since it began a week ago. Typically, it's not such a jolt to the system but I was a bit more relaxed this off-season.

Did I throw the winning touchdown pass in last season's Super Bowl? Yes. Was it one of the best trick plays ever executed? Yes. Did I let it go to my head? Also yes. It's not a contract year for me and most of the Upstate Cosmos have remained intact—there's no harm in letting loose and having some fun.

I didn't know what it meant to be drafted to an expansion team—literally a new one created from a pool of current NFL players. Teams like this don't usually see success in their early seasons but we fucking set the bar. The Upstate Cosmos: one year in the league and one Super Bowl earned.

Being a long snapper has its perks, like not getting violently tackled during most of the game, but it also means I'm on the sideline for most of the moments. The ones you watch back and remember every millisecond of the play. My bones will never forget the trick play—it's ingrained in me at a cellular level. And my dick.

The amount of women I've spent time with this off-season is staggering, even for me. I don't typically have relationships but do enjoy a month-long situationship. Now, take month and swap it for three days and you'll have my off-season in a nutshell.

As I walk toward the table, Emilie stands and my breath catches in my throat. My eyes dance from the nape of her neck, all the way down her spine, to her lower back.

Fuck. She's gorgeous. Nothing new.

She sees me and her face lights up, like the twinkly lights she loves to see on a rooftop bar.

"Zack!" Her voice is packed with what feels like enthusiasm. "Why are you walking like that?" She stops and looks me up and down, her brows furrowed. I pull her in for a hug, lightly pressing my lips on her cheek.

"There's no way you're this sore from training camp?!" She grabs my elbow and looks back, her hazel eyes greener than normal tonight as they catch mine. Emilie always has a knack for answering her own questions.

"You did good," I praise, looking around the room at the packed event. Pink creeps into her cheeks, scrunched with a smile.

"You think?" She rubs her hands on the front of her dress, looking around the room.

I lightly shake her elbows bringing her attention back to me. "I know." She smirks at me, and her look could bring light to the grayest day.

She looks for the date she'll never find. "Who did you bring?"

"Well, about that..."

Chapter 3
Emilie

I CAN'T HELP BUT laugh at the bit of chocolate frosting on the corner of Zack's lip. He's going on and on about his latest restaurant adventures. The man thrives on finding new places to eat and telling me about each mouth-watering detail. As a fellow foodie, I don't mind. Since he ended up dateless, he sat at the empty spot at our table.

I had no intention of bringing a date, since I helped plan the event. Plus, it's not like I had anyone to ask. The dating pool is a cruel hurricane, and I'm sick of being sucked in. I recently deleted my dating apps and have been trying to focus on myself; or at least not focus on John or Jack or Peter, who work in finance and all lie about being over six foot tall.

"You have a little..." I touch the side of my lip. Zack then uses his tongue to catch the rogue frosting and heat rushes to my cheeks. His eyes find mine and my flushed cheeks, and I know he's about to say something dangerous.

Ting! Ting! The clinking of a glass breaks through the room. Tripp stands on the stage, microphone in hand.

"Before we open the dance floor, I just want to say thank you, from the bottom of my heart. This event is more than what I ever dreamed of, and I couldn't have done it without all of you. *When We Play* could reach so many kids and families," Tripp's voice cracks, and he wipes the corner of his eye. Aww's fill the room. "Before I turn into a blubbering mess, I want to thank some special people. First, my mom, Wendy. Without her, there is no Tripp Owens, wide receiver for the Upstate Cosmos."

Polite claps fill the room as Wendy gives a small wave from her table near the stage.

"Next, Willow, the love of my life, for showing me what true love and support looks like." I look over to see Willow, eyes glistening with her own tears. For some couples, this whole thing would be insufferable and over the top—not for Willow and Tripp. Their love is the kind you dream of, bright and honest.

"Last, and certainly not least, Emilie Hayes. I could've never pulled this off without you. And you were right, the chocolate cake was the way to go."

The crowd laughs and claps. Zack screams an enthusiastic "Woo!" and claps much louder than is necessary, which makes everyone laugh a bit deeper.

"The dance floor and the bar are open. Thanks again for coming and don't forget about the silent auction." Tripp waves and walks off the stage.

I slowly turn to Zack and shake my head from side to side.

"What? I'm proud of you." He shrugs his shoulders, and it's impossible not to smile at him. "Want another drink before we hit the dance floor?" He stands, snaps his fingers, and shakes his shoulders.

My stomach drops.

This is the type of behavior I need to be careful with. These are the things Zack does to make me think he's interested or sees me as more than a friend. Zack doesn't date and I have a new rule: don't date unless it has long-term potential. The butterflies in my stomach don't get the memo—fluttering even faster when Zack gives me his favorite smirk, the one with one corner of his mouth pinching up accompanied with a wink.

Here's the thing: dancing isn't dating. Plus, Zack is a great dancer—I'm guaranteed to have an amazing time.

I nod, and Zack practically skips to the bar. My heart squeezes when I see guests leaving their seats to look at the silent auction items or make their way to the dance floor. I sit back, thrilled people aren't running for the exits.

Willow and Tripp are one of the first couples to hit the dance floor, and they curl into each other, dancing like they're the only people in the room. I want to roll my eyes, but they are so wrapped up in each other I can't get enough after watching their love story live.

I let out a sigh, happy and fulfilled in this moment.

"Emilie!" a too-loud voice interrupts. I know who it is before I even turn around. The mere sound of him speaking is like nails on a chalkboard.

Mitch—my ex and future brother-in-law. Who else could find a way to ruin such a perfectly wholesome moment?

Eliza stands next to him, wearing a satin emerald dress which clings perfectly to her damn near perfect silhouette. I stand and reach for my sister. She hugs me like an acquaintance she's supposed to remember but can't. I kiss her cheek.

We've always been hot and cold. I stay in her orbit because no matter what, I do hope we can have a rewarding relationship later in life—or that's what my therapist tells me is a solid goal. Some days are easier than others and anything with Mitch has a dash of extra tension.

"A lovely event," Mitch says.

"*When We Play* is grateful for your donation." I try to mask my annoyance.

The thing is, I don't think Mitch is trying to upset me but his mere presence is irritating. It's been years since we were together but it still bothers me. My therapist encourages me to have a conversation with him one-on-one about the whole thing, but I just don't have the mental space for it.

"Can you introduce us to Willow and Tripp?" Eliza asks, looping an arm with Mitch's and leaning her head on his shoulder.

I turn my head, watching my friends out on the dance floor. "They're busy," I gesture to Willow and Tripp being the cutest thing you've ever seen. "Maybe another time."

But probably not.

"Did you look at the silent auction items?" I ask, desperate to change the subject.

"Yes, we bid on quite a few." Eliza laughs, scrunching her nose while looking at Mitch, who is now glancing at the auction tables.

I smile but internally scoff, thinking back to how Mitch viewed money and success—it's why he and my dad have always gotten along.

"Who did you come with? Or are you flying solo?" Mitch trying to be subtle is hilarious.

I don't need a man to feel validated or complete, but fuck, it'd be way better to flaunt a gorgeous boyfriend right about now.

I've held out long enough, and as I go to open my mouth, a low hand touches my back, someone sliding in next to me.

"Sorry, love. The line was atrocious." Zack hands me a glass of champagne, placing a gentle kiss on my cheek.

Mitch and Eliza both have their mouths hanging open, heads falling forward as they take in all of Zack in his black tie glory. The man is a showstopper. I try to mask the surprise, lean into the moment, and let this play out.

"What did I miss?"

Chapter 4
Zack

I love a good "what the fuck" moment and it seems we've got a solid one on our hands.

"This is my sister, Eliza, and her fiancé, Mitch." Emilie's words are syrupy sweet, enough to rot your teeth. I know who they are courtesy of Tripp, who gave in one day and had to tell me some gossip he'd heard from Willow.

Pulling the hand from Emilie's back, I go for a handshake. Eliza's hand feels like a limp doll while Mitch is trying to show me he can hang—even when I know he can't.

"You're Zack Andersen," Mitch stammers, voice quiet and a bit too fast, like there's not enough room for the words in his mouth. "You threw the game-winning touchdown in the Super Bowl."

"You must be the backup quarterback?" Eliza asks, taking me in, from my blonde hair down to my Tom Ford dress shoes.

"Nope, just the long snapper. Definitely a big fan of the trick play."

"You came here with Zack Andersen. How does that happen?" Mitch asks, looking to Emilie and wearing an enthusiastic smile.

"Why wouldn't she come with me? She *is* my girlfriend." The words are smooth and confident from my mouth. Emilie laughs next to me, enough for me to feel her body move with it.

Skeptical eyes from her sister and surprised ones from Mitch fall on Emilie. "You never said anything..." Eliza presses.

"Yeah, that's all me." I put a hand on my chest, claiming responsibility before I take the same hand and thread my fingers into Emilie's. She doesn't miss a beat. "I wanted to keep it quiet. You know, the press and all that."

"So, you're coming to the wedding?" Mitch asks.

Shit. I didn't see that coming. Emilie's fingers squeeze mine, too hard. I try to keep my face steady.

"October 17th. Cancun, Mexico."

I don't know what I did to deserve such luck in this life sometimes, but I know that is our bye week for the Upstate Cosmos. That date is burned into my brain because I plan a trip every single season.

"I'll be there, " I reply as Mitch loudly claps his hands before I can even get the words out. I can feel Emilie's hazel eyes on me.

"You only RSVP'd for one," Eliza protests to Emilie.

Emilie shrugs her shoulders. "Did I? Well, whoops."

"Zack Andersen is coming to our wedding!" Mitch jostles Eliza, her forehead scrunched and lips in a thin line.

"We're going to get a drink. I'm sure we'll see you at a family dinner soon," Eliza snaps as she begins pulling Mitch toward the bar.

I wave to Mitch who is still looking back at me, his arm dangling like it's barely attached to his body.

Emilie turns to me, taking a long drink of her champagne. I bet she wishes it was an Aperol Spritz—doesn't matter if it's spritz season or not, she'll take one. I'll never forget when a bartender in Vegas gave her such shit for ordering one at the Super Bowl after party.

"What the fuck was that?" She smiles, but her voice is sharper than I like.

"Right? I can't believe you dated that guy."

Emilie gives me her fakest laugh, using a hand to smooth out the front of my suit jacket. "Not that. What did you just do? How did you even know who that was?"

"Tripp gave me the short version a few weeks ago. And I've overheard bits and pieces when we've been out." I cheers her glass with mine. Emilie doesn't move, her golden eyes like knives. "Don't worry, I have a valid passport and a bye week."

"Of course you do." She drinks the rest of the champagne before setting the empty glass on the table behind us.

"What's the problem? We hang out in Mexico. I can be the doting, professional athlete boyfriend while your sister marries your ex. I think I'm the perfect distraction."

Honestly, it seems like a great time. It won't be the first instance where I've helped make someone jealous.

Emilie is trying to keep it together. She picks at her palms, and her chest rises and falls quickly, matching her breath. I don't have all the details but it's clear Emilie has a complicated relationship with her family, which is hard to relate to. My parents, who were high school sweethearts and are still married, plus my baby sister, are some of my favorite people.

"The problem is that my sister is a sleuthing snake. If we're not dating, she'll find out, and she'll find a way to twist it and make it some terrible thing I did to her."

I have half an idea forming, maybe not even half.

"Okay, so we'll date."

Emilie's eyes widen. "*We'll date*? How many drinks have you had?"

"I'm sober, Emilie. We'll pretend to date, that way your sister won't find anything amiss."

"You want to pretend-date me?"

"Why wouldn't I? We'll try out all the new restaurants on my list. You already come to the Cosmos games with Willow. It'll be fun."

She scoffs and shakes her head, looking around the room, before stopping at the floor. It kills me to let the silence stretch.

"This is a big deal. Things between Eliza and me are already rocky and complicated."

"I understand."

"That means you won't be able to—" Emilie's eyebrows scrunch, and her eyes dart around the room, like she's trying to find the right words— "do whatever it is you do with whoever you do it with."

Well played. She's being as vague as possible, but I get it.

"Is that something you're willing to give up?" Her mouth is pressed in a line so thin I can barely see her red lips.

That isn't something I considered with the very loose idea in my brain. I can do that, probably. For Emilie, I can try.

"To jog your memory," she says, with her arms crossed and a slow but painful look. While taking a slow breath, she tilts her head. "The last time we were out, you were practically having a threesome on the dance floor. *That's* what you're giving up."

Nothing vague about that. I'd like to tell her that was a one-time deal, but that would be a lie. This specific instance had me between two sisters, both with chocolate colored hair, and they couldn't get enough of making me their sandwich. I kept catching Emilie watching me, and she made sure I saw her roll her eyes while she wore a smirk. Nothing like a little light judgement when I probably deserved it.

"Done and done. Let's deactivate the dating app right now." I pull my phone out, going to the exclusive app which only allows celebrities and athletes to join. Emilie watches as I go to my settings and click the big deactivate button.

Emilie bites her lip. "We're really doing this?" she asks.

I answer by reaching for her hand and leading her to the dance floor. A slow song is playing so I put my hands on her lower back, and she wraps her arms around me.

How hard can this be?

Chapter 5
Emilie

I'm home after a meeting with Willow and now I'm thinking about how much my life has changed while working with her. She's one of my best friends and one of the biggest celebrities in the world—I never would've dreamed of meeting her, let alone having her become one of my closest friends.

It also let some of my other friends show their true colors, ones I was already wary of. Making and keeping friends, as a woman, is so hard.

Living in New York was the first nail in the coffin. Michigan is technically home, and I don't make it back often. My last trip there was telling in the worst ways, considering they kept asking me weirdly personal questions about Willow and acted like I owed them something.

Not a good sign.

It's been a few days since the ridiculously successful *When We Play* event and now I'm thinking about Zack. If we can pull this off, I'm sure my old friends will resurface. That's how they broke the radio silence the first time, when they saw pictures of me and Zack at a Cosmos event last year.

I stepped onto the red carpet, wearing the type of dress which fits in a way that makes you hold your head a little taller. My heart raced as someone recognized me: That was Willow's assistant, Emilie! The press shouted, shifted their lenses, and took a few pictures. I had done the PR training and knew that when you came to an event like this, you stood on the carpet, let people get a photo or two, before you slinked into the background.

Zack Andersen stepped onto the carpet, and I felt the energy shift. I had met him briefly at a Cosmos game. He had always been kind, welcoming, and damn, he was hot. He didn't just pose on the red carpet—he danced. He actually shimmied and shook his shoulders between poses; he was having the time of his life.

He was long and lean, the silhouette of his suit showing off his shoulders that were just broad enough for his frame. Zack Andersen was a smoke show. I knew I shouldn't have objectified the man for the way he looked, but I was practically drooling. His dirty blonde hair was longer on the top—the man had great hair. Why was I thinking about how it'd feel to run my fingers through it?

When Zack saw me, he gave a little wave and immediately moved closer to where I was on the carpet. Before I knew what was happening, he had pulled me in, and the press was eating it up. He let his arm wrap low around my back, lightly touching the top of my hip. I was only 5'6" but with the heels, I was closer to his height.

The thing was, when he touched me, it felt right—the type of energy I expected from Zack. I smiled up at him and slowly shook my head, not needing to say a single thing with my mouth. His eyes told me he knew he was wild, but he loved it.

My heart beat like a sprinter pounding their feet into the track, and I forgot to breathe. When I remembered, it was like breathing in vanilla and bourbon. I wondered if he had a drink in the limo on the way here?

Those eyes, the type of blue you dream about, looked like they were on an expedition for my deepest, darkest secrets. With a look like that, he wouldn't have needed to search for long—I'd have told him anything he wanted to know.

I smile while thinking about that night. Not because Zack swooped in and had some fun with me on a red carpet, but it's almost like he sensed I needed to belong. I showed up with Willow and Tripp, who clearly had their own thing going on. It was nice to have a connection other than them.

Zack and I hung out a lot that evening. That's when I learned he's a fantastic dancer, and an even better time. I also learned I couldn't fall in love with Zack Andersen. Not only would it most likely be one sided and a disaster, but I had some rules to follow.

I'm almost twenty-six and at this point, I'm only dating people I think I can see myself with long-term. Well, it's a new thing I'm trying out. It's not that I'm dying to get married or anything, but I don't want to waste my time on someone who doesn't view me as a potential forever destination. I've been burned by being the stop along the way too many times.

Not sure how this Zack thing fits in with it, but since it's fake, I think it's fine.

There's a knock on the door, one I expected. Zack is coming over so we can make a schedule, a game plan—something to show we might be able to pull this off.

I open the door and Zack grins, holding two iced coffees—both my color, indicating the right amount of cream and sugar—and shaking them for effect.

"Hi, lover!" he says, too loudly, and kisses my cheek. I roll my eyes and let him come inside. "Got your coffee order from Willow."

Zack's hair is messy, darker than usual and a bit damp, like he took a shower at the training facility and came here right after. He's wearing a black t-shirt and bright pink shorts—the man loves a pop of color—and it's hard not to stare because of that short inseam.

"I can feel you staring at my shorts and this is a compromise. I got the color I wanted but the length you recommended."

How could I forget? Zack and I were online shopping during the break between sets at Willow's concert a few weeks back. The opener wrapped up just as Zack pleaded with Tripp to help him find the perfect pair of shorts, and when Tripp was uninterested, I was the next best thing.

Yes, I did help him pick out these shorts. And let me say, on behalf of anyone attracted to men, I did everyone a favor with the length.

"I like them. Also, we'll never lose you in a crowd, so that's a win." I pick up one of the iced coffees, pop a straw in, and take a long drink.

"Some of the guys were giving me shit but I love this color, so they can get bent." He grabs the other iced coffee and reaches out for a cheers.

Zack walks to the loveseat and falls in. Even though the living room has multiple places to sit, I typically end up cozy on the corduroy loveseat—the first piece of furniture I bought when I knew I'd be staying in the apartment long-term. "Alright, let's plan our fake relationship."

"Don't make fun of a good plan. Listen, I know you thought you were doing a good thing, and you did, but if this blows up, my family will be even more insufferable than they already are."

I can't even put into words the things they would say. The microscope I'd be under.

Zack nods. "Tell me what to do, Captain." He gives me a weird salute that if it came from anyone else, I'd tell them to get lost.

"I propose going out during the week, when our schedules allow it, hitting your restaurant list. Obviously a weekend when it works—really give the press the chance to get photos of us. Since it's August, this should be doable until the season starts, yes?"

"Yeah. One hundred percent doable," he smirks and it has me shaking my head. "We should probably be seen together after all the Cosmos games you come to. Shouldn't be hard, since you're typically there any-way," Zack offers, shaking his iced coffee, the ice rattling in the cup.

"Easy."

A lightbulb turns on behind his eyes mid-drink, and Zack leans forward, trying to swallow the coffee as fast as possible. "AHH! You need to wear my jersey!" He sets the coffee down on the table in front of us so he can grab my hands. "Please do that, just like Willow does for Tripp."

I can't fight the stomach flip but I can reason with my brain: this isn't real.

"Speaking of Willow and Tripp, what do we tell them?" I ask.

Zack rubs his fingers together in thought. "I think we should let them in on the whole plan. I can handle Tripp, but I'm a tiny bit scared of Willow. I know she'd castrate me if I ever did anything to you, so I'd prefer being upfront." He puts his hands up like he's surrendering and sits back into the loveseat.

"I agree. I couldn't keep that from them. But that's it, we don't tell anyone else. That's the first rule." I point a playful finger at Zack, but he and I both know he's the one with the loose lips.

"Got it." He nods in understanding. "What about PDA? Can I touch you when we're out? What's the line?"

I really didn't think about PDA. Zack is always touchy feely, and he's never made me feel uncomfortable.

"We'll know if it's within reason." I try not to blush as I catch his denim blue eyes. "As long as it's in public."

"Within reason?" He scrunches his forehead. "There's lots of things we could do... within reason..." He moves his eyebrows up and down with a small smile, his eyes still locked on mine.

I give him a playful push. "Quit it. You know what I mean." He throws his head back with his boyish grin, and it hits me.

I'm going to fake date Zack Andersen.

Chapter 6
Zack

I love making Emilie's face red—the closest to her hair color, the better. Currently, she's making a list of rules and plans in a shared note on her phone, one she's already shared with me and confirmed I can open. Don't ask the woman a single social media question because she'll think you're technology illiterate for the rest of time.

"What about social media? Should we post about each other?" I ask.

"Yes, but if you use any nasty 2000's rap lyrics as the caption..." She throws a look at me, one that says, 'I've been on your socials.' I like the idea of her looking. "Rule two, let's run social media posts by the other, just to make sure we're comfortable."

I have no issue with what she'd post; she's too much of a good girl to ruffle my feathers. Now, I've been in trouble more than once with an accidental post that was meant to go to a single person, or something the PR team views as borderline and asks me to take down, 'just to be safe.'

I'm the long snapper, no one's really paying that close of attention. Well, maybe they are, but to be honest, I barely care.

"Agreed, but I don't want any more rules. Two is enough. I won't be a dick and I'll play nice, ok?"

Emilie nods, setting her phone in her lap while locking the screen, and picking up her iced coffee.

"Now, when is family dinner?" I ask, thinking back to her snarky sister grilling Emilie at the event. "Need to get it in my calendar."

"I would never subject you to that, Zack." She catches my eyes, pausing. "Seriously."

"No, I want to come. At some point before the wedding, whenever you're comfortable." I like the idea of meeting her family, mostly to understand her better. She's always acted like she's only got herself, when it's just not true. I'm guessing her family has something to do with that.

"Fine. Remember, you asked for this." She chews on her straw, one of her nervous habits.

She's right. I did. I'm a little afraid to admit why.

⚬ ✕✕✕

"THIS IS TORTURE. WHY do you do this to yourself?" a breathless Riley, blonde hair pulled into an almost too-high ponytail, whines while resting hands on her knees. Even though we're at the Cosmos facility, it's just the two of us. Everyone is still squeezing in the last of summer before football takes over.

My baby sister is one of my favorite people, but that doesn't mean she's not dramatic as fuck.

"Don't act like you've never done burpees before." I turn to her right before I jump, finishing my own.

She whips her head to look at me, the sweat dripping down her nose. "Not after every squat variation you could think of."

The timer goes off, letting me know the circuit is over. I take a swig from my water bottle filled with an electrolyte drink. It's some sort of powder, which makes the water saltier than any flavor they promise, but it's not too bad.

It tastes better considering this company is one of my newest sponsors. The ending play in the Super Bowl is still paying off in sponsorships and women. Well, now I guess it's woman. One. My now fake girlfriend.

I wipe the sweat from my forehead and tease, "We've done much harder workouts than this."

"Why the torture today?"

How do I say that the most cardio I've done during this off-season was a threesome with two ex-gymnasts? We're close but not *that* close.

"I'm just trying to get ready for the season." I'm also trying to keep myself distracted from the fact that I'm keeping a secret from my sister and I hate that.

Riley slumps down on a yoga mat, spreading her limbs out like a starfish. Her chest rises and falls quickly.

"When's the next flight?" I ask, trying to distract her from the personal hell she seems to be going through.

"I just flew back from London, so I'm off the next two days. Then I'm on a six-day streak, so I won't be able to do this again until at least next week." Her eyes are closed as she speaks. "Which is good, considering I don't know when I'll be able to walk again."

I start to stretch, using my own yoga mat. "Yes! I'm in serious need of Riley's-tales-of-the-sky." I clap my hands and rub them together.

Riley is a flight attendant and loves it. The thing I love most about her job are all the ridiculous passenger stories. Last week, they had to remove a man because he wouldn't stop standing up and reciting his poetry. He seemed mentally sound, especially because he *explained* to the flight attendants that this was a new attempt at guerilla marketing. Apparently, he's an indie author and was hoping on loads of press.

I mean, that probably wasn't worth going on the no-fly list, but what do I know? Maybe being an indie author is harder than I think.

"What's new with you?" Riley asks as she continues stretching.

What a question. I haven't had much time to think about what this thing with Emilie means. It's been a week since she and I basically shook hands on a fake relationship. My brain feels like a tornado, random thoughts just swirling around, crashing into whatever is in its way.

I've gone over the interaction a thousand times, and I can't believe I went all in and invited myself to her sister's wedding. All in the name of pissing off her ex. Showing him up. All I know is I saw them talking to Emilie and it took one awkward look around from her to know I had to help.

Fuck that guy. Who marries the little sister?

Just then, I get a text message from Kass Blonde Lawyer. All it says is "hi" before she sends a picture of her tits. I've never been more thankful that I didn't open this next to Riley.

"Not much," I lie, which is much better than, "Well, you see, I've decided to start fake dating someone to help make her ex jealous. It requires a passport and social media approval. Also, someone just casually sent me a nude."

My sister can typically call out a lie before it even falls out of my mouth, but she buys this one. I blame it on the lack of oxygen making it to her brain.

I *will* tell her, just not right now. Maybe I'll run it by Emilie, since it's the first rule she set? I was so nervous about what she was going to propose that I sort of forget about needing to keep Riley in the loop.

She rolls her eyes. "You're so boring."

Sure. That's it.

Chapter 7
Emilie

First dates are hard. Fake first dates might be harder.

Tonight Zack and I are going out, and I'm counting on the press to do its thing. Since we're supposed to have been together for a bit already, I need evidence of our relationship timeline. For my family to think this is real, which is non-negotiable, I have to kick that timeline into gear.

That means going with Zack to a new restaurant opening for The Trivium Food Company. It's a small-plate centric spot in Tribeca, taking common American style foods and putting a modern or bougie spin on it.

Out of all the things Zack has on his calendar, this one is an easy yes. I already follow the owner on social media and have been drooling over the food pics.

Even before last season's championship, Zack seemed to get invites to things like this all the time. Whether it's live-streaming some part of the event—paired with unhinged commentary—or posting on his socials with the type of caption that makes you raise your eyebrows, he never fails to deliver. With Zack, you never know what you're going to get, but you can almost bet it will be a good time.

What do you wear to a fake date? I stand in my walk-in closet, hands on my hips, sweat starting to break out across my forehead. Why does it feel like I just worked out when all I've done is pull clothes on, only to take them off three minutes later?

Zack is also zero help.

Me

What are you wearing?

Zack

my new pink shorts

be serious

how do you know I'm not being serious?

That's the thing, I don't. It wouldn't be all that surprising for him show up in something casually trendy and cool. However, I do know that Zack loves to shop for clothes. I can't imagine he doesn't have something he's been itching to pull out.

there's no dress code

doesn't help it's 100 degrees outside

it's only 93

ONLY 93 is saying it's only like being three steps into the depths of hell

do you need a snack? Seem kind of hangry

no, I need to start getting ready

I'm wearing shorts, but they're Tom Ford.

and a button up shirt. Casual

but figure it out because I'll be at your apartment in 40 minutes

I look at the clock and can't believe it's already that late. Trying to pick out clothes puts me in the twilight zone, where time makes zero sense.

Luckily, since it's miserably hot, my hair is going back in a low bun. There's no way I'm trying to manage and tame these lion-mane-like curls for this humidity. Plus, I don't want to see pictures of Zack, in all his Tom Ford glory, standing next to Mufasa from The Lion King.

I want to look hot. I want Eliza to see these pictures and gasp, "Wow, she was telling the truth." I need to look like I belong with someone like Zack.

After washing my face, the cold water has me catching my breath and waking me up before I sit at my vanity to put my makeup on. I can't put my finger on it, but I've always loved makeup. My mom, too busy with whatever high-brow club she was trying to be part of, never made the time to show me what to do—everything I knew about makeup I learned from stolen copies of Seventeen and Cosmopolitan.

I remember the first tube of red lipstick I bought. How I snuck it into the house, like it was something I wasn't supposed to have, and showed it to Eliza. We spent the next ten minutes putting it on each other. Cautiously I put the color on her lips, careful not to go outside her lip line. I took my time and when all was said and done, I was proud of how good I did—her fair skin untouched with any of the crimson.

Eliza wasn't nearly as careful, and she made a mess of her attempt. Just as I was looking in the mirror to see if I should wash my face and start fresh, my mom opened the door to Eliza's room.

"Oh, Eliza. Red is your color. Good job, honey." She beams at her youngest daughter. Eliza's eyes sparkled in gratitude as she purses her lips.

As I turn to face my mom, she pivots her attention to me. Her eyes go from my own to my lips and back to Eliza. Her lips sit in a tight line as her forehead scrunches in distaste.

"Emilie, you look like a mess. Wash that off and have your sister show you how to do it." She turned and shut the door. Tears crowded my eyes. Heat flooded my cheeks. She left before I had a chance to say, "Eliza, did this! She's the messy one. I'm the one who did a good job."

My trip down memory lane ends when I glance at the almost-final look staring back at me. The makeup is natural but highlights my features: long lashes, high cheekbones, and bow-shaped lips. I hold my new go-to red lipstick and apply it, just as carefully as I did that first time with my little sister. I blot my lips, even though much of the color doesn't come off—we love a no-smudge moment.

I decide on a light blue linen dress. With a halter top tie and a collar, it's unique enough to not fade into the background—the dusty blue a beautiful contrast to my fair skin and bold, red hair. For jewelry, I choose my diamond studs—a thank you gift from Willow—and a gold tennis bracelet.

Two last decisions to make: a bag and shoes. I shift my weight from foot to foot as I stand in front of shelves full of my options. My phone tells me I'm running out of time—Zack will be here any minute. I close my eyes, take a deep breath, and shimmy my shoulders in an attempt to shake off the indecision.

When my eyes pop open, I go with my gut—the first pair of shoes and bag that catches my attention—and probably what I would've picked five minutes ago: strappy gold heels and my classic white Chanel.

My hands touch the soft leather of the purse, and my cheeks immediately pull into a smile. I don't have many things I'm emotionally invested in, but this bag is rare—in a special way. This is the first thing I bought when I met with my financial adviser, another gift from Willow, and they basically told me it was time to stop hoarding and start investing.

You're in great financial shape. Let your money work for you. You have no debt.

My parents could no longer hold financial stability over me, like a lifeboat I may or may not need. All my hard work, the late nights and lack of sleep through college, all in the name of paying my own way, came to fruition when the adviser raised his eyebrows, surprised at what I had in my bank account.

Go and treat yourself. It appears you never do that from what I see here. So, I went and bought a bag that I dreamed of for years: a cream quilted Chanel with gold hardware. It immediately lifts my mood and gives me "you've got this" energy.

Which is exactly what I need when I think of tonight.

A knock at the door—which must be Zack since you can't get past the doorman without being on a schedule—wakes up the butterflies, which have been fluttering around ever since we agreed on this as our first outing during our new *arrangement*.

I open the door with my free hand, the other still holding my gold heels.

"Woah," Zack admires, pausing outside the door. "That blue... I need something in that color." His eyes rake over my entire body.

Heat creeps into my cheeks. I wave him in, turning away to hide the blush, and realize putting on my heels is the perfect ploy. I slip my feet in, still needing to secure the straps. Shuffling over to the barstool, one of my go-to spots—I love being in or around a kitchen— I finish putting the heels on.

Immediately, I regret my decision. I can't quite pull my leg up to secure the straps without showing Zack all my lady business. Which, fake dating or not, no one wants an unannounced full-frontal shot.

Zack stands, hands in his charcoal gray shorts—sporting a delectable inseam—and a patterned button up. I can't help but roll my eyes because this is the type of shirt that would be all wrong on someone, but on Zack, it's a perfect fit. Naturally.

Zack runs his hands through his thick hair, floppy and blonde, and walks a couple steps closer.

"Need some help with those?"

Chapter 8
Zack

I DON'T KNOW WHAT it is, but when Emilie's cheeks flush red like that, it makes my dick twitch. The color spreads across the bridge of her nose, hitting her cheek bones.

For fuck's sake.

"Please," she answers, her shoulders relaxing as her back rests on the bar behind her.

Emilie kicks her feet out, the gold straps sticking out behind her foot.

I lightly reach around, realizing each shoe has two straps, much longer than I thought they'd be.

"They wrap around my ankle before buckling on the side." Emilie's soft voice makes me look up at her.

She's wearing that red lipstick, the one that makes her lips look completely fucking kissable. It's never too much with Emilie; she knows exactly what she's doing—one of the only reasons I ask her opinion when it comes to clothes.

I lightly take the thin straps in my hands and wrap them around her ankle. My knuckles brush her skin, and it's as soft as I thought it'd be. I hold my breath. The clasp is delicate; I move my head to get a better look.

I'd be lying if I wasn't thinking of what it'd be like to kiss up these legs. I sneak a look up and see her, lips pursed, leaned just a bit forward to see what I'm doing.

When I successfully manage each strappy heel, Emilie kicks her feet, probably making sure they're not going to fly off. My breath, which was held hostage in my lungs, finally escapes as soon as I create a little room between us.

"What do you think?" Emilie stands, doing a quick half turn while kicking up one of the heels. "Not too boring?"

Ha! Boring is never a word I'd use to describe her.

"Definitely not boring." I bite my lip, taking her in from the red hair pulled back down to the tip of the heels. "You're really something."

Emilie smirks and grabs her white bag from the table. I offer her my hand, fake boyfriend things and all, and she shakes her head before taking it.

THE TRIVIUM FOOD COMPANY is my favorite kind of place: good food, better drinks, and an eclectic menu. Serving small plates only, most of their food spins a classic on its head.

"Up next, we have a soup designed to make you think of dipping your french fries into vanilla ice cream." Our server, Tori, lifts the top of a dish and steam escapes. She reaches into a small sack-bag, kind of like what you'd get at elementary school for a field trip, and pull out a small container of fries, before laying them out—just so—on the plate.

"Dip the fries in the soup, at least for the first bite." Tori sets down two tiny spoons for Emilie and me. "Enjoy!" She claps her hands, almost every inch covered in tattoos, and heads back to the kitchen.

I take a deep breath and it oddly smells like sweet vanilla, and of course, salty potatoes.

"These are like, ridiculously thin. Perfectly straight. " Emilie picks up a fry, examining it. Sitting across from me in a booth for two, she takes the fry, dips it into the soup, and pops it into her mouth—careful not to drip anything on her dress.

"MMMMMohmygod," Emilie moans, closing her eyes. I'm surprised I can hear her because most openings like this are chaotic and obnoxious. Seems like Trivium has it figured out.

Wanting to see what all the fuss is about, I dip my own fry into the soup before putting it in my mouth. It's bizarre because it's exactly as they've described: vanilla ice cream, but soup? Hot vanilla ice cream? It feels like it shouldn't work but it does, and it's fucking fantastic.

"How the fuck do they do that?" I ask, dipping another fry in the soup. All of a sudden I'm calculating how many fries are left compared to the soup ratio—I don't want to use a spoon.

Emilie replies, "It doesn't make sense but I love it. You know?" Another fry from the plate bites the dust before I can blink.

When we both reach for the last fry, it's like the press gods have shined their nosey light upon us, because a photographer is getting shots at our table. Typical for an event like this—let everyone eat and as the food wraps up, come out of the woodwork to get the PR shots.

"It's like that Disney movie! The one with the noodle and the dogs," I joke. Lines crinkle the corner of Emilie's eyes as she lets out a small laugh but doesn't give up the crispy potato.

"I'm the lady." She leans in, her eyes golden in the dim light. "And you can be the tramp." She pops her lips at the end, hitting that P hard. It makes me laugh and tip my head down, giving her the perfect opportunity to snatch the last fry.

Shaking my head in defeat, I joke, "You're cold."

She shrugs her shoulders and finishes her drink. Like clockwork, Tori is at the table with fresh drinks for both of us: an Aperol Spritz for Emilie and a vodka soda with orange for me.

"Look how cute we are. A couple with the same garnish." I shake my head, teasing, before picking up the rocks glass. I feel the bubbles on my nose before the smooth vodka and light citrus hit my tongue.

"Meant to be, I guess." Her hand reaches over and squeezes mine, her fingers soft and nails painted her usual inky black. Emilie moves her fingers back and forth over my knuckles before catching my eyes. When she raises her eyebrows and a corner of her lip in a smile, my stomach bottoms out.

The way it sometimes does when she looks at me like that. She's got one hell of a smirk and, fuck, if that red lipstick doesn't make me think of where she could leave smudges on me...

Stop. This isn't legit. Plus, Emilie isn't the type of woman to waste her time on someone like me, romantically at least. I'm the fun friend, a good time, the one you call when you need a break from the heavy.

I'm just the guy who couldn't keep my mouth shut. This whole fake dating thing seems like it could be fun—certainly no regrets here—but it feels there's more at stake than me showing up as a plus one. Maybe Emilie wishes I would've left it alone, or that someone else would've stepped in?

"Do you know her?" Emilie asks, interrupting my self-deprecating rant.

I look to the woman who is clearly approaching our table. I shake my head. At first, I think she works for Trivium, but she's not wearing a uniform.

She walks right by our table, leaving a folded up piece of paper near my drink glass.

"What in the world?" Emilie laughs and leans forward. "What does it say?"

I open the wadded up piece of paper to find a scribbled phone number.

Emilie sits back and shakes her head. "Does that happen a lot?" she asks, looking to see if the woman is around.

"Sometimes," I tell a little white lie.

I leave out the part where, when I go out with the team, I sometimes get so many numbers that I'll draw one out at the end of the night, and that's who I go home with.

I don't think Emilie would be impressed with my version of phone number roulette. I mean, sometimes I embarrass myself when I think about it. Part of me knows I'm smarter than the antics and it's always louder than the part questioning my plan for an end game.

Finishing the rest of my drink, I take the unsolicited phone number, ball it up, and put it in the leftover ice.

"That's cold, Zack," Emilie jokes, barely able to stifle her laugh when she takes a drink of her spritz.

I laugh at her cheesy pun, put my head in my hands, and peek through my fingers at her. She's chewing her straw, glowing, and looks so unbothered.

Why would she be? No one saw it happen and this is just for looks.

Right?

"Ready?" I reach my hand out for Emilie to take. I turn to find her a step or two behind me, her legs on display thanks to that fucking blue dress. The one she'll be wearing in my dreams, which may or may not involve her removing it slowly. Not that I'll tell her that.

The press buzzes about twenty feet from us. They're outside the front door of the restaurant, perched and ready for their shots. At openings like this, there are only a couple floating around inside. It's like an unspoken deal: we'll let you eat, with minimal disruption, but be ready for the exit, baby.

She slips her fingers in mine right before we walk out the front. The contact warms me from the inside but puts my brain on high alert. How is it that this is the first time we've done this? It's effortless and not at all like we committed to being in a fake relationship a week ago.

You'd think with today's technology, we'd get rid of the incessant click of cameras. How haven't we fixed that? It's a barrage of clicks, flashes, and the occasional snap from the asshole who needs more of your attention.

When we know everyone has a picture of the two of us holding hands, Emilie steps in closer, turning her body and leaning into mine. Her hand touches my stomach, and before I can adequately appreciate her fingers touching me like this, she turns and looks up at me.

Not looks—fucking beams. Her lips, still bold and red, wear that smirk as her eyes find mine. She scrunches her nose before turning to face the paparazzi.

Zack! Over here! Is this your new girlfriend?

Who is she?!

Wait, that's Emilie Hayes! Willow's assistant.

Zack! Emilie! Over here.

They are eating this up. Damn, we're good at this.

Just as we've fulfilled our paparazzi quota, I tip down and put my lips on Emilie's temple. She leans in further, our body like magnets.

Something pulling us in, a string, something I could almost reach out and grab.

Something definitely not fake.

Fuck.

Chapter 9
Emilie

"WHAT IN THE WORLD is happening?" Willow opens the door with her phone practically hitting me in the face.

If I had to guess, it's one of the many articles showing Zack and me at Trivium last night. Damn, I might work hard but the press works harder. My plan was to tell Willow and Tripp about the whole situation this morning but clickbait got to them first.

Playboy Zack Making a Play for Emilie
Who is Emilie Hayes, Zack Andersen's Girl of the Week?
Stars Align for Zack Andersen and His New Girl

"I'm not a girl of the week. That's insulting," I groan, rolling my eyes and pushing in to Willow's home. I practically lived here last year, especially last summer. Willow and I were new to working together but became fast friends.

I'm carrying donuts and coffee because this isn't something you drop over a calming beverage, like Willow's go-to peppermint tea.

"I tried calling Zack, but he didn't answer," Tripp says, standing up from the bar in the kitchen.

I set the carrier full of coffees down and place the bag of donuts next to them. "You two, chill. Coffee first and details second."

While I hand out my breakfast peace offering, a task I wish took longer than twenty seconds, I try to catch my breath. Why does it feel like I'm talking to two disappointed parents?

Taking a long drink of my iced coffee, I stand across from Willow and Tripp, both sitting at the bar.

"You don't need to worry, it's not real. I mean, it's like, real as in I was at Trivium with Zack last night, it's not a hologram or anything."

Willow shakes her head. "No babbling."

"It's fake. We're in a pretend relationship because Zack opened his big, beautiful mouth at the *When We Play* event. Zack was all white knight, trying to help me. He told Mitch he was my boyfriend and then Mitch was all, 'You're coming to the wedding, right?'"

The two of them are dialed in, hanging on my every word. I take another long sip; the caffeine is a necessity today.

"Ummm, Lo. This kind of, might be, our fault." Tripp is the first one to speak.

Willow leans on the bar, looking at him, a little less in adoration and a bit more in annoyance.

"What?! It is. We were complaining about Eliza and Mitch at the bar, remember? Zack was definitely there when they came up to her," Tripp gestures to me, voice soft.

"It also sounds like you gave Zack some Mitch details a few weeks ago." I cross my arms, pretending to be mad.

He throws his hands up. "I knew it. I shouldn't have said anything. That's my bad, I'm not typically—"

I let a smile hit my lips. "I'm totally kidding. I don't care that you told Zack." Tripp's shoulders relax, and Willow is trying not to laugh. "Back to the details. He has a bye week the week of the wedding. So, he's coming with me to Mexico. How perfect is that?" I smile through the awkwardness.

"My brain can barely compute this." Willow puts her head in her hands.

"No one is at fault. I could've corrected Zack. I didn't need to go along with it," I tell a small lie. There was no way I wasn't going to continue the thing that was having Eliza look at me how she did. I'd like to say the petty version of myself doesn't exist anymore, but truth is, she's always right below the surface.

"Listen, this isn't a big deal. We already hang out, I go to all the Cosmos games, and it's going to be fine. He'll come with me to the wedding, help me deal with the disaster that is my family, and then we'll have a quiet break-up after. Or something."

I put a piece of donut, cinnamon sugar apple cider—even though it's August— in my mouth because this is the first time I thought about how we'll end this thing. How long is long enough to seem real, but not long enough to think we're two wounded lovers? I make a mental note to ask Zack.

"Or something?" Willow asks. "You're the queen of a plan and you're telling me you don't have this part figured out yet?"

Damn it. Willow knows me too much for her own good. Or my own good. Who's to know?

I sigh out a breath. "We'll figure it out."

"I know you will, but I'm just protective of you. You deserve to have a real boyfriend with real feelings, not whatever you're trying to do with Zack."

It stings, but I also don't buy it. I've not had a serious boyfriend since Mitch, and it makes me wonder if that isn't something meant for me. No matter who it is, what kind of guy, it never felt right. I don't expect it to be easy but I'd imagine, at some point, you let the mask fall a bit—the one that's carefully constructed to be the most appealing version of yourself. Mitch was the last one who let me get that far and it still felt like raw skin from a fresh sunburn.

Maybe it's me? Is there something that makes it hard for someone to want to tie themselves to me for longer than a few nights?

I reach over and squeeze Willow's hand. I'm so thankful for the way she cares about me.

Tripp scrolls on his phone before picking it up and showing it to me. "You're doing a hell of a job. This doesn't look fake at all."

His screen shows two pictures, side by side. The first is a picture of Zack and me during dinner. We're leaning in—I don't ever remember being that close—and both of our fingers on the last french fry. The second is us in front of the restaurant before we left. I'm turned in, still looking up at him because my heels are still no match for his 6'3" frame, my hand touching the front of his chest.

A breath gets lost on its way to my lungs, and I hide it as best I can. Even though I've seen every rendition of every angle of the same photos, they're still jarring. It's because we look like a true couple, not able to get enough of each other.

They take me back to when we were out front of Trivium. While the press interaction was less than a minute, I lived through it in slow motion, on repeat, before I could get any sleep.

Sleep has never been easy for me. My mind runs and gallops when I try to wind down—at this point, I hope it picks a good hole to fall into. Last night, thinking about Zack and me and how we might pull this off, was one of the best scenarios as far as my brain getting stuck.

It was me, placing my hand on his front, feeling the soft fabric of his Versace shirt on his hard muscles. His hand reached around and landed on the top of my hip, his fingers moving back and forth, almost like he was getting comfortable. Then it was him, looking at me, his eyes the perfect shade of blue. Only for a few fleeting seconds but it felt like he was peeking at the corners of myself, the ones I keep tucked back.

He was *really* looking at me.

I let out a breath, keeping my face neutral in front of Tripp and Willow. Keeping myself as unbothered as possible is key to the two of them letting this go.

"Everything will be the same. Except the randoms won't be sitting at our table. And Zack and I will hold hands and sit by each other, things like that."

Tripp lets out a laugh, one I'm grateful for. "No randoms for Zack? After the off-season he had? Nothing will be the same." He bumps into Willow's shoulder.

My skin prickles, and I roll my shoulders—up, down, and back—trying to release the tightness. I reach for my iced coffee, needing a drink to swallow past whatever is stuck in my throat.

Chapter 10
Zack

"Andersen, why the hell are you waddling like that?" Coach asks as I move spots on the field for my next practice circuit. He's already turned and walking away from me. Clearly a rhetorical question then.

It's because I'm a fucking slacker and currently paying for every day I did something other than move my body or lift a weight. I was a dickhead during the off-season, and now my muscles are revolting.

Snickers and laughs from my teammates cut in before I can answer. "That new redhead teaching you a thing or two?" someone asks, and I know it's going to be a thing the minute I see Tripp's eyes flash and catch mine.

Yup. Here we go.

I follow Tripp as he approaches whoever made the redhead comment.

"No comments on the redhead," he points at the group as they smirk back at him. Tripp has always had dad energy, like someone you didn't want to disappoint, but it also makes him a perfect target. "She's my friend, Willow's assistant, and kind of works for the non-profit. Leave it alone," he commands while turning back.

"Zack's the one—" one of the wide receivers, Julio, starts to say.

"Don't even say it," Tripp interrupts. Julio presses his lips together, raises his eyebrows and awkwardly turns away, moving to his next practice set.

Trying to diffuse any tension, I joke, "Don't worry, I'm just a little sore."

"You're not making it better, Zack," Tripp says while walking past me and toward his receiver core.

It's hard to believe this is only the second season the Upstate Cosmos have been around. Some billionaire thought New York needed another football team — she was in the minority — so the expansion draft last year brought this team together. After winning the Super Bowl in our first season—thanks to me, or really, my special teams coach finally convincing our head coach to let us try a trick play we'd been dreaming about for an entire season—we've managed to keep most of the team intact.

I like it here. It's much better than Florida, my first NFL team and where the expansion draft plucked me from. Honestly, good riddance. The fans were great, you could even say spectacular, but nothing would compensate for the nightmare that was humidity. Nothing like feeling like you're breathing in the sweat of your teammates when you're trying to play football.

Before Florida, I played college football at a small Division 2 school in Illinois. Full ride scholarship and all the playtime I'd need to make it to the NFL as a special teams player.

Now I'm one of those guys who talks about the seasons. Here's the thing: I don't fucking care. At least I can breathe here, most of the time. Right now it's a bit challenging because Tripp shoots me a look which screams, "I'd pay someone to tackle you right now."

> you're kidding right

> thought she was just a friend?!

SCREENSHOTS OF PHOTOS OF Emilie and me follow Riley's messages. *Fuck me.* I didn't have a chance to bring her up to speed. We're those annoying siblings, the ones that tell each other everything. I set my phone down, pulling my shirt on, my skin still hot from the shower.

I reach for my phone, about to text Riley back, when Emilie sends a message.

> forgot to mention, talked to willow and tripp this morning

> wasn't great but also wasn't a disaster

> also my sister is poking around about you so

> no telling anyone else

I can't help but roll my eyes. I hate keeping things from Riley but the least I can do is what Emilie asked. Her situation is higher stakes than telling my little sister. Riley will get over it, and if not, we can fight about it for the next few years.

> secret club

> i like it

> can confirm tripp is not happy

There's no way I can leave my sister on read, so I open our conversation and my brain aches. This is why you shouldn't tell lies because how the fuck do you keep them straight? I text Riley back, trying not to grin at the pictures of Emilie and me, which was the last thing she sent.

As soon as I put my phone in my pocket, trying to get away from my sister, Tripp is walking toward me like someone put his tennis shoes in the showers or pissed in his cereal. The locker room is conveniently empty. Wonder why people didn't want to hang around?

"You really know how to clear a room," I laugh at Tripp.

"Just remember, whatever you're doing with her, she's not someone who will disappear when you get bored." His voice is stern, but still full of care and caution.

Ouch. That stings. Doesn't mean he isn't onto something. I've not been known to ever really pursue someone for more than an evening. But this isn't even that; it's not real.

"It's just for the wedding and then—"

If Tripp rolled his eyes any harder, they'd get stuck looking at his brain. "I heard the same thing from Emilie this morning. Don't need the speech. Just be careful." He lets out a breath, an emphatic pause. "She's important."

His eyes latch onto mine, and I hear the message loud and clear: don't hurt Emilie.

Tripp squeezes my shoulder and is out the door before I have a chance to say another word.

⚬ ✕✕✕
↳ ooo
o

"I'M JUST SAYING, IT'D be nice to hear things from you before the women at Pilates ask me about it." My mom shrugs her shoulders as she sits back with a cup of tea.

"Mack, he's a grown man. Give him some space," my dad says before placing a kiss on her cheek. She leans into him as a grin starts to form, knowing it's coming before his lips touch her skin.

They've been like this my whole life—in deep, deep love. I used to joke about how disgusting they were and had my fair share of get-a-room-paired-with-an-eye-roll tantrums. It only took a sleepover at a buddy's house, and an uncomfortable after-dinner fight between his parents, before I started to realize how lucky I was. I'll never forget how they spoke to each other, how the pit in my stomach grew.

Mackenzie and Christopher Andersen set the standard high for what forever could look like. They loved and supported Riley and me in big ways. Even though they both worked demanding jobs—my dad as a pilot and my mom a marketing executive—they did their best to show up for us.

They still do, as they sit in my apartment, bringing over lunch from my favorite deli from our home neighborhood—about an hour away.

Mom continues her prodding. "I'm just saying, we finally get you back for a long period of time and you've got a mystery girlfriend? When do we get to meet her?"

"I'm sure you've met. She's always at Cosmos things." I try to sidestep the pointed request.

"Don't act like you don't know what she means. She wants to ask her at least fifty questions, preferably over a meal. You know, really get into it," my dad teases, sarcasm dripping from his words as my mom nudges him playfully.

I'm a jackass. I should've called my parents as soon as Riley texted me about Emilie.

Truth is? I love family dinner. When I was away for college or living in Florida, I'd come home every time I had the chance. The guys would give me such shit for not staying back to party or hang out, but it was worth it.

"Once Riley's back in town, we can come over for dinner," I reply, watching my mom's face light up like she found something she's been looking for.

My heart picks up, thinking about bringing Emilie to my family home, which means the world to me. I offered to buy my parents a new place when I signed my first big contract with guaranteed money, but they refused. My mom always used to say, "There's too much love in these walls to give it up." I would pretend gag but secretly sigh in relief, knowing our home meant as much to them as it did to me.

There's something special about being able to go home to your bedroom. Not that I'd show Emilie my bedroom. I mean, yes, I would show it to her, but there wouldn't be anything for us to do in there.

"Why are your cheeks so red?" Mom puts the back of her hand on my forehead, like she's feeling for a fever.

And because I can't say, "Well, I'm thinking about bringing my pretend girlfriend back to my room, and it's kind of hot but it shouldn't be," I answer, "It's kind of hot in here. I'm going to turn the AC down."

I walk to the thermostat before they can look too closely and find a tell—point out they know I'm lying.

"Are we on for golf next week?" I ask my dad. We try to get out a few times a month, just the two of us.

My dad is looking at his phone, not paying attention.

"Chris, did you hear Zack? Are you golfing next week?" my mom repeats.

My dad's cheeks tint pink before he puts his phone face down. "Ah, sorry. Next week won't work. I'll check my work calendar." He offers a smile.

He seems distracted, but who am I to talk?

Chapter 11
Emilie

WHY CAN'T I TAKE a full breath? I throw the blankets off and practically jump out of bed. Tapping my phone screen, it says it's after midnight. I've been lying here for over an hour yet I'm nowhere near sleep.

I can't put my finger on what's wrong, but I don't feel right. It's like my skin is a size too small, and there's too much pressure on my bones. I feel like I'm sideways in a world that's completely upright.

I walk through the apartment; the rhythm of my steps is consistent, a stark contrast to my erratic heartbeat—it frantically flutters and flips. My limbs feel weightless, kind of how I'd imagine space to be.

Space. I hate space. Oblivion. Darkness. So much nothing. Nothing to hold on to.

Fuck. This is taking a turn for the worse.

I bite my lip hard, needing to feel the sting. It's there in a reassuringly painful way. My brain tries to run but keeps stumbling, getting stuck on the things that I hide from during the day. The thoughts I'm able to manage, most of the time, and tend to only come out at night. I pinch the skin of my forearm, like how I wish I could squeeze the intrusive thoughts which are a rabbit hole away from bringing me to my knees.

After countless laps around the living room and kitchen, I pause and check my pulse. *Count and feel.* Count the heart beats, feel the blood move through my body.

I am here.

This is real.

I am safe.

I grip my phone, my safety net—what if I have to call 911? Tapping the screen, I see that only three minutes have passed, even though it feels like it's been almost an hour. Fuck. It feels like I'm floating.

Sitting on the edge of a chair in the living room, I put my head between my knees. I suck in as much air as my lungs will allow and hold. Each second that passes, I keep the breath, and my heart rate slows from a sprint to a skip.

I try to take a deep breath but the corners of my mouth resist—the skin cracking and strained. My tongue pushes against the roof of my mouth, then my lower lip, and it feels like there's no room for it. Is it swelling? Can I swallow? Is this what an allergic reaction feels like?

My mind runs through the last few hours, trying to find the culprit. The traitor.

The trigger.

When I come up empty on a reason why, I practically jog into the kitchen, desperate for cold water. My hand swings the cabinet door open, definitely too hard, and I grab the first glass I can find.

Shoving the glass under the faucet, I only let it fill up halfway before chugging it. The tightness in my chest lessens with each swallow, proving my throat isn't closing. I wipe my mouth with the back of my hand.

Buzz. A text message comes in.

Zack

> look at this shit

He sends an article, and while I've seen this picture in twenty different versions, the headline is a new one: ***Zack Andersen Fumbles His Look While Date Scores Big.*** A perfect distraction. It's like he knew I was spiraling.

I skim the article from our night at Trivium, which calls out Zack for wearing something boring, lazy, and uninspired. Meanwhile, my outfit gets 4.5 red-bottom shoes, indicating a successful outfit.

it wasn't boring

I mean obviously, you look good but

I thought WE looked good

Me

how did you even find this?

woah didn't expect you to be up

FJ sent it. Convinced the guy has a Google alert set up and just waits for something like this to send in our group chat

Fritz, or FJ, is an equipment manager for the Upstate Cosmos. And Zack is probably right. While they are all close friends, they love to pick on Zack when given an opportunity.

we did look good

don't let the low brow clickbait get you down

why are you awake

Instead of telling the truth, something like, "Well, I'm in a crippling obsessive-compulsive disorder episode and the intrusive thoughts feel like they could choke me," I tell a little white lie.

Nightmare. Can't fall back asleep.

I see the bubbles, indicating Zack is typing, come up and disappear a few times. And then the phone rings.

"Hello?"

"That article is going to keep me up. That's my nightmare," Zack says, his words quick and choppy.

I feel my lips slightly shift from the firmly pressed line to the smallest start of a smirk.

"Why did you call?" I ask, genuinely wanting to know the answer. My mouth is dry, and I cough, covering the hoarseness of my voice.

Zack sighs. "Not being able to sleep is the worst. I thought I could tell you a story and maybe bore you right to sleep." Even now, late at night, Zack feels like he moves at an energy level I can only tap into on special occasions.

This isn't how I expected my night to go.

"You don't have to do that—"

"I know I don't. Maybe I'm the one who needs a distraction from that fucking article," Zack scoffs, which makes me almost laugh. "Two things. One, do you want to talk about your nightmare?"

There's nothing to talk about, so I reply, "No. Not really."

"Valid. Two, do you have breakfast plans for tomorrow morning?"

Tomorrow. Wednesday. The middle of the week.

"No plans."

"Want to come with me to my favorite breakfast spot in the morning? I could meet you at your place, and we could walk together."

Zack lives close by, maybe a ten minute walk. There's no reason not to go to breakfast, minus the fact that I might be dead tired, depending on how the rest of the night goes.

"Breakfast sounds good. As long as it's not some fashion revenge tour. I need tomorrow to be low-key."

I almost trip over my words. I'm still taking in the distraction from my overactive brain.

"Definitely an athleisure type of spot," he confirms. When I don't say anything else, Zack continues, "Why don't you go get cozy? And have you ever heard about the one where I went to an amateur male stripper night?"

For some reason, I'm compelled to listen. I walk to my bedroom.

"No, I haven't heard that one, but I don't want any more nightmares." I fall into my bed and pull the covers to my chin.

Zack laughs, light and clear. "Oh, this is a funny story. Promise."

He launches into the story, his voice inflecting up and down in a way you'd hear someone read a children's book, not like he's talking about getting naked on stage.

"Really, it was poor marketing on their part. I thought I was showing up to a boy band dance contest. Rules were simple: dance to any boy band song of your choice and the winner got $500."

"What was the pull here? You don't need $500."

"Shh. This is my story," he lightly scolds on the other line. "It wasn't about the money but here's the thing... I love a boy band moment. It seemed like it would be fun. Anyways, the thing they left out was that the dancing was a strip tease."

I prop my phone up on my pillow, Zack's voice still easy to hear, and let my body relax. My bones, heavy and tired, feel comfort with the weight of the blanket. I place one hand on my chest, feeling secure in the rising and falling of my own breaths. I will myself to sink further into the mattress, the pressure welcome and like a warm hug. My eyelids flutter, struggling to stay open, until they finally lose the fight.

And I fall asleep to the sound of Zack's voice.

Chapter 12
Zack

"Want to walk around the park before we head back?" I ask Emilie as we stand outside the breakfast spot. I put out a hand, an invitation.

She holds her iced coffee like it's a life source. I brought her one when I met her at her apartment, and she ordered another at breakfast this morning.

It's early but there's still a person lurking with a camera, documenting this entire interaction. Doesn't bother me—take those pictures and post them. Kind of counting on it. If one thing's clear, I need to make this work—pull it off—for Emilie.

The way she sounded last night is hard to get out of my head. It was like you could reach out and grab the panic. Emilie has always been consistent, together, and one step ahead of most. Hearing her like that was the equivalent of nails on a chalkboard.

The sun hits Emilie's face and she pulls her sunglasses on, abandoning the top of her head. One corner of her lip pulls up as she reaches for my outstretched hand, her fingers slipping into mine.

The smile that takes over my face has no business being this bright. Emilie is always holding someone's hand—it's kind of her thing. Could be a stranger on a plane, Willow, or someone in the suite during a game.

Chill the fuck out, Zack. This is nothing.

I pull her closer as we walk through the park entrance. It's early enough that it's decently empty. We walk in silence for a few minutes.

Birds chirp as a breeze runs through the trees, rustling the leaves still bright and green at the height of summer.

The wind tones down the August air, making it the perfect temperature.

"What's your favorite month?" I ask.

"January."

I don't know what I expected her to say but it wasn't that. My face must give me away.

She shrugs. "I like the start of something new. Fresh start. January makes me feel like I can accomplish anything."

"January makes my stomach hurt." I mimic keeling over, my free hand touching my core. "It's the heat of the playoffs. Do or die. All or nothing. Win or go home."

Emilie turns to me. "I can see that. The contrast of how we view the same time of year...it's interesting."

"I *am* interesting," I joke and bump her shoulder with mine. I can't see her eyes behind her sunglasses but I'm betting I got a signature Emilie-eyeroll.

"You're something," she says, a smile still pulling at her lips.

Ding. Her phone goes off.

"Who keeps the sound on their phone? I feel like I haven't heard mine in years." I poke her.

"Someone who feels mentally hung over," she pokes back. Emilie lets go of my hand to grab her phone. I don't need to see much to know she doesn't like what she sees.

"Everything good?"

She sighs, stares at the message for another minute, and then puts her phone back. "If by good you mean annoying. Then, yes."

I respond with nothing but big, fat silence.

"It's my family group chat. AKA hell in the digital world."

"That bad?" From what I've gathered, the family situation isn't great for Emilie. I don't need to pry. She'll tell me if she wants to.

"Consistently horrible. Currently, my sister is passive-aggressively complaining, in our family group chat, how my last minute plus one has thrown off her entire seating arrangement. What will we ever do with an odd number of attendees?!" She puts her hand on her forehead for emphasis before reaching back for mine.

Her fingers tangled in mine. I like it. Too fucking much.

"Family dinners have been even more insufferable than usual."

I can't relate to this. My family is like a puzzle with just enough pieces to keep it interesting, but they always fit together. That's how we've always been.

"Well, you should bring me. I'm known to make things more... sufferable?"

"That barely makes any sense." She laughs. "I wouldn't subject you to that. Hell, I wouldn't ask my worst enemy to subject themselves to that."

From my experience, Emilie rarely does anything she doesn't want to do. Family shit is always weird, though.

"Lucky for you, you don't even have to ask. I'm there."

She turns her face to mine, our pace slower than before. It's like she's trying to see if I'm making a joke or being serious.

I shrug and offer a smile. "I'll have to meet them eventually. Right?"

"Right..." Her voice trails off, like a question, and I can hear her brain waves.

She tosses her empty coffee cup in a trash can, and we stop, looking over the park. I pull her closer to me, our sides pressed together. My hand goes from her low back to softly rest on her hip. My finger instinctively draws small circles, like I've done this a hundred times before. Like it's the only right choice to make.

Emilie turns her head toward me, looking up. I give her a small smile, taking in her details—ones I already know. The freckles that smatter the bridge of her nose. Her lips that honestly look like someone drew a heart where they'd go.

I'm trying to pay attention. With Emilie, it feels like I should.

"What are you doing?" she asks, pulling me back to the moment. Our noses are almost touching. I must've leaned in, looking for more things to catalog.

A camera. Out of my peripheral vision. Consider my ass saved.

I put my finger under her chin and lean close to her ear. "There's a camera, right over there." It's almost like she relaxes just enough for me to feel it.

I press a for-show kiss on her cheek.

Or at least that's what I tell myself it is.

Chapter 13
Emilie

"WHAT THE HELL DOES a girl gotta do to get a heads up that you're banging an NFL player?"

I almost spit out my coffee as Keegan puts her phone down, a picture of Zack and me walking hand in hand filling the screen. Just like in college at the University of Michigan, Keegan always knows how to make an entrance.

"You're late," I retort while watching her situate her bag and sit across from me. The coffee shop buzzes around us; people working with headphones and having their own conversations is a reprieve from prying eyes or ears.

"Ma'am, no. You don't get to tell me I'm late when you've been withholding information." She claps her hands for each syllable. "Spill."

I don't want to lie but it's necessary. The less people know the truth, the better.

"It's casual. Just sort of happened." I sip my coffee, holding the mug like it's precious, as I deliver the most boring and vague answer I can think of.

Keegan rolls her eyes, almost too brown to be real, and grabs her own mug. She sips the foamy cappuccino and her eyes land on mine.

"How long has it sort of been happening?" She narrows her eyes over the steam of her mug.

It's been two weeks since the event, when this whole thing transpired, so I'm careful when I answer, "A few weeks."

She nods and takes another sip before saying, "Zack Andersen doesn't seem like your type."

Joke's on her—I don't really have a type.

She tucks a strand of short blonde hair behind her ears. "I mean, he seems kind of like... an equal opportunist." Her voice rises at the end.

I give her a side-eye.

"I'm just saying. He seems to bounce around. One interest to another."

"He's not bouncing now," I reply, hoping it's true. "And it doesn't matter, people can bounce wherever they please." I shoot her a knowing glance.

I don't care who people sleep with. Unless we've come to an agreement, committed to one another, it's none of my business. Love is love and orgasms are orgasms.

Zack does have a bit of a playboy reputation but it's tired. Who cares who he hooks up with if he's single? I'm aware that if this was a woman, the headlines would have a much different connotation.

My brain runs through the list of names I've seen Zack with. Models, professional athletes, actresses, baristas; he doesn't discriminate. It's always him, his messy blonde hair which always seems to work, and he's usually wearing that smile.

Ugh, don't go there. Don't think of *that* smile.

Keegan snaps me out of it. "Please tell me he's coming with you to Eliza's wedding," she pleads, her brown eyes look like they're filled with honey in this lighting.

I'm thankful for the topic shift. "Obviously," I say, like it's a no-brainer and not a thing Zack walked into. "He has a bye week. Kind of wild how our schedules lined up." That part is true. No idea what the odds are for something like this to line up, but it feels like it has a tinge of meant-to-be.

I switch topics seamlessly. "Tell me about the store. How's it going?"

These are the magic words, as Keegan launches into the boutique store she opened last year. Her business degree helps her succeed when it comes to the finances and books, but her eye for detail and fashion savvy keeps her buying the trending pieces before they trend. Her brain is beautiful, and I love listening to her talk about the store with such passion.

I adore the store. I brought Willow there last year, and the press helped bring some well-deserved buzz to Keegan. I'm so proud of how far she's come.

She's telling me about this new lingerie line she started carrying when my phone buzzes.

Zack

I know it's last minute but come out with me tonight

there's a bar I've wanted to go to and finally got Tripp and Willow onboard

you in?

That's just like him; three rapid fire texts, back to back to back. My stomach flips and the feeling catches me off guard. *Come out with me.* I read the texts in the way I imagine him speaking. Now I'm back in my bed, my heart beat slowing from the panic.

How did he know I needed a distraction? Zack texted me when I was about to hit the point of no return and instead, because of him, I could sleep. My chest warms at the unexpected comfort.

"Emilie! Sis. Look at you!" Keegan squeals, both hands hitting the sides of the table.

Heads snap toward us.

I shush her. "What are you talking about?"

"You, blushing, smiling. Let me guess—Zack?" She gestures to the phone. I roll my eyes even though she's spot on.

I shouldn't be blushing or letting my mind wander. There's nothing to think about when everything is fabricated.

I nod as I text him back. The grin I'm wearing pinches at my cheeks. It's too damn easy to play this part.

> Me
>
> meeting at 6, as long as it's after

> I'll be at your place at 9

The wave of warmth that runs over my skin at the thought of him picking me up. Ugh, swoon. I smile at Keegan because I can feel her watching me.

Buzz.

> can't miss out on a good photo opp

I don't let my face show the drop in my mood. Damn it, Emilie. Why are you doing this to yourself? The scolding isn't enough to take control of the situation and lessen the sting. The reminder. Even though I know none of this is real, there are these moments, glimmers, where it feels like it might be more than what we're giving ourselves credit for.

It's not fair to Zack for me to do that, put that on him. We have a clear agreement, with rules and expectations. There's nothing sexy about that.

Hell, it's not fair for me to fall into the pit with shards of anxiety and jealousy waiting at the bottom. I put my phone in my bag, not needing any other messages from Zack or anyone else at this point, and sip my coffee, wondering where my self-awareness escaped to.

Chapter 14
Emilie

WE WALK HAND IN hand, Zack obnoxiously swinging our arms back and forth, as we approach the bar. I prefer to hold hands, whether it's with friends or partners, or in this sense, fake partners. My therapist tells me it's a sensory thing, while I think it's about needing to feel wanted. Maybe we're both right.

"How was the meeting?" he asks.

Honestly, since Willow started her own label, it's been a dream. "So good. It's been so fun finding new venues for the second set of dates. Everyone I talk to is excited."

Willow recently wrapped up her first leg of the new tour, and I'm currently planning a second. I love being in control of where she's going to play.

"Sounds like we need to have some fun then," Zack says, his voice smooth and convincing, like he's daring me.

I look over at Zack and catch him looking at me, smiling. He's wearing a black shirt, jeans, and these Nike sneakers I know he had to pull strings to get. Even in the most casual of clothes, he looks good enough to eat.

I also went with sneakers tonight, but paired them with a pleated red skirt, which hits right above the knee, and a black top which hugs my shoulders with a wide neck. Keegan picked it out, straight from her boutique, and the woman doesn't miss.

The top dips a little low, enough to see my cleavage, but we're going out. Plus, I feel good in it. Keegan has a knack for picking out things I'd never choose for myself, but I end up feeling like I belong in it.

We approach the door, knowing Willow and Tripp are already inside, and the security guard waves us in. The bar is dark but has strategic lighting placed throughout, which makes it feel intimate, but also not like you're locked in a basement.

Walking into the VIP area is still something I'll never get used to. The second the security guard saw us, someone was waiting to take us to our table. We walk up a short flight of stairs and to the spot—cozy benches with plush velvet pillows and some fabric intentionally draped to create a barrier between one section to the next. Willow and Tripp are sitting next to each other, waiting.

"Hey, love birds!" Tripp jokes when he sees us. Willow gives him a playful shove in response.

Playing the part with Zack has been too easy over the last three weeks. That isn't lost on me as Zack leads me in front of him, his hand grazing my hip before I sit down. I so badly want to look at the places where his fingers touched the fabric, almost like he smeared me with paint, but I show some restraint. Now, all I can think of is his hands on me and how I'm not wearing tights under this skirt.

"Ready for some fun?" Zack says close to my ear, his lips practically in my loose curls, as he sits next to me.

Fuck, I need a drink.

THE BAR KEEPS BRINGING samples of signature cocktails to our table, and it's clear I haven't eaten enough today. I'm only on my second Aperol

Spritz but I'm a tad tipsy, the buzz of the alcohol running over my skin. When the bartender brings a basket of truffle fries, I practically throw myself in front of them.

Zack and I reach for the same one—what is this phenomenon of us doing this with fries?—and laugh. This time, he puts the fry in his mouth and leaves most of it out, leaning toward me. I don't know if it's the drinks, or Willow laughing hysterically, but I bite—literally. I bite down, our noses close, our lips almost touching, for my portion of the french fry.

"I can't believe he shares food with you," Tripp says, loud enough to be heard over the packed bar. Even the VIP area has people spilling out from their booths and tables.

I shoot Zack a look that says, "Huh?"

"Just because I don't like *your* grimy hands touching *my* food doesn't mean that goes for everyone."

"You've never let *me* have any of your food," Willow chimes in.

Interesting. The flush pinches my cheeks, part cocktail and part Zack looking from me to Willow and Tripp.

Zack leans into the whole thing, wrapping an arm around my shoulder as he pulls me in. When he kisses me on my forehead, Willow and Tripp start cheering, and I can feel my face getting as red as my hair.

"Alright, I'm going to get another drink. Anyone need one?" I ask and am almost walking toward the bar before I get all the words out. I know the server will bring us more drinks, but I think I need a break.

It was all getting too easy. The leaning into the touch. Our legs bumping into one another. The quick glance but catching one another. Over and over. The way I kept stealing looks at his mouth.

I fill my lungs with air, holding the breath as I lean on the counter.

"She'll take an Aperol Spritz," a voice from behind me says. But it isn't Zack.

Colton.

Goosebumps cover my arms as he lightly presses a hand on my low back. "It's been a minute, Emmy," he says, too close to my face, before putting a piece of my hair in between his fingers and lightly tugging.

I hate that nickname. Emmy. I only let him call me that because the sex was good enough to make the exception.

"My situation has changed," I reply, giving him a small smile before intently watching the bartender make my drink. Colton isn't the guy you date, but he is the guy you have casual sex with when you cross paths. He's respectful, safe, and a good time. He's also who I would call when I got frustrated enough with dating disasters.

My belly used to flip when I'd see him out—his look telling me everything I needed to know about where we'd end up. But now? There's absolutely nothing besides the itch to get back to Zack.

"How so?"

I look over to our spot just as Zack glances over to me, hands running through his hair, almost like he knew I was thinking about him.

Colton clicks tongue and laughs. "I saw that. Didn't quite buy it," he jokes.

Alarm bells go off in my head, and I do my best to keep my face level.

"Nothing for you to buy," I shrug, not angry or annoyed, just telling the truth. Out of everything at stake, my casual hookup isn't high on the list.

"Whatever you say." He leans his forearms on the bar and looks at me. "My number's the same," Colton murmurs while the bartender puts my drink on the bar.

Walking back to my friends, I can feel Colton's eyes on me—the same way I always could. This time it makes me want to walk faster, get out of his line of sight.

"Who was that?" Zack asks as soon as I sit next to him. Willow and Tripp are having their own conversation. I take a drink and the bubbles dance on my tongue, balanced by the comfortable bitterness of the Aperol. "An old friend."

"One you don't play with anymore?" Zack asks, leaning in closer. His eyes are intense, the warm light of the bar showing off their depth—like the bluest of waters you picture in your mind.

"I've got someone else to play with." I put my fingers on the front of his shirt and gently tug him toward me until his nose is right in front of mine.

It might be the drinks, the run-in with Colton, or the smirk that won't leave Zack's face whenever I look at him, but there's no air to breathe. My lungs are tight. I need a break.

"I'm going to the restroom," I say, on my way before the words are out of my mouth.

On my way to the hallway, I try to catch my breath and am thankful we're in the VIP area. Since I'm not with any of my counterparts, no one stops me—they don't know who I am. Thank god.

The hallway is long and dimly lit, except for lights that line the floor and the tops of the ceilings on each side of where the wall meets. Luckily, there's no one down here standing around—in the VIP area there is never a line for the restroom, which is a definite perk.

My back hits the wall and I tip my head, looking at the line of lights, and close my eyes for a few seconds. *Breathe in, hold, and out, hold.* I repeat the exercise a few times and get the urge to open my eyes.

Zack. Coming this way.

"You good?" he asks, his voice soft.

I'm not sure, which is unsettling. It's not that I always have the answers but I typically have them when it comes to me and my feelings—hyper self-awareness and all that.

Before I can string together an answer, or an excuse, Zack steps closer, putting his left forearm on the wall. My breath stops in my throat. I'm frozen.

What is this?

He uses a finger, the one not an inch from my head, and lightly touches my chin, tipping it up to him. Zack turns his head and slowly starts to lean in.

Is he?

Fuck.

It's in this moment that I know, I want nothing more in the world for him to kiss me.

Chapter 15
Zack

I'm too close. Too fucking close. This is the cruel game I've been playing all night—and I'm not the only one.

I chalk it up to the rules she set. Maybe there's not much at risk, since this has an expiration date? No chance to get caught up?

Fuck. I don't know.

What I do know is Emilie is a magnet, pulling me to her, which explains how I ended up in a dark hallway. Whoever she was talking to at the bar was about to follow her in and that wasn't going to work for me.

I'm practically breathing her in—citrus and vanilla. Her eyes reflect the lights on the ceiling; they're like dark honey with emeralds encroaching on the edges. That's how close I am.

"What are you doing?" Her voice is breathy and shallow. I feel her swallow, my finger still underneath her chin.

I move in, my lips grazing her cheek before I whisper in her ear, "Someone was about to follow you in." My eyes look to the side, giving her a clue.

For a second, it feels like her back arches and her hips move forward, maybe by half an inch but it feels much more than that.

Emilie darts her eyes to the guy who was at the bar, who is currently standing around like he has his dick in his hand.

He thought he was going to pop in here with her? Not tonight, my guy. Game over.

"Colton is harmless," she murmurs in my ear as I'm dipped down, still leaning into her.

I move my face back enough to take hers in. "Old boyfriend?" I might come off as a jealous prick, and that's really saying something for a fake boyfriend, but I don't give a fuck.

Emilie's body moves with a snicker. "Jealous?"

Yes.

"You didn't answer my question," I reply, the muscles flexing in my jaw.

Her lips pull into a lopsided smile and she sinks further back into the wall. "Not a boyfriend." Her eyes are looking into mine like there's an answer to something she's been needing. "More like a fuck friend."

Fuck friend? I didn't expect her to say that.

"Whenever we crossed paths and were available, we'd hook up. Nothing emotional." Her voice is matter of fact, like she's telling me about the weather.

My dick twitches at the thought of her naked. Her skin, creamy and bare. Those perfect tits on full display. The curve of her thighs up and around her ass. I wonder what she looks like when she comes undone?

"Any other fuck friends in this bar? Boyfriends? Anyone else eager to follow you into a dark hallway?"

Emilie shakes her head no. "Well, no one besides you." She winks, and I swear to god I can't help the devilish laugh that escapes me. I pull my head back and shake it, desperate to get a grip.

The push and pull. The push of the fabricated nature of this whole thing but the pull of the way she looks at me, how her skin feels touching mine, the way my hands feel as if they belong on her.

"Just me, huh?" I tease, tucking a strand of hair behind her ear before grazing her jaw.

Her eyes blink slowly. "Just you," she answers, quiet enough that I can barely hear her. But I feel her lips move—that's how close I am.

Our mouths are a sigh apart. A single shift from either of us and they'd be touching. Fuck, I want to kiss her. Maybe I should?

Her chest rises and falls, quicker than before. The result of us, like this.

"Are you going to kiss me?" Emilie asks, catching me off guard.

I almost answer her with a kiss. A resounding yes. But her eyes glance to her right, just for the briefest of seconds. I follow suit and see Colton, still awkwardly standing around.

This changes things.

I lean in, and before our lips could hit, I move my head to the side. "Here's the thing," I murmur, my voice low and raspy. "The first time I kiss you won't be in front of any of your old fuck friends." I can feel her suck in a breath. "Or when we have friends waiting for us to get back." I tip my head into hers.

"Is that so?" she asks, her voice shaky in a way you could only hear if you were really listening for it.

"Fucking positive. You only get one first kiss, and I plan to make the most of it." I barely know what I'm saying but I don't know if I could ever just kiss her once, in a dark hallway.

"I'm the kind of guy who likes to take his time."

But because I can't help myself, my lips graze from her ear lobe down to the crook of her neck, where I plant a soft kiss.

Emilie presses into it.

And I *almost* give in.

Chapter 16
Emilie

Willow and I walk hand in hand to the high-security entrance. Even though I've done this before, today feels different. Charged.

Granted, it is the Upstate Cosmos' first game of the season, and it's at home since they're the reigning Super Bowl champions. It might only be their second season in the NFL but you'd never be able to tell from their fan base.

Seth, Willow's head of security, walks a few steps ahead of us. Even though the security here is more than sufficient, he needs to be in control. I know he'll stand outside of the suite for most of the game, just like he always does.

We love him, though.

Since it's the home opener, I thought Zack's parents would come but apparently they get too nervous and don't attend many games.

Today, I get that. My stomach feels like it's tied in a knot, and with each minute closer to kick-off, it pulls tighter. I went to almost all of the home games last year and yes, I wanted the Cosmos to win, but now it's different.

We walk into the suite and are greeted by familiar faces—mostly WAGS, wives and girlfriends, of other players. They take me in wearing Zack's jersey tailored into a dress and paired with a charcoal gray slip underneath, the lace peeking out at the bottom. I'm wearing Cosmos blue glitter boots—a perk to being Willow's assistant. Stylists, brands, and anything you can think of will send her things to wear on game day, and sometimes I benefit.

I walk to the glass and try to spot Zack. He's easy to find in the special teams core because he looks like a kernel of popcorn in hot oil. The man's energy is unmatched—that's how it's always been on game day.

Zack stretches with a teammate, and I swear I can hear his laugh from here. Seeing him on the field has my nerves fighting for their life. There's no denying I'm nervous but also ridiculously excited.

Today's going to be fun.

The stadium fills with fans, waves of Cosmos blue in all sorts of formats—everything from face paint to custom jerseys. I love the energy before a home game. It's almost like a living, breathing thing.

The Jumbotron is showing warmups, cutting from one group to the next. Football is bizarre to me considering it's rough. Dangerous. But it's also like a carefully choreographed dance, each player with their own responsibility and timing to make it all come together.

It's fascinating. It always has been. No matter how busy I was during my time at the University of Michigan, I never missed a home football game. There's something special about The Big House on a Saturday.

I will say, the Upstate Cosmos' home games are the only thing that's come close to that feeling.

The smell of truffle popcorn hits me, and I know my favorite snack has entered the chat. I have no idea what they do to make it so addicting; like, I could eat an entire bucket on my own. Hell, I've probably done that at some point. I pop some of the buttery, savory kernels in my mouth and look to see Zack on the Jumbotron.

He's snapping the ball to different teammates. It's kind of wild to me that his job is this niche—hold the ball and basically get it anywhere from six to fifteen yards to a teammate behind you. Typically, long snappers only touch the field for punts and extra point attempts, but I bet the Cosmos will try and use Zack as a decoy this season.

He has shown he's capable of legitimately throwing the ball and hitting the intended target. Teams will always suspect a trick play when the ball is in his hands, or if they bring him out for a play, even though it's just to pull the attention from the actual play call.

The screen cuts to the highlight I'm sure everyone in this stadium has seen: Zack throwing the game-winning touchdown and Tripp catching it. Everyone cheers like it's happening in real time. My chest warms at the thought of all these fans being proud of Zack and Tripp.

Zack walks near the sideline, his hands gesturing like he's trying to pull more energy from the crowd, and they deliver. Fans scream and holler when Zack gets closer to their area.

That's when he sees the suite. He goes from getting the crowd hyped up to putting his hands on his hips, weight on one leg.

He's looking right at me. My breath catches in my throat and it's as if he knows what he's doing to me because he waves toward the suite. Anyone in here who is paying attention starts to clap while some put their hands on my shoulders, playfully jostling me.

And then Zack blows me a kiss. Not only does the suite get loud, but the Jumbotron cameraman has his lens on us. Just in time to see me smiling, ear-to-ear, and putting my head in my hands.

Willow reaches for my hand, squeezes, and catches my eyes. She smiles—knowing and pointed—in a way a friend does when they have something to talk to you about, not now but later.

How in the fuck is the camera this good? My blushing cheeks, almost matching my crimson hair, are on display for 76,000 fans. The stadium erupts in cheers, and Zack joins in, clapping and walking back toward his teammates.

Before he gets too far, he looks back at me, that Zack Andersen smirk at full voltage. The same lips I was begging to kiss. The same mouth I wanted on mine a few nights ago.

The same man who has an innate ability to make me question things I thought I was sure about. Like, how I couldn't date Zack for real. Out of the question. Not in the realm of possibility.

But now? I'm not so sure.

THE UPSTATE COSMOS WIN their first game of the season. My cheeks ache from smiling, and my bones are a happy kind of exhausted. It was the screaming fans that really drove this home; the energy surges to the tip top before dipping and coming back again, sometimes all within a single play.

Since Zack is a special teams player, his performance is measured in mistakes, which is sort of brutal. There are no yards to rack up, points to score, or receptions to aim for. Today, it doesn't matter because he was perfect.

I find myself standing alone, taking in families finding their player, in their own bubbles. Willow and Tripp already left—I said I'd get a ride with Zack.

I pretend to focus on the toes of my boots. Glitter reflects the light and it's like a disco party on the tile floor. There's no issue with me spending time alone; it's more that I don't want to encroach on anyone's moment.

My solo-disco-party is short-lived when arms wrap around me.

"One and oh, baby!" Zack picks me up, my back to his front, and his chin finds a spot in the space between my shoulder and neck. My stomach flips like I'm at the top of the rollercoaster, waiting for the drop.

When Zack sets me down, I turn and wrap my arms around his neck. "Everyone was great today. Good job," I beam.

It's not lost on me how natural this feels. Him picking me up. Me hugging him like I've done it a thousand times.

He grabs my hand and steps back. The man spins me in a circle, letting out a long whistle, like we're on a movie set.

"You look so fucking good," he says, "Like, it's unfair." And just when I think my cheeks couldn't get any redder, he looks to the people around us and asks, "When has this jersey looked better?! Anyone? Nothing? Right. Just as I suspected."

The people around us laugh at Zack. Some of them start to clap, and if I could show someone a ten-second clip which encompassed Zack Andersen as a person, I'd show this one.

He's wearing a salmon pink suit and a white dress shirt, with the first few buttons undone. Most guys change into something more comfortable or choose to do something leisurely, but Zack loves a fashion moment. His bangs fall forward—this is what I call the 'heartthrob hair cut'—and his eyes are bright blue, just like the jersey I'm wearing.

"Let's take a selfie." He pulls his phone out.

I step into him, putting one hand on his stomach, and it's met with hard muscles. My throat is dry—I need water. He tips his head closer to mine, makes sure we're both in the frame, and takes a few pictures.

"Turn around. I want a picture of my jersey." He smiles in a way that makes it impossible to tell him no.

I turn, my back on full display.

"Can't get enough of yourself, can ya, Zack?" a teammate asks, all in good fun.

Feeling like I gave Zack enough time to get the picture he wanted, I turn back, just as Zack says, "When you get someone this gorgeous in your jersey, you soak it in any way you can."

Charming as fuck. He always is.

"French fries and ice cream?" he asks.

There's only one answer to that. "Absolutely."

Zack intertwines his fingers with mine, and warmth spreads over my entire body. It's his hand in mine. Him calling me gorgeous. Him looking at me like that.

We walk to the exit, and Zack reaches for the door but pauses before he opens it. He doesn't ask if I'm ready or warn me about what's on the other side. Instead, he looks me square in the face and says, "Fuck. I can't get over you in my jersey."

When he opens the door, the first thing anyone sees is me beaming at him—a million watts, no shame. He's looking at me like I'm something special, something to keep. His eyes fall to the lace, where it hits mid-thighs. Now he's looking at me like something he wants to devour.

Get it together, Emilie.

My mind zones out the sound of the press vying for Zack's attention, asking borderline inappropriate questions about the two of us. It's almost like everything is muffled and my brain has run out of room—no computing power left.

That's what his fucking smirk does to me.

Right as we're through the paparazzi, a blonde woman—someone I don't know—is standing there with her hands on her hips, clearly waiting for Zack.

"Oh, fuck," he groans as soon as he sees her.

She's hard to miss, considering she might be one of the most beautiful humans I've seen in real life. Model status. The kind of features that people dream about, the kind artists paint.

"Baby, you never called me back," the blonde woman says, taking a step toward him, like he's not holding my hand.

Does she not see me standing right here?

"No, I haven't." Zack looks at me, reinforcing the point, and she turns, recognizing my presence for the first time. Bold.

"I thought we had fun," she pouts—like actually puts out her bottom lip.

Zack squeezes my hand, obviously uncomfortable. "We did have fun, but I thought I was clear, no strings."

"Thought you didn't do relationships?" she asks, looking not at me but at our hands intertwined.

The call out to Zack not doing relationships stings. To be fair, I've never met one of Zack's girlfriends or dates who managed to stick around for more than a week.

He shrugs. "Guess that changes when the right person comes along."

"I found us a third, if you ever change your mind. She's the Calvin Klein model that's all over the city right now." This bombshell offers up a threesome like she has an extra coupon for a free coffee and is trying to give it to a stranger. Also, I think I know what model she's talking about, and all I can think is 'wow.'

Zack laughs. "I'm going to pass, Cassie. Thanks, though." He starts walking past her.

"Here," she says, putting an envelope into his chest. Where the hell was she keeping that?

He looks at her, and her hand touching him, before he takes the envelope and we keep walking.

Zack doesn't say anything as we get situated in the car—the envelope is sitting on the console.

"So, that was Cassie. She seems fun." I clap my hands and set them in my lap. "What do you think she gave you?"

"Don't know. Don't really care."

"She waited for you in a parking lot with an envelope. You're not at all curious?"

"Not really. I'm not interested," he says, his voice calm and level. "You can look if you want."

And because I have no chill and have been curious since I saw the envelope in her hand, I take him up on his offer.

Kind of wish I hadn't.

In my hand are three nude photos—actually printed on paper—one of them has a lipstick kiss on it. I need to wash my hands.

"That's Cassie for you," Zack says, like we're talking about if it's going to rain or not, but we're planning to stay inside no matter the weather. Like it doesn't matter

"Does this happen a lot?" I ask, not sure if I really want to know the answer.

"I mean, yes and no. I get a lot of pics sent to me, digitally. Printed nudes are kind of aggressive, but I'm not dumb enough to throw them away. I'll shred them when I'm home."

"Two things. One, you and I have very different lives. Two, this is kind of disgusting."

"I've not been texting her. She sent me a nude the other day, when I was working out, and I just deleted it and moved on. No big deal."

I nod in agreement. Because it shouldn't be a big deal. I mean, for someone like Zack who has experiences like this often?

But why does it feel like I've been sucker punched?

Chapter 17
Zack

"Miss fidget, what's your deal?" I ask as Emilie rolls her shoulders and stretches her neck for what seems like the eighth time in the last three minutes. We're in the car, driving to her parents' house for dinner, and she hasn't stopped moving since she got in.

We've been doing the fake dating thing for a month, and it's time to meet her parents.

She turns, with the fakest of smiles I've seen from her to date. "I'm fine. Just mentally preparing."

"What's your middle name?" I ask, trying to get her mind off whatever it's stuck on.

"James."

I expected Marie, Ann, Rose—certainly not James.

"Emilie James. That's unique. I like it."

"Thank you. People loved telling me it was a boy middle name... like letters have a gender association." Her words would roll their eyes if they had them. "What's yours?"

"William. That would make me Zachary William Andersen. I got to learn almost all the letters of the alphabet real quick."

"You're the first Zack I met with a 'K' instead of a 'c' or 'ch.'"

"Well, my first name doesn't actually have a K, it's your typical CH spelling. But I came home from school one day demanding the different spelling; apparently I had an affinity for the letter K. My parents said yes. The rest is history."

"Stop, that's adorable. My parents would never. They even changed my nickname. Like friends started calling me EJ and they told me Em or Emmy was a better fit for a girl." Her voice trails as she looks out the window.

I fucking hate that.

My hand finds her knee. I squeeze, and she looks over with a semi-sad smile on her lips. Maybe sad isn't the right word—maybe tired would be better? I know family relationships are complicated but hers seems like it's always been that way—even when she was a kid, when it's supposed to be easy.

"Well, EJ, if you want to leave early, say the word and we're out of there." When I use the new nickname, her eyes damn near sparkle.

"Thank you, Zack with a K."

"YOUR HOME IS LOVELY. It must've been special to raise a family here," I say, taking a sip of the red wine Ethan, Emilie's dad, handed me as soon as we got settled.

The vibe is tense. Eliza and Mitch sit on a couch next to Elaine, their mom. Ethan sits alone, and I sit next to Emilie on a love seat. The room is set up for social gatherings but it feels like the people currently present aren't.

"Oh, we lived in Michigan. Moved outside the city when Eliza went to NYU. She got an early acceptance into the law school."

"Wow! You're doing the law school thing?" I ask, trying to bring Eliza into the conversation.

It's like I can feel Emilie's shoulders move up to her ears as she drinks her wine.

"School wasn't for Eliza. Not a good fit for our girl. Instead, she works at Ethan's practice as an administrative assistant." Elaine smiles at Eliza. "She and Mitch do *very well* for themselves."

Emilie coughs, covers her mouth, and takes a drink of water. I nod because I have no idea how to respond to that.

I've been here for fifteen minutes and I'm starting to understand. I can't necessarily put my finger on it, but it's clear Emilie doesn't fit here.

"Emilie, have you heard from Jen?"

"No, Mom. Not since I went back to Michigan for a girls weekend that was a disaster. I don't anticipate I'll be hearing from Jen, or any of them, for a while." Her voice is pointed, defensive.

"Oh, you can't just throw away friendships, Emilie. Those girls have been with you since high school."

The rage radiating from Emilie is something I could reach out and grab. Instead, I reach for her free hand, the one not holding her glass of red wine like it's a life source.

"They didn't want to hang out with me. The only reason I got an invite was because I work with Willow. They wanted concert tickets, or a lunch date, or who knows what else."

Fuck. That stings.

Elaine rolls her eyes and scoffs. "Don't be dramatic. You don't have many friends. It'd be a shame to lose someone like Jen. Her dad and yours still play golf at the club when we're back in Michigan."

How does this keep getting worse? Doesn't she see how uncomfortable this makes her daughter? I try to think of a time I saw my mom do this with Riley, and I'm at a loss. They've had their fair share of mother-daughter fights growing up, but this is different.

"I won't be friends with someone who doesn't want me just so it's more comfortable for Dad and his golf partner." Emilie's words are sickly sweet, dripping with sarcasm, and the smile she wears goes from ear-to-ear.

My eyebrows raise with each word that comes out of her mouth, and I look down at my shoes. I'm trying to wrap my brain around the idea of someone not wanting Emilie. That just doesn't track with what I know about her.

"Well, I can't get Willow tickets, but if you ever want to see a Cosmos game, I'm sure I could hook you up."

Honestly, I don't want to give these people anything besides a reality check, but I'd do anything to change the topic of conversation, and the offer kind of just fell out of my mouth.

I'm desperate to change the vibe; the air is thick like smoke you shouldn't breathe in.

"Wait a second... I just got it," I slap my knees, sit up straighter with the realization. "You all have 'E' names." Eliza slowly blinks, while Mitch looks confused. "Big fan of the fifth letter in the alphabet or a coincidence?" I shrug my shoulders.

"Yes, we all have first names that start with the letter E," Elaine replies, her words like a scratch on a record player you want to run from.

"Oh man, you guys were on fire last week. Great first game," Mitch chimes in for the first time tonight. He pulled himself from his phone for long enough, and I don't know if I'll ever him like him more than I do in the next few seconds.

"Appreciate it. Hoping for a good season."

"Have any trick plays drawn up like the Super Bowl?" her dad asks.

"We might have something up our sleeves." I give them the generic answer before drinking the rest of my wine. I'm for sure not about to share playbook secrets with these people.

"Are you really coming to the wedding? With Emilie as a date?" Ethan asks, like Emilie isn't sitting next to me.

"As long as she'll still have me." I turn to her, hitting my knee to hers.

Her mom chimes in, like the ray of fucking sunshine she is. "So, you're dating. Exclusively?" The doubt gets stronger with each syllable.

Emilie doesn't move. She is frozen.

"Yeah." I try not to sound weird but it's fucking hard because this conversation is bonkers. "I've always had my eye on her, to be honest."

"Tell us about your first date," Eliza jumps in, trying to pin us against a wall. I know Emilie mentioned this as a possibility, but I thought she was exaggerating.

"Eliza. What are you doing?" Emilie chides, eyeing her sister with what I'd call comfortable distaste.

"Oh, I love this story. Let me tell it." I put my hand on Emilie's knee and give it a squeeze, before leaning forward, my forearms on my knees. "I knew from Tripp and Willow how obsessed Emilie is with this bakery. It's a couple blocks from her place and she always orders the same latte and gets a croissant. I heard her mention to Willow, one time when we were all out somewhere, that she wished she knew how to make croissants. So, I called the bakery and asked if they'd do an after-hours event, just her and I." I pause to steal a look at Emilie, and she's trying not to look surprised. I lean back to tell the rest of the story, so I can look from Emilie to her family.

"When I told her our date would have leftovers, she agreed. They taught us how to make croissant dough, and they gave her the recipe for the latte she's obsessed with."

"Croissants take more than one day to make," Eliza sneers, speculating that I'm not telling the truth.

"We learned that. We picked them up when they were ready a few days later." Before I can get the end of my sentence out, Emilie wraps her arm around my arm closest to her and lays her head on my shoulder—just for a few seconds.

Eliza and Mitch watch the two of us, like they're waiting for us to slip up.

"Best croissants I've had to date," Emilie croons, her chin on my shoulder.

"Did you hear that Mitch got a promotion?" Elaine says to what I'm assuming is Emilie. The change in subject is jarring. Like, they won't let her take up even the smallest amount of space, even though it was a question someone else asked.

My brows furrow and irritation hits me like a wave. Emilie squeezes my arm. I look to her and she shakes her head in the smallest 'no.'

"No, I didn't. Why don't you tell us about it, Mitch?" She enunciates every letter in his name like it's a dare.

Mitch launches into a boring rendition of his new responsibilities. Her parents laugh and ask follow-up questions. Eliza leans into him and smiles like the dutiful fiancé. He looks at me a few times, I think to see if I'm still listening, which I am—unfortunately. Emilie wears the fakest of smiles, one she's probably practiced for years.

The difference in how they speak to Eliza and Emilie is absolute bullshit. The long awaited sunshine versus the persistent thunderstorm. It's like Eliza can do no wrong, but Emilie can do nothing right.

MY SKIN ITCHES WITH each minute that passes. We're finally almost done with dinner; Eliza and Mitch have been going on and on about the wedding and I've been staring at my plate, trying to count the ridges on the edge.

"Emilie, where'd you get that dress?"

"Oh, it's a designer that Keegan is working with. Isn't it fun?" Emilie's eyes brighten when she looks down at it, and then to her mom. The fabric, flowy and light pink, is the perfect shade to match her light complexion and hair. It bunches in at her waist, showing off her figure, and isn't too short—it hits about mid-thigh.

"I do like the color. I feel like you should've sized up though, yes?" Elaine smiles through the backhanded compliment.

I set my fork on my plate and reach over to Emilie, placing a hand on her knee. Who says shit like that? Let alone a mom talking to one of her kids.

"I love EJ in this dress. It's one of my favorites." I look at Emilie, not her poor excuse of a family. She beams when I use the nickname I learned about in the car. Everyone crinkles their brows when I say "EJ."

It's the smallest act of defiance, a subtle "fuck you" for the people who are supposed to treat her with kindness and respect. Instead, they make things difficult.

"Like I said, the color is spectacular." Elaine tries to smooth me over but it doesn't work.

I make it a point to dramatically look at my watch. "I didn't know it was so late. Emilie and I actually have to get going. I've got something at the Cosmos facility tonight."

Emilie doesn't look surprised when I stand up from the table. Instead, she looks relieved as she grabs her purse. Biting my tongue with these people, who are supposed to love and support Emilie, is fucking hard.

"If you ever want to come to a Cosmos game, let EJ know and I'll take care of it." It's not that I ever want to spend more time with these people, but my mom taught me to be kind to people even when they don't deserve it.

Emilie smirks when I call her EJ for the second time tonight.

"Count me in!" Mitch screams. To be fair, he doesn't seem that bad, until you remember the whole him marrying his ex's little sister thing. It says a lot that he's my favorite of the bunch.

After some lukewarm goodbyes, I hold Emilie's hand as we walk to the car.

"That actually could've been worse," she says, eyes fixed on the sidewalk in front of us. "I mean, I know it wasn't great, but I've definitely had worse interactions with them." Her words fall out of her mouth, quick and a little breathless. Maybe this is for her benefit, like she's trying to convince herself?

Before I open the car door, I stop and turn toward her.

"What's the matter?" Concern etches her soft cheeks and golden eyes. I scoff. "Are you okay?"

"That actually wasn't that bad. I mean—" She starts down a path which probably ends at some sort of excuse or reasoning. But before she gets too far, I quickly pull her to me. My arms wrap around her mid-back and squeeze. I breathe her in, vanilla, when I tip down and put my head on her shoulder.

When she hugs me back, I feel her exhale. She leans in, holds onto me, and my heart cracks a little.

"You deserve better than that. Whatever the fuck that was."

I feel her take a breath, her front flush to mine.

"Thank you."

When she doesn't let go, I keep holding on, trying to make up for all the times she's been cast aside, not valued.

Who knows if there's enough time to make up for all those other ones, but damn it, I'm going to try.

Chapter 18
Emilie

I'D BE LYING IF I hadn't been thinking about Zack much more than one should when it comes to a fake boyfriend. It was the way he went to bat for me with my family and did it without question or issue. He treated me with such kindness; not that he hasn't before, but this was different.

It was the way he told me about the best first date I've never been on. He had a story lined up, quick and convincing. If he'd asked me out on that date, it would've been hard to say no.

Plus, Zack can hold his own with them. I know enough that his family is probably lovely; full of love and adoration for one another, instead of the transactional relationship I'm used to. Part of me is embarrassed he knows where I came from.

I feel like Zack has seen a lot of me, but the part that's reserved for the energy my family takes is different. Obviously, I love them. But they require significant boundaries. It's not like one day something changed and I was then second best. Over time, I became too vocal, too loud, and wanted to do things other than what they'd planned. All the while, Eliza never told them no. She fit into the perfect mold they dreamed up for a daughter. There's not much room for the woman who still wants to hold hands with her family at twenty-five.

For fuck's sake, she got them to up and move to New York—my dad's practice and all—for a college she ended up dropping out of. The real kicker? They talk about Eliza's NYU acceptance like it's this massive accomplishment.

Eliza is smarter than she lets on and that infuriates me. We've never been close as adults. One day she was my kid sister, who needed help cutting the tops off her strawberries and mixing the milk and butter for the Mac and cheese after school. Then in the next moment, she was her own human who didn't need me anymore.

I've not shut the door on us having a better relationship, but her marrying Mitch will always be something that stings.

Mitch. God. He is two years older than me and stuck his hooks in when I was a junior in high school. He went to our rival high school and loved to come around with his buddies to work up whoever he could. We didn't date until I was a senior—I was the girl with the college boyfriend, probably another reason my so-called-friends flocked to me. He had all the connections for the things we were too young for.

Things seemed fine until I was in my fourth year of college. I was living in a house off-campus; really it was a glorified closet, but rent was the cheapest I could find and I got along with everyone. I felt safe.

Mitch hated where I lived. He'd drive over in his shiny silver BMW, and talk down to me and everyone else, like he knew better. He especially didn't like that other guys lived in this house, not that I'd ever done anything to make him question my loyalty. This was also the year that Mitch got the internship with my dad's firm, and that's when I knew it was over.

He had signed up for a life I for sure didn't want. I'd seen it play out. My parents arguing, loud and aggressive, until one day there was no more arguing. They move around each other like two acquaintances out in public—smiles that are kind enough and minimal conversation.

I wanted someone who loved me, and I always wondered if Mitch was dating me to get close to my dad but chalked that up to watching too many movies. And really, the question I should've asked was maybe he was trying to get close to my sister.

I'll never forget that Thanksgiving. It was the last one we had in my family home, before they sold it and moved to New York. I thought I was going to be stuck at my internship, but when I still had time to make dinner, I thought I'd surprise my family.

Mitch and I had broken up six months before. It was my decision, and for a while he kept in touch, acting like nothing had changed. He told me that I'd make a mistake and I'd be crawling back before I knew it.

I walk up to the door of my childhood home, excitement seeping into my bones. It'd been too long since I'd been home last, work and classes getting in the way. I turned twenty-one a month ago, and my parents sent flowers and a bottle of champagne—not able to make the trip to see me.

None of that mattered, because I was going to be able to spend one of my favorite days with my family. They were never the warmest of parents, but something about the holidays seemed to thaw them a bit.

I'm greeted with the smell of rosemary and freshly baked bread—a recipe from my grandma that's only ever made for special occasions—and hang my heavy winter coat on the door. Late November in Michigan is always a gamble, but this year it's brutally cold. My mom walks to the foyer, probably after hearing the door shut.

"Surprise!" I say, a little more enthusiastic than I know she likes, but hell, I'm excited.

Instead of hugging me, she puts her hands on her hips. "Emilie, I thought you couldn't make it." Her brows scrunch in confusion.

I step in wrapping her in a hug, kissing her on the cheek. "I made it work. Ugh, it smells so good in here. Hopefully I didn't miss dinner." I'm walking into the dining room, my mom following me.

"I really wish you would've called," she says, something on the edge of her voice that I just can't place.

"I mean, do I need an invite to come home?" I ask, looking over my shoulder at her.

"Well, it's just..."

I don't hear what she says next. I'm one foot in the dining room when I see them: Eliza and Mitch. Eliza leans into him, and he's playing with the end of her perfectly straight strawberry blonde hair.

Mitch? Eliza. Mitch and Eliza. No. How? What?

My stomach flips, and I feel like I might throw up.

Their eyes are bigger than the dinner plates set in front of them. Eliza slowly gets herself upright, locking eyes with me for a single second before looking back to Mitch.

She doesn't say anything.

"Why are you here?" I ask, my voice like something that's been run over and pressed into the gravel.

Mitch clicks his tongue before shrugging his shoulders. "I didn't think you'd be here. Listen, we wanted to tell you, but it's still new and—"

"Not that new. You're at my house. For Thanksgiving." I look around the dining room which has housed some of my happiest memories.

"Listen, I'm sorry. I was going to call you."

"To convince me that us breaking up was a mistake or to tell me you were dating my sister? Two conflicting ideas there," I say and try to catch my breath. I want to cry but I absolutely will not give this man any more of myself.

"I'm sorry," he replies in a way that feels for show, as he stands at his hands in his lap. There isn't a single emotion behind it, kind of like a kid who is being told to apologize but doesn't know what they're apologizing for.

"What about you?" I look at Eliza. Flawless Eliza. She couldn't look more unbothered.

"It's not like it was planned," is all she says before getting up and sauntering to the kitchen. She doesn't tell me she's sorry. She doesn't do anything.

"Perfect timing, Emilie. Dinner time," my dad chimes in, walking into the dining room, holding the platter of turkey.

"I don't know if I should stay." My voice is quiet, and I hate it.

My mom puts her hands on my shoulders, not to console me but to lead me toward a place at the table that she's set while I've been trying to wrap my head around this whole thing. "Emilie, this is your home. Sit down. Eat."

And that was it. We didn't have any more conversations about the fact that my sister was dating my ex-boyfriend. It wasn't that surprising, considering my parents are terrible communicators and would rather avoid than address.

There have been many small shifts over the years but sitting here, at a time that's supposed to be full of connection and joy, I know this is going to be major. I've worked on allowing myself to take up space, in almost every avenue of my life, but I don't think I have it in me to do it here. There truly isn't any space for me.

I spend the last Thanksgiving, in the only home I'd ever known, fighting back tears.

My phone buzzes, a message from Keegan.

Keegan

disaster at the store currently

need to raincheck our cooking class

Me

What am I going to do? You can't go to a two-person cooking class alone—it's quite literally designed for people to cook together.

> don't go alone and don't cancel

> invite your new mans

I roll my eyes but it is my best bet on short notice. Zack should be wrapping up practice any minute. It's a Tuesday night, and I know tomorrow is his day off—this is kind of perfect.

Since it's time sensitive, I hit call next to his name, which he's edited to add a blue heart and the sweating emojis. He had the eggplant at the end and that's the only one I removed. As soon as Zack answers the phone, I ask, "Hey, do you have plans tonight?"

I can hear the wind whip outside; he's probably walking to his car as he says, "No plans. Unless it's dinner with your family, and then I am very busy. With things. Important things I could never reschedule."

I let out a real laugh and put my hand over my mouth.

"No, not dinner with my family. How do you feel about a cooking class?"

"What a perfect way to celebrate our one month anniversary!" he says on the other line but I can't tell if he's kidding or not.

WE WALK INTO THE cooking space, and the reactions are perfect. This is the last class of three, and people typically come with their partner. Keegan and I signed up for this long before Zack and I were... whatever we are, and people expect me to walk in with her, not Zack Andersen, golden boy from the Upstate Cosmos.

I point him to our station where everything we need for tonight's dish is ready and waiting. Zack makes it a point to introduce himself to the six other couples before settling next to me. A wave of pride washes over me with each handshake, each selfie he takes, and every person he makes smile. Zack is like a ray of sunshine wherever he is.

Our Chef, Beau, who currently cooks at a Michelin restaurant in the city, is French and walks in like Zack may as well be Keegan and claps his hand—bringing the room to attention.

"Yes, Chef," the room calls back, and Beau laughs. It's definitely a joke but it never gets old. Zack looks at me, like I didn't let him in on a critical piece of information. I give him a smirk and a side-eye, as he stands razor straight, his entire focus on Beau.

"Today, we're conquering cacio e pepe. Yes, it's an Italian dish, but so many people in America get it wrong, the Italians will not be offended by this Frenchman teaching you to get it right." He rubs his hands together.

"We'll start with a generous pour of Chablis, the purest of the Chardonnays. Now, you may be thinking, Chef, is there wine in the pasta sauce? And I'd say, cheese-us Christ, the wine is for drinking!" He picks up his glass, some of the white wine sloshing up the rim, and the room laughs. "Forgive the pun, I couldn't help myself. Cacio e pepe translates into cheese and pepper. The wine is for pairing and enjoying yourself while cooking today."

Zack follows suit and opens the bottle of wine waiting for us, pouring each of us a glass.

"Cheers," he says, handing me a glass before clinking his into mine. When he wraps his arm around me, I hold my breath. His hand rests on my hip, and I melt into him as Chef Beau goes through an overview of the recipe.

My cheeks feel like they'd be hot to the touch, being this close to Zack. No matter how many times it happens, I'm always a little nervous. Kind of like when you first start dating someone, and you're testing out the PDA waters.

Zack dips down slowly and whispers, "This is way better than our last date." He puts a period on the sentence in the form of a kiss on my cheek. His lips are full and like velvet on my skin.

Now I'm back in the hallway at the bar when he told me "the first time I kiss you won't be in front of any of your old fuck friends." Like it was inevitable.

My stomach flips as I think about what it'd be like to have those lips on mine. On other parts of my body. Would he kiss me slowly and leisurely, or would it be delectable chaos?

Emilie, quit that.

I take a long drink of wine to try and cool the flames in my belly.

Chapter 19
Zack

Did I think a cheese paste would be part of my plans tonight? No, I didn't. But when Emilie called, I couldn't say yes fast enough, especially because I was supposed to get dinner with my dad but he had to reschedule.

"A cheese paste? What the hell is that?" I whisper as I ask Emilie what Chef is talking about. Apparently, cacio e pepe is a real dick to make, and many people end up with a clumpy, cheesy mess.

She laughs and playfully shoves me in the ribs. "Listen, he's going to tell us."

Emilie is definitely a rule follower. There were a few times I tried jumping ahead like half a step, and she'd gently put her hand on mine and shake her head no.

"Oh, you're one of those good girls." Before the words exit my mouth, I'm holding back a laugh.

"Wouldn't you like to know?" She doesn't take her eyes from Chef as he's showing us how to make cheese paste, which I hope tastes better than it sounds.

Fuck. Yes. I would like to know.

"Isn't it fun to be bad every once in a while?"

"Again, wouldn't you like to know?" This time she turns to me, her eyes daring me to keep going.

"Maybe I would, EJ." I use her nickname, the one I know she likes, and I find that we're too close for a public cooking class.

I feel her breath on the side of my face as I lean over her shoulder. My dick has forgotten we're in public, and I quickly think of anything else to get myself under control: ice baths, TRX bands, wall sits with weights on my legs.

I pay attention to Beau because, even though he's a handsome man and probably feeds his lovers like royalty, he's not Emilie. Good thing I did—turns out, cheese paste is hard. Basically, cacio e pepe doesn't use butter or milk to create the creamy sauce. It's just pasta water, pecorino cheese, and pepper.

I'm using our glass bowl, trying to get the paste on the outside so we can toss the pasta, while Emilie is finishing the pasta. Chef made us all fresh pasta before the class—what a guy.

"My fingers are starting to cramp," I whine while I hold a chilled metal spoon, using the round edge to help with the paste consistency.

"Oooh. Bad sign," Emilie gloats as she delicately stirs the pasta.

I bite my lip and won't give her the satisfaction of a laugh—even though that was a good one.

"Don't mangle the cheese with those hands," she says as I'm putting pressure on the inside of the bowl.

"I bet you think about these hands," I tease, as I'm so laser focused on not a piece of this bowl showing through this cheese paste situation.

"What if I do?" Emilie quips, and my body freezes. I slowly turn and catch her looking at me. Her curls are wild today, just how I love 'em. She shrugs her shoulders before draining the rest of her wine, her hazel eyes looking at me through the glass.

Fuck, does she think about my hands? About me? Touching her?

I grab the bottle of wine and pour more in her glass. I close the space between us, but she doesn't look up from the pasta she's stirring. With a finger under her chin, I tip her face up until she has no choice but to look at me.

"What if I thought about my hands in these curls, pulling them?" I wrap a crimson curl around a finger for emphasis.

Emilie's eyes are on me, and it's just the two of us. The rest of the room fades in the background, like I'm living a fucking rom-com, and I don't question it.

"Quit looking at me like that." Her voice is quiet through her devilish grin.

"Like what?"

"Like I'm on the menu," she enunciates as I continue to twist her hair around my fingers. We keep leaning in, getting closer and closer.

Fuck.

"Your cheese paste is damn near perfect! Très bien. It's good." We immediately step back from one another, as Beau has our bowl in his hands, inspecting. "Do you want to tell everyone your secret?" he asks.

"Well, you see, got those championship hands." I wiggle my fingers, and the group laughs.

The moment is over, but it feels like this whole thing is just getting started.

"THIS IS THE BEST part of cooking class." I spin a bite of pasta on the spoon, like Chef showed me, and take a bite. The sauce is smooth and peppery—not too rich—and might be one of my new favorite dishes. It's probably a saving grace that cheese paste is kind of a bitch to make because I could easily eat this a few times a week.

Outside of the cooking space, there's a small patio with room for seven tables—one for each couple. Twinkly lights are strung from the roof of the building to the one next door, creating the perfect vibe.

I get it. This seems like such a fun thing to be able to do.

"Where do we sign up for the next session?" I ask between bites. "You know I'm here as long as I don't have anything for Cosmos."

"You want to sign up for cooking classes with me?" Emilie makes her voice small, a mound of pasta on her spoon, waiting to be devoured.

I'm chewing some of the best pasta I've ever eaten. Fuck, this is so good. The cheese paste was difficult but worth it.

"Why wouldn't I? This was so fun. Didn't you have a good time?" I ask her, now questioning if it's just me who would do this again.

Typically, I'm pretty sure of other people. Sometimes, Emilie makes me scratch my head. Is she too good at playing into the fake relationship? Is she not having as much fun as I am? Does she think about me the way I think about her when we're not together?

"I'd love to do a cooking class with you. The next time they announce one, it's you and me, okay?"

You and me. Me and Emilie. I like the sound of that.

"Need those championship hands, I guess. This is so good." She slurps the end of a noodle from her spoon.

"They're yours," I say, dipping a piece of fresh bread in oil courtesy of Chef.

I swear she blushes, or maybe I'm making it up.

"Thank you for inviting me. I like learning new things," I say, trying to express my gratitude for the last minute invite.

I have a lot of opportunities, but as of late, they're mostly based on my looks or something to do with football. I like to learn new things and tonight was perfect. Somehow, Emilie made it even better.

"Me too," she replies, grabbing my hand and giving me a classic Emilie smile. God, she's so fucking beautiful. I don't know how someone hasn't married her yet.

Woah. Maybe I need to cool it on the wine.

"I have a question," Emilie starts, her eyes struggling to meet mine but her cheek pinched in a smirk. "How did you think of the first date story? When we were with my family."

I take a deep breath, weighing my options. Tell her the truth or make something up. "Promise not to laugh?" I ask.

She nods.

Doing my best to hide the nervousness in the truth, I say, "It was the first date I would've asked you on. The thing I thought you'd say yes to. I knew you'd never turn me down if it meant you got croissants at the end." I shrug my shoulders and rub my hands together.

I change the topic immediately. "Let me get your photo. This whole thing," I gesture around the aesthetic space, "is perfect for social media."

Emilie smiles at me over a massive bite of noodles, and with the warm light and the candles on the table, she looks like a fucking goddess. I take a few photos of her, all of them good.

"Let's take a selfie," I suggest. Before I can get up to move to her, she's already sliding in, sitting on my lap.

Good god. Emilie is sitting on my lap. I pray to the gods of erections that my dick plays nice. I don't need to make this weird.

"Is this okay?" she asks.

"Fuck yeah. You can sit on my lap anytime." Man, do I mean it. I want to wrap her up and keep her here.

I put my arm out, and we take a few photos. She kisses me on the cheek for a few seconds, and my heart feels like it could leap out of my chest.

No surprises here. That's what Emilie does to me.

Which is unfortunate, considering this thing has an end date.

But what if it didn't have to?

While I'm daydreaming, she almost falls off my lap, and I use my hand to catch her, grabbing her hip, which is actually her ass. Good god, these curves should be against the rules.

"Woah. You good? Are you cheese drunk?" I ask, trying to distract myself from the fact that my hand is on her ass, and she didn't immediately stand up or slap my hand away.

She turns to me, giggling, cheeks turning red—could be from the chilly air, the wine, or maybe she's embarrassed.

I don't break eye contact as her laugh dies out—I swear, her eyes have me under some sort of spell. The air between us is sparks and electricity. When I think she's going to stand up, get off my lap, she puts a piece of my hair between her fingers.

"You're always playing with my curls. Figured it's my turn." She plays with a few strands, before putting her whole hand through my hair.

I'm frozen. I'm afraid to move my hand, jostle her, or ruin the moment.

Fuck. Why does that feel so good?

I hold back a moan because, while that's my first reaction to her hand running through my hair, I know that is one hundred percent not something I should be doing in public.

"Now you'll be thinking about *my* hands," she says, her mouth too close to mine. We keep doing this, ending up in this position, but neither of us are giving in.

Someone drops silverware at another table and the clanging sound has Emilie up and back in her seat like she was never in my lap.

"Let's make sure we have a good one." She grabs my phone to look at the selfies we took. Emilie swipes for a few seconds and then pauses, before giving the phone back to me.

"Good?" I ask.

"Good," she replies, her voice almost flat.

I don't know what it is, but something's changed. The air feels stale compared to the crackle I felt a minute ago.

I will Emilie to look at me, but she doesn't. No matter how badly I want her to.

Chapter 20
Emilie

Me

no to that caption

Zack

come on it's so good

she's got a thing about pepe (cacio e pepe)

no to the dick joke via social media caption

how about this

i've got a pepe for your cacio

that's just another dick joke

fine, I'll be good

and by good i mean boring

excited for your dinner?

with my sister and all her friends?

I SHAKE MY HEAD and put my phone in my bag. It's alarming how easy it is to fall into things like that with Zack—calling him after something just to dish on what happened, as an example.

Tonight, he's traveling for an away game. I'm bummed I'm home this weekend and not watching the Cosmos play. It's not like I've ever been to an away game, but Zack has turned into my go-to when it comes to plans.

Part of me wonders if Zack has any regular hookups where he's going. I have no business wondering about such a thing but I can't help it. When I was looking at our selfies after the cooking class the other night, someone named "Kass blonde lawyer" sent him three texts while I was looking.

This is a bad look—for me, not for him. He's done exactly what we planned, and then some. Besides Cassie waiting for him in the parking lot after his first home game, there hasn't been anything—or anyone—else.

I wasn't trying to snoop or be sneaky, it just sort of happened. He didn't flinch like he had something to hide when I wanted to look at the photos.

Emilie, stop. He's not yours, not really. He's given you more than enough.

Before I saw the texts, I thought he was finally going to kiss me. It feels like we've been dancing around it for weeks. I still can't get over what he said about the first time he would kiss me, how it wouldn't be in front of a fuck friend.

Fuck, why did Colt have to be at the bar that night?

At this point, I'm agonizing over what it would be like, his mouth on mine, our lips finally touching. Would he put his hands in my hair? Or would he lightly touch my face? Maybe he'd bite my lip?

I walk into the restaurant, the buzz bringing me back to tonight: apps and drinks to celebrate Eliza. In lieu of a traditional bachelorette party, she elected to foot the bill at one of the most exclusive spots in New York.

The only ask was for everyone, besides the bride, to wear black. I've got a pair of vintage Chanel trousers and a black sleeveless V-neck vest, with three buttons and little pinstripes. With only a bra underneath, my curves are on display and I feel fantastic. Enough so that I'm excited to get a picture to send Zack. Our affinity for clothes and fashion is an unexpected bonding experience.

"Thank you for coming," Eliza says, hugging me tighter than she's done in years. It catches me off guard.

"Of course, wouldn't miss it." I smile at her and her friends at the table. I've only met a few of them in passing, and with my mother declining, there's no one I really know.

Eliza smiles at me as she sits back down, and she's stunning in a white halter dress. It's basic and beautifully plain to show off her natural features.

"Is there something on me?" she asks. I must've been staring too long.

"No! I love the dress. Looks great on you."

With the compliment, her eyebrows go back to their normal position as her back hits the chair behind her. She's nervous, which doesn't make much sense, considering these are supposed to be her closest friends. Maybe it's the wedding in general—the whole thing has to be stressful.

"Everyone, this is my sister, Emilie." Eliza introduces me as I take the only open seat.

Like moths to a flame, the attention shifts, and almost everyone's eyes are on me.

"You lucky bitch. I can't believe you're friends with Willow and dating Zack Andersen. We are not worthy," the platinum blonde woman next to me says while lifting her glass of wine into the air. The rest of the table laughs.

My skin itches, but in a place you can't scratch. I take a long drink of the water in front of me.

"Tell me, is Willow really as nice as she seems, or what's the deal?" Platinum asks as the entire table leans in.

"She's not going to dish on her boss slash friend." A brunette, with some of the longest hair I've seen and not been grossed out by, hits Platinum's shoulder and pairs it with an eye roll.

Platinum takes a big breath. "Fine. I've heard Zack's dick is *massive*. Tell me it's true."

I let out a horrific cough sound, truly caught off guard by this person, and reach back for my water.

Our server comes at the perfect time looking for my drink order. Platinum sits back in her chair, giving me space, but I'm truly not sure it will ever be enough—unless it's on the other side of the room.

If there's one thing I respect, it's a girl's girl—someone who likes to build up women. There's enough going on in the world that we don't need to compete with one another, unprovoked.

Miss Platinum Blonde does not seem like a girl's girl. Also, who asks a stranger a question like that? Hard pass.

Eliza leans over to say something to her, and it doesn't seem like Platinum likes it too much when she responds with, "I'm kidding. Chill out."

I introduce myself to the other women at the table, and no one else asks about Zack's penis, so I feel like that's a win.

I can't wait to tell Zack that one.

Once we all have a drink, Platinum stands up to make a toast.

"Here's to the bride!" she cheers as she clinks silverware on her glass. "Eliza is one of my closest friends, and I'm so excited to spend some time celebrating her and Mitch. The next chapter is going to be a fun one. Also, she's going to be so gorgeous on the beach in just a few weeks."

Aw, this is nice. Maybe she's not all bad? In the spirit of being a girl's girl, giving everyone a chance, I turn over a blank page in my mind. I can certainly give her a chance.

"Here's to Eliza and Mitch and their happily ever after!" Everyone offers a small "woo" or clinks their glass before taking a drink.

"Emilie, don't be afraid to bring some extra single Cosmos to the beach. You seem like you have good taste in men." She winks at me, pointing at Eliza as half the table pretends she didn't just say that.

I take back everything I said. No chance.

A teeny tiny pit opens in my chest—jealousy which has no right to take up space like this. Zack isn't mine; not really.

I drink half of my Aperol Spritz then and there.

※

THE REST OF THE night is low-key, as in we order Eliza too many cocktails and the table too much food.

I'm currently eating a bacon-wrapped date stuffed with goat cheese, when someone says we should open gifts.

Eliza opens some gorgeous, and some not-so-much, lingerie, along with your standard bride items like a silk robe embroidered with her name and a sun hat for lounging on the beach.

When my gift is the only one left, I pull a gold envelope from my purse and hand it to Eliza, her cheeks pink from too many drinks.

Now if my sister wasn't marrying a fairly serious ex-boyfriend, maybe I could've gone the lingerie route. One of my favorite types of gifts to give are experiences, which is what I've done for tonight.

"You're kidding! How did you pull this off?!" Eliza shrieks while reading the paper tucked inside the envelope. I smile at the excitement dripping from her voice.

I pulled some strings and was able to get in contact with the Chef from her favorite restaurant. Technically, Keegan was the one with strings, but she pulled them on my behalf.

"It's a gift certificate for one of my favorite Chef's, from my favorite restaurant in the city, to come and cook dinner for Mitch and me. But it's at our house!"

The table lets out a collective "aww" and I know I did a good job.

"Emilie, thank you. Very thoughtful." She puts the note back in the envelope and into another gift bag.

My sister and I haven't been close in a long time, but my chest warms at her reaction. No matter what happens, she *is* getting married. I don't want to do something I regret later.

"Emilie, is Zack coming to the wedding for real?" Platinum asks, her words high pitched and too loud, as she takes the empty seat next to me.

"He's coming with me to the wedding, yes." I drink the rest of my spritz, no intentions of ordering another.

"He's so hot. How did you do that? Land a man like that?" she asks.

What the fuck? I nervously laugh, looking at my freshly manicured nails, deciding what to say next.

"I don't know if you think this behavior is funny, or acceptable, but it's not. My free tip for the evening is don't ask strangers about their boyfriend's dick size or insinuate they're not attractive enough for their partner. It's not a good look."

With each word, she sits further back in her chair. I feel like she's about to launch into some defensive rant about how "that's not what she meant" or whatever bullshit she's used to leaning on for getting away with comments like this.

"I'm sorry, I didn't—" she says.

"That's enough," I cut her off, pointing a finger . "Thank you for apologizing. Now, excuse me." I stand and walk to the bathroom, more annoyed than anything.

When I swing the door open, I see Eliza standing at the sink—it's just her and me.

"Some of your friends are really on one tonight." A nervous chuckle escapes as I check my reflection in the mirror. "Sorry, it's not for you to worry about. All is well."

"I haven't talked to some of them in months. Tonight's a little weird, being back together." Eliza washes her hands, her eyes down. "Honestly, I think you're the reason some of them came tonight. They've been asking me about Zack, and Willow, and even Tripp. I don't think they really care about this." She gestures to herself before showing me her engagement ring—a two carat princess cut diamond on a platinum band.

My heart drops. This is a feeling I know all too well and no matter how much time passes, it still stings. Realizing people don't want you, or view you as a steppingstone, is truly the fucking worst. The irony is that them not wanting you is mostly a reflection of themselves, and not of you, but it never feels like that when you're on the receiving end.

"You know you don't have to keep them around, right? Like, you can make new friends," I insist.

Her sigh is frustrated. "I'm not like you, Emilie," she tells me, and it's not the first time. But this time, it feels like it *might* be a compliment.

She offers me a sad smile, one where only a single corner of her mouth barely pulls up.

Eliza walks out before I have a chance to say anything else.

Chapter 21
Zack

One of my favorite traditions is my dad coming to my first away game. Since my first college football season, he's always made the trip—no matter how far or bad the matchup. When it started, I'm guessing it was supposed to be him and my mom, but she got too nervous and backed out.

The family always jokes about how she's too gentle for football. Even though I'm a special teams player and am rarely in a position for actual injury, she's only seen me play a handful of times after high school.

My dad and I always grab dinner, or whatever sort of meal we can. One year, I'm pretty sure it was just a platter of chocolate chip cookies and a beer from the mini-bar, around eleven pm, the night before the game.

It may not sound like a lot, but it's one of the things I look forward to every year. Now I'm able to get him great seats, or a field pass if he wants. I don't care where he sits, but I play with a different type of energy knowing my dad is there.

We're playing an early game, so my dad and I are planning to get dinner afterwards.

I'm in the locker room before everyone else—I like to get there early and do everything I need before the entire team is here. Before I turn my phone off, two messages come in.

Riley

Classic Riley, always thinking something is wrong or constantly worried. She's always been a bit of a hypochondriac, which has proven to cause more harm than good. Like the one time she convinced me, and my parents, that I had spinal meningitis. After a painful spinal tap, and a ridiculous amount of undue stress, turns out I had a normal cold with really swollen lymph nodes that were sore when I turned my neck.

I'm pretty sure that's what sparked Riley going to therapy—which she desperately needed. We all went with her a few times, on our own, and as a family. Her therapist helped explain what it was like to be Riley; the anxiety of every single day, the things she'd worry about—sometimes make herself physically sick about.

We all learned a lot, and I'm thankful.

My phone buzzes again—this time, it's Emilie.

Next, a picture of her wearing my jersey comes through. She's currently wearing it out in public, at what looks to be a sports bar. Fuck, that's so hot.

I immediately save it, just like I did when she sent me her fit for what she wore to her sister's bachelorette non-party. She's the kind of person who *wears* clothes, like they were made perfectly for her—doesn't matter what it is.

Seeing her in that suit vest, with nothing underneath it, had me thinking *some thoughts*. I dreamt about her taking it off, a single button at a time, but woke up before she completely removed it. I've thought about her tits much more than is probably appropriate for a fake girlfriend.

Nerves sit low in my core, like they do before every game. I recognize them, and my love for the game. I turn my phone off and soak up a quiet minute in the locker room.

WE PULL OUT THE win, thanks to a fifty-eight-yard field goal as time expired—a play I contributed to. It's so surreal to look up in the stands and see Cosmos blue throughout the stadium during an away game. Doesn't matter that it's only our second season as a team in the NFL—Cosmos fans travel.

The elevator opens to the lobby, and I see my dad waiting near the doors. When he sees me, he lights up, and it's a look I wish I could bottle and keep forever.

"Mr. Undefeated. Come here." He wraps me in a hug, hitting my back like men do.

"Hell of a game," I respond, a hand on his shoulder. "Thanks for coming."

"Always," he says, but he's looking around the lobby. Sometimes he's nervous when it comes to fans approaching us when we're out. I don't blame him—the public can be wild.

"You good?"

He rolls his shoulders back and responds, "Yeah, totally. All good. Let's get to dinner."

We walk the short four blocks to the steakhouse I picked for dinner, while my dad goes through the highlights from the game. His voice is quick, full of life, and it takes me back to our after-game chats. If there's something my dad loves, it's talking about football.

Before I know it, we're eating fresh bread at the restaurant.

"Emilie still in the picture?" he pokes, and I welcome the change of topic. Not because I don't love talking about football, but having a beer, talking girls with your dad, is an experience I don't take for granted.

When I nod yes, he keeps going. "When are you bringing her over for dinner? You know your mom is just salivating to host. Plus, it's been a minute since you met someone like this."

I bite. "What do you mean?"

"Just that it seems like she's kept your attention. And you've spent more than a few drunken nights with her. That's all."

This makes me pause. I've always had an open type of communication with my parents when it comes to relationships and partners. My parents were always telling Riley and me about safe and consensual sex, making it an open topic for conversation when most of my friends had a parent throw them a box of condoms and tell them "not to get anyone pregnant."

It catches me off guard because he's right. I've not had serious relationships, rarely bringing people home to meet my parents, which isn't weird when you're in college and an athlete. My time was spent at football and making sure my grades were solid enough to keep doing so. It's weirder when you're almost twenty-seven.

"Zack, it's fine. I didn't say that to make you feel bad about previous decisions or nights, or whatever," Dad scrambles, sensing my reaction. "It's just that we're happy to meet her. When you're ready."

I believe him. It's not that he said what he's thinking—I'm lucky to have him be honest with me—it's just making me wonder if I'm missing out. On real people. Genuine connections.

We both take a long drink before he says, "Tell me something about her."

"She's so smart. Probably too smart for someone like me," I make the small self-deprecating joke that I whole-heartedly believe. "She's the kind of person who can learn almost anything and do it like she's damn near an expert."

I launch into how she's helped Tripp and Willow start a new non-profit and a record label. How much she's figured out. How no task is too small. How she'll lend a hand even if she's drowning, personally.

I only stop when my food arrives. My cheeks are probably warm, a touch embarrassed from the rambling.

"Damn. She sounds like quite the woman." My dad looks at me over his plate, beaming, matching the smile on my own face.

Dinner is quiet, with both of us hungry enough to clear our plates. Dessert is a must, and when we can't choose, we get the crème brûlée and bananas foster.

"Is there anything else I can get you?" the woman who brought the dessert asks, but I already have a forkful of pie in my mouth.

I shake my head, and my dad chuckles at my full mouth.

"*Anything* at all?" She puts both hands on the table, leaning over a bit with her eyes on me.

I know this bit. She's trying to get my attention. When she says anything, she means in the bedroom when she's done with work. I've dabbled in anything, but not tonight, not now.

"Nope. All set. Thank you." I look at her briefly before focusing back on the dessert.

She takes a piece of paper from her cleavage, puts it on the table, and says, "Here. If you change your mind, any time you're in town." She gives me a wicked smirk before turning and walking away.

I grab the number, put it in my pocket, and make a mental note to throw it away when I get to the hotel. I press my lips in a thin line, waiting for her to be clear from our table, and glance up to see my dad's eyebrows scrunched as he looks at me.

"Wild times," I say, hoping to put an end to this.

"Are you kidding me? What are you doing?"

"Do you want to start with the pie? That's cool—"

"No, not the fucking dessert. With that woman. You just went on a rant about Emilie. Praising her up and down. Smiling like an idiot talking about someone you could be in love with. Start a life with. Do big things with."

"What are you talking about?" I'm confused. What happened?

"Don't interrupt me." Dad points a finger at me, and it feels like I'm in trouble so I do my best to listen and not move, even as an adult. "You're better than this, Zack. Your mom and I worked hard and taught you to be a respectful human being; one you could trust, one whose word meant something." He stops, sits back in his chair while crossing his arms and maintaining eye contact.

"This is about that?" I gesture to the woman who walked away. "For an interaction I didn't ask for or entertain?"

"You took her number." His voice is cold as ice.

"Yeah, to throw it away. I don't need some creep picking it up and calling her. You did teach me to be a respectful human being and that's what I was doing." I mean to stop but the words are flying out of my mouth before they get the memo. "I am someone you can trust. I'm someone Emilie can trust. It's fucking bullshit that you're upset with me over an interaction with a stranger I didn't ask for."

"You're not going to call her?" he asks and this part stings. I don't know if he believes me.

"No, I'm not going to call her. Here, you take the number and throw it away, call her in a week to see if I was telling the truth, whatever you want to do." I pull the piece of paper, small and wadded up, and give it to my dad.

He sighs a long breath out as he stares at the piece of paper.

"I just want you to have everything you deserve. People you deserve. Emilie seems like someone who falls in that category."

My brain is trying to make sense of this whole thing, and that's when I remember what Riley said. She noticed something about my dad not being quite right—this conversation falls in line with that.

"Is everything okay? Are you about to tell me you're sick or something?"

My dad has the spoon in the crème brûlée, tapping the torched sugar topping.

"What? No! I'm not sick. Healthy as a horse. " He knocks on his chest for emphasis. "When you get older, you think of these things more, or maybe I'm tired from the flight." He takes a bite of dessert. "Sorry, didn't mean to jump to conclusions there. That's not fair." He offers me a smile.

We sit in silence for a minute before he says, "Hey. I'm proud of you. You know that, right?"

"Thanks, Dad. I know you are."

I appreciate the change of subject because, while it's clear something is going on, he's not ready to talk about it.

Chapter 22
Emilie

When We Play is hosting an event for city kids and that means I'm spending my Friday night watching professional athletes run around like *they're* kids. This event was my idea, and I'm thankful the Cosmos let us alter their practice schedule and steal facility time during the season. It's after school on a Friday, so that means they just shifted practice to end earlier.

The point is to do a little press for *When We Play* and the Cosmos, while kids get instruction on specific football positions. Obviously, we have Tripp and a few wide receivers, Ben Gambill showing how to drop back and throw a pass as a quarterback, and then Zack, with all things long snapper.

It might be a weird mix of players and positions, but it's who we could get to bite on a Friday night volunteer opportunity.

Once the kids check in, they get their own Cosmos jersey, and it's making my heart hurt how cute they are. Boys and girls, aged eight to twelve, run around showing off their new team wear. There's even an option to wear eye black like the team does during real games.

I've never really thought about having kids. After high school, it was college, and my path was unconventional. My parents offered to pay for my tuition, but I didn't take it. I didn't want the experience to be tainted, or held above my head in any way, shape, or form. Plus, since I wasn't going to law school, I knew I was already on the wrong foot.

Instead, I worked my ass off—in school to get great grades and out of school to scrape together every penny I could. I learned how to get by with three hours of sleep. Obviously, that didn't leave much room for partying or hanging out. I tried to get to every sporting event I could, but that was the extent of my consistent social life.

College took me longer than most, but I graduated with minimal debt and honors, and I'm proud I did it that way. I heard from a friend of a friend about an assistant opening, which turned out to be for Willow, and things have never been the same.

Now, I watch a girl, probably ten years old, learn how to properly hold a football that is almost as big as her. She laughs as she runs, zigzagging through the course, and some Cosmos players fail to catch her.

My ovaries. They hurt. Bad.

This lightheaded feeling washes over me, and I put my hand on my chest to feel my heartbeat. It consistently thuds, no spaces or anything out of sorts. I suck in a deep breath, letting the air stretch my lungs.

I recognize the feeling, the uncomfortableness of it all, because I've not considered this life-altering topic: a family. Now, I always envisioned myself with a partner I'd grow old with—whether we got married or not would depend on them. I'm not someone who has to get married.

Honestly, all I want is someone who can love and support me.

I find myself wondering if there should be kids in that same vision. Oof. Sweat beads on the bridge of my nose. This isn't where I thought I'd be, mentally, while working this non-profit event. Luckily, I did most of the set up and now I'm responsible for getting candid pictures of the athletes.

Last but not least is Zack's section. Currently, he's showing a group of kids the correct stance prior to snapping the football. He's turned it into a game—whoever stays up the longest wins. He runs around, in between the kids, and he's making them laugh with impressions and just casual Zack shenanigans.

He goes as far to take a pom from the dance team and is shaking it near their ears, trying to get them to fall from the tickle. That certainly seems like it should be against the rules.

Next, he's showing how to block when it comes to punt returns. He acts like the offensive player, whoever is returning the kick, and the kid's fake block him but he acts like the human version of a pinball.

Zack's eyes catch mine, all alive and bright, clearly in his element. He fits so effortlessly in every situation I've seen him in. Doesn't matter if it's a bunch of ten-year-olds, a press conference, the general public, or a lackluster dinner with my family. My hand immediately goes to my heart, to feel my heartbeat, and this time it's racing.

"Hey! Earth to EJ." Zack is clapping and waving his hands, bringing me back to the moment. He's always seeming to turn up when I need him.

"Sorry, what's up?"

"Nothing, you just looked like you were on another planet, a really sad one. You good?"

No. I wouldn't use the word good to describe myself. My anxiety has been rough the last few days. Intrusive thoughts pinched my brain last night, and again this morning, and I'm mentally exhausted.

"All good," I lie as I look at my watch. The event is about over; time to take the group photos.

"You still need a ride home, right?" Zack asks, placing a hand on my lower back just for the briefest of seconds as we walk toward the group of kids being wrangled for the photo. Those hands. His fingers. I wish his hands were all over me and we weren't at a children's event.

I nod, my head feeling like it's full of thick clouds, because I have no idea what my voice would sound like at this moment.

"Good thing the stadium had the roof on today," Zack says as we exit the stadium.

Buckets of rain drop from the sky, gray and ominous. We drive slowly in the parking lot as it fills with the water that's coming down too fast.

The thing about the Upstate Cosmos is they're not really Upstate—the stadium is located just outside the city, far enough to have the room but close enough to still deal with the horrific New York City traffic.

My phone vibrates with a notification: severe thunderstorm warning. We're about to turn out onto the road when I show it to Zack.

"You good with driving slow, trying to get back to your apartment?" he asks, putting the car in park, giving me time.

The alternative is to post up at the stadium, and that doesn't sound appealing. "Yes, let's try to get back."

We drive painfully slow, and I keep my eyes on the radar. There's not any lightning or thunder yet, just heavy rain. There are some parts of the interstate with standing water; cars driving too fast don't see it until it's too late—we've seen a handful of them hydroplane.

My heart races, and my body's tired. I'm not typically concerned about weather, since New York doesn't get anything too severe: no hurricanes, earthquakes, and a tornado would be extremely rare. But given the last few days, and lack of sleep, my nerves are shot. I crave my apartment, my bed, my own space.

The thoughts, which I have no energy to shove down, are getting louder. What if you drove into oncoming traffic? What if that car side swipes us? Is my car door locked? Is my seatbelt really buckled?

Zack slams on the breaks, putting his arm out in front of my chest, as a car spins out in front of us. If he hadn't been driving with enough space between the car in front of us, we'd probably have hit them.

"If these people would slow the fuck down." he says, his chest rising and falling with nervous breath. "You okay?" He looks over, and I nod.

My phone, which I'm holding too tight, vibrates. When I turn it over, I thought I'd see another weather alert. Instead, it's a barrage of social media notifications. I open the app and my stomach drops.

Zack Andersen NSFW Video Leaked.

The post shows a still of Zack, completely nude, parts of him censored, with a blonde draped over him. They're clearly both naked and it's not hard to guess what they were doing. Without thinking, I scroll the comments: 'what about @ehayestrueblue,' 'omg so much better than @ehayestrueblue,' 'thought he was a good one – poor emilie.' It's everyone commenting and mentioning my handle which has my phone blowing up.

I can't do this. Any of this. The weather. This thing with Zack; I'll just call it off and go to the wedding alone. I'm too rundown to pretend anymore. Pretend that this doesn't hurt.

Since I love to torture myself, I click on the short clip. It's Zack, naked, and a woman naked around his waist. They laugh as he walks her toward the wall. When they're kissing, hands all over each other, I turn my phone over and cross my arms against my chest.

"You look like you've seen a ghost," Zack offers, looking over at me, sensing my mood change.

"How much longer?" I ask, not wanting to get into this right now.

"I'm guessing fifteen minutes." He focuses on the road.

I turn and act like I'm fixated on what's outside my window. I can't see much but dark gray and water. I focus on the raindrops falling on the window until we get to my apartment.

Chapter 23
Zack

SOMETHING'S WRONG WITH EMILIE. She's been off, even at the event—kind of like she's smiling but in a way she knows she's supposed to. She's on edge, and I keep catching her putting her hand on her chest. It makes me want to figure out what's going on, find a way to bring her back to me.

Not that's she mine, not really. Tell that to my brain before bed or my dick when I think of all the times we've been together and always found ways to touch.

After seeing how her family treats her and how she's practically accepted it, I want to protect her. I know she doesn't need it but, fuck, I want to do it anyway.

This weather is wild; standing water fills the road, and I'm trying to get us home safely. I'm trying to get to her apartment, but some of the roads are impassable, completely flooded.

Finally, I'm on her street, but the flooding ahead means we'll have to walk.

"I'm going to park where it's not flooded, and we're going to run to your apartment, ok?"

She doesn't say anything, but instead zips her purse and her *When We Play* quarter zip.

I park the car when she says, "You don't have to come with me. I'm fine." It's like an order and not a suggestion. She has her hand on the door handle and opens it before I have a chance to do anything.

Scrambling, I unbuckle, feel for my key fob in my pocket, and run after her. It's not flooded on the sidewalks, not yet at least, but the sky is getting darker and the rain shows no sign of stopping.

I catch up to her at the entrance to her apartment building. Emilie tries to shield herself from the rain, coming down sideways, as she tries to enter the keycode to get in. She has her apartment key in the same hand. I try to stand in front of her, blocking the rain. "Can you give me some room?" she snaps.

What the fuck?

"Give you room? It's a fucking monsoon. I'm trying to help," I practically yell as the wind whips through, loud and threatening.

"I don't need your help," she says as she drops her keys.

I reach down, pick them up, and stand in front of her. "You don't, huh?" She finally gets the code right, grabs the keys from me, and opens the door to her building without saying a word.

The lobby is empty, the doorman not even around.

"Apparently, I've pissed you off. Tell me what I did so I can fix it," I insist, shaking the water from my hands.

She whips around, her curls wet on the side of her face. She sighs, opens her bag, pulls her phone out, and puts it right in front of my face.

Well, fuck. It's a still from a night out with Cassie. I take the phone from Emilie, letting it jog my memory. I remember that night, and I knew I was being reckless. It's not a full-fledged sex tape, but she asked if we could record some of it, and I said yes. All of this is consensual.

The timing isn't ideal.

She grabs her phone from me and turns.

"Wait, Emilie." I reach for her arm and get just enough to stop her.

"Maybe that's why Cassie showed up at the game? She was looking for another Zack Andersen cameo."

I take a deep breath. I don't want to go on the defensive but she's making it hard. "That video isn't recent. It's from last year when I had that stupid blue streak in my hair for one of my sponsorships."

Never thought I'd find a good thing that came from someone temporarily putting a Cosmos blue dye in my hair, but I guess it's solid for timestamping a NSFW video that shows up much later.

"You know, this was your idea. The whole fake dating thing. You showed up, unannounced, and it wasn't something I asked for, but that's just how you are. No one tells Zack Andersen 'no.' You're so charming and cunning and FUCK. Why did you even do this in the first place? I can't wait to try and explain *this* to my family."

Emilie is full-on ranting. I watch her lips move, trying to catch the words flying out of her mouth a mile a minute.

"Let's go inside and let me explain this." I try to keep my voice calm and level.

"Explain what? Your sex tape that's taking the Internet by storm? God, it's so cliché I can't even take it. The fake version of us isn't even worth it." She starts to laugh and looks at the ceiling, her hands resting on her hips.

The cliché comment stings. I take a step closer to her, my eyes glued on hers. "First of all, don't do that—tell me I'm a cliché. Believe me, I get it. I don't need to hear it from you." Emilie scoffs and turns her head to the side, breaking eye contact. I follow with my head so she must look at me. "Second, if this," I point between the two of us, "is so fake, why are you so pissed off?"

"You know what my family is like and they already weren't convinced, and now I'm going to look like an even bigger idiot at this wedding and—"

I can't even let her finish. "Your family? Get the fuck out of here. You're the realest person I've ever met, and I *know* this is not about your family."

"You don't know everything about me." Her arms cross over her chest as she looks up into my face.

"I don't. But I do know you had a chance to end this at the gala, tell Mitch and Eliza I was kidding. I know you didn't have to bring me to your family dinner. I also know that you don't do a damn thing you don't want to. You wanted in on this, too."

"You didn't give me much of a choice when you just show up and announce you're coming to this wedding." She looks around, like the answer to the question is hidden somewhere in this apartment lobby.

"You're fucking kidding me. You *always* have a choice. Plus, you were the one with all the rules and stipulations. You clearly thought this through."

I close the distance, our faces even closer, rage dancing in her eyes. Now would be the most ridiculous time to kiss her but I can't help but stare at those lips. Those perfect fucking lips. It's like months of almost touching her, having her, thinking about what it'd be like, is coming down to this moment. Again, the timing couldn't be worse.

"And you didn't answer my question. If this is fake, why are you so fucking mad?"

Her eyes flash with surprise.

Just as the power goes out and the city sirens wail.

Chapter 24
Emilie

I WHIP THE DOOR open to the stairwell, almost hitting Zack with it, before he holds it open and follows me inside. Nothing like the power going out when you live on the twelfth floor.

We take the stairs in silence, using the lights from our cell phone to guide the way. I don't ask why he's following me. I don't tell him not to and he doesn't remind me that his question still hasn't been answered.

Why am I upset?

It's hard to check in with myself. My brain is foggy from lack of sleep, I'm shivering from being soaked with rain, and I can feel the intrusive thoughts on the verge of staking their claim for the evening.

What if you fell backward, taking Zack with you, and hit your head? How long would it take for someone to find us? What if you were both unconscious? How awful would it be for the person who stumbled on us?

I've always had a soft spot for Zack. Ever since the first time I met him, when he looked at me in that way that made me count. Whatever we've been doing the last six-ish weeks has blurred the lines.

It's not lost on me that I've probably always wanted more but I'd never ask for it. I would reason with myself on how it's absurd: people like Zack don't end up with people like me. Now I'm the cliché.

We get to my apartment door, and I open it, my knuckles white from clutching the keys. Zack walks in after me and locks the door behind him.

I start with my wet clothes, losing layers, tossing them in a laundry basket.

"The sirens. It's a thunderstorm. Sixty mile per hour wind gusts and hail," Zack says, also taking off his wet clothes.

I go to my closet, now only in my bra and panties, and my body shakes so bad it's hard to think about anything else. My body feels light and hazy, like I'm about to pass out. The tears come, and I try to keep quiet, but it doesn't work.

"Emilie. Are you okay?" Zack questions, right outside the closet.

I don't have it in me to lie anymore. "No. I'm not okay."

"Can I come in?" he asks, as I crouch down to the floor, arms around myself.

"Yes," I choke out, trying to catch my breath.

Next thing I know, Zack is beside me on the floor, wearing a hoodie I borrowed from him and was waiting to return, and his briefs. He set his phone tilted on the ground to light up at least some of the closet. He grips the sides of my arms and leads me out to my bed, sitting me down. In my closet, he finds sweatpants and a crewneck.

"Arms up," he says, his voice gentle and caring, as silent tears trickle down my cheeks.

I do what he says, and he puts the crewneck on me. He picks up an arm, looking for a hair tie on my wrist, which he finds. He pulls my hair into a bun, trying to keep my new top dry.

Then he's kneeling in front of me, putting my legs into the sweatpants before standing me up and pulling them on. When I think Zack's done dressing me, he comes back with two pairs of long fuzzy socks—a pair for each of us.

"We should be in the center of a room, away from windows. I think we should go in the living room. I already pulled down all the blinds and curtains. You good with that?" he asks.

I nod, tears still falling. He grabs my hand and walks me to the living room. When I think he's going to set me on the couch, he wraps me in a hug. Tight. My body still shakes as he rubs circles on my back. I hold on to him like I need him to breathe.

Right now, maybe I do?

I put the side of my face on his chest as he sways us back and forth. One hand rubs the side of an arm while the other holds my back. The pressure is perfect. I don't know how he does this—gives me what I need without asking for it.

I don't know how long we stand like this, alternating positions but still holding onto each other in my dark living room. Long enough for my shaking, and tears, to stop and for the warmth to come back to my bones.

Zack reaches back, placing his hands on the sides of my face. "Do you have candles anywhere? Any power banks for our phones?"

I point to the closet near the apartment door. "There's an entire emergency response kit in there." Zack smiles.

When we're set up on the couch, with almost every blanket I own, and a few candles lit in the apartment so we can make our way around, Zack gets to the bottom of the bag and pulls out two iPads, looking confused.

"They're charged with movies and stuff to watch. Sometimes I can't sleep and need the sound or the distraction of something familiar."

"Jackpot!" Zack says enthusiastically with a fist pump.

He puts the iPads on the coffee table and leans back, looking at me. I'm practically curled into the couch, knees to my chest, and looking straight at him.

"I feel like we need to finish our conversation, but I'd like to call a time-out. The power isn't going to come back on until tomorrow, at least. All I know is I don't want to leave you. I want to stay here with you tonight. As long as you're comfortable with that."

His eyes are eager, honest. In this moment, there's nothing to hide.

"Time-out granted. And please don't leave me tonight," I beg, being as vulnerable as I can. The thought of being here alone could send me straight for a panic attack.Zack opens his arms, and I practically crawl into his lap. He wraps one arm around my shoulders and uses the other to reach for my hand to hold.

We sit like this without saying a word, soaking in the silence of the apartment. There's things that have gone unanswered, and I know we'll pick it up when it makes sense.

All I know is right now, I feel safe.

Chapter 25
Zack

I WAKE UP, CONFUSED about where I am. Then I see Emilie, sleeping on my chest. I'm careful not to move her as I check my phone for the time—it's after 2 AM.

I had to delete all social media apps from my phone, because the notifications wouldn't stop. I looked at just a few to see there's quite an uproar about me cheating on Emilie. I didn't. I wouldn't.

After I deleted the apps, I blocked Cassie's number. It doesn't take a rocket scientist to know how the video got out. She didn't get the attention she wanted from me so then hit me where it hurts, especially when she saw me leaving with someone.

Maybe Emilie has real feelings for me? Maybe I fucked this up before there was a chance to even see what's what? Maybe I'm overthinking all of this.

She called me a cliché. Fuck. I don't want to be a cliché, but I know that the fun and chaotic version of me is who people like best. Maybe I've leaned into, and stayed too long, in the way I've been categorized by people who don't really know me.

Being yourself is fucking hard. It's easier when you're putting on a show, and people don't like you, or want to push back on something.

Maybe it's time to be vulnerable?

Maybe it's too fucking late.

Emilie brings me back to the moment, gasping for air and practically jumping off my chest. She looks at me, her face painted with a look of terror.

"It's me. Zack. We're at your apartment. You're safe." I stand up and get in front of her.

I wonder if she had a nightmare. She moves away from me, her hand on her wrist and her eyes on the clock. Her breathing is loud and erratic.

"Are you... taking your pulse?"

She doesn't speak until she's finished. "Yes."

"Is that something you do often?" I don't know what's going on.

She tries to breathe in air but it's too fast, too shallow. Instead of answering me, she practically runs to me and grabs my hand to put it on her chest.

"You feel that, right?"

"Your heartbeat? Yes. I feel it."

"Does it feel normal?" Her eyes plead, and she grips my hand that's on her chest.

"What does that mean?" I want to understand her, reassure her, but I'm not sure I know how.

She moves away from me, both hands on her chest. Emilie paces a small spot between the kitchen and living room. I don't understand—this doesn't seem like a nightmare but I don't know what it could be.

Emilie puts her back on a wall and slides down until she's sitting, putting her head in between her knees.

I sit next to her and lightly put a hand on her back. "EJ, what can I do?"

She looks at me over one of her kneecaps, and her paled face breaks me. It looks like she's in agonizing pain. I put pressure on her back as she breathes deep—I feel her hold air in and slowly let it out.

"Tell me you're real. This is real."

I squeeze her shoulders. "I'm real. You're here with me. This is real." I say it like I'm trying to convince someone. "Did you have a nightmare?"

"Sometimes my life is a nightmare," she answers, which leaves me even more confused. "It's my brain. My stupid fucking brain."

"I think you have a beautiful brain," I insist, tucking a curl behind her ear.

She takes her time to compose herself. "If you could hear it, you wouldn't say that, " she says, her voice dripping with sadness. "It's not nightmares. It's my obsessive-compulsive disorder, OCD. But not OCD like I like to keep things clean or neat and organized."

Emilie leans back against the wall—I keep my eyes on her but don't say anything. I want to give her the room to keep going.

"It's intrusive thoughts. These things that my brain tricks me into thinking are true or are possible. Sometimes they are so horrible. I'll wake from a dead sleep and just fall into this loop." She wipes tears from her eyes with the back of her hand, which I immediately grab and squeeze.

"Like today, in the car, I thought about driving into oncoming traffic. What would happen. What it would be like. How much it would hurt. The sounds that would fill me ears. I woke up and felt like my heart wasn't beating, that it just stopped. That's one of the most common."

God. That sounds terrifying. Now I'm thinking about the night that I called her, she said it was a nightmare. It wasn't. It was her thinking she was dying or not alive or something else horrible.

"People make it out to be this quirky personality thing, but it's like your brain telling you fucking horror stories of hypotheticals most of the time." Her voice trails off and she cries into her hands.

I stand in front of her, my hand on one of her shoulders until she looks up at me. Emilie's hazel eyes are dark, red rimmed, and wide. I put my hands out for her to grab. When she takes them, I help her stand and wrap her up in a hug that's borderline too tight. I think about her, alone in her apartment, pacing, checking her pulse. The pain she deals with and doesn't say anything.

"You probably think I'm crazy," she murmurs into my chest.

I'm alternating between rubbing her arms and holding her tight to me. "Absolutely fucking not. I think you're strong. I can't imagine what it's like to feel the way you do."

She leans back a little, catches my eyes with hers. "You think I'm strong?"

"I've always thought that. You've always been a force, but joke's on me—you're battling yourself, every day, on top of everything else I see you do." I put a hand in her hair, putting a curl around my finger.

"A force." She doesn't sound like she believes me.

"I'm here. This is real. And you, Emilie James, are a force." I kiss her on the forehead before surrounding her body with mine.

Fuck, they say everyone has things going on you can't see, but I never thought about this with Emilie. She has always seemed so put together, accomplished. She's still those things, but now, it's much more impressive.

If I felt protective before, there's no words for what I feel now. Like my only goal should be to take away some of the pain and hurt she's feeling. I want her to know how incredible she is.

No matter how much her brain tries to convince her otherwise.

"Can we go back to sleep? In my bed this time?" Emilie's voice is delicate and unsure.

"Whatever you want." And I mean it.

We gather the blankets and get her bed back in order. I let her show me what side she sleeps on, and I get under the blankets on the other side of her king bed.

She sets up one of the iPads on her bedside table.

"Do you care if I play something? It will help me calm down and fall asleep."

I think it's adorable and proactive she keeps charged iPads in her emergency items stash. "Whatever you need."

Emilie puts on Friends, which must be one of her comfort shows, and snuggles into my side.

I stay up until the rhythm of her breathing tells me she's asleep.

Chapter 26
Emilie

Even the weather seems to be on the Cosmos' side. If they were scheduled to play on Sunday, the game would've had to move or be rescheduled. Luckily, they got the Monday night slot.

It's Monday afternoon, and the city is back to normal. The flooding has receded, the subway is back on schedule, and I'm sitting at my favorite coffee shop with an iced coffee.

My schedule with True Blue Records is flexible—I do what I need to do, when it needs to be done. Willow and I meet at least once a week, when it works with both of our schedules. I'm supposed to be working on finding new openers for Willow's next tour leg, to share with her for our meeting on Wednesday. The fact that she fought to do a smaller, more intimate tour, has allowed me to learn this part of the business.

When she interviewed me for the assistant position, one of the questions she asked was, "What do you want to learn?" I answered with a quick, "What *don't* I want to learn?" It sounded a little cheesy in the moment, but I meant it. I crave the new, whether that's learning, places, or things to explore. Willow has taken full advantage of that answer and I've learned more in the last eighteen months, in an industry I'm unfamiliar with, than I ever did in a year-long college internship.

Right now, all I can think about is Zack. The video. Our fight. Him staying over. Me spilling my guts about something only a handful of people know about. I'm like emotional vegetable soup.

On one hand, with a little space, I feel awful about the leaked video. Zack didn't ask for that, and I'm fairly certain it came from a place of "let me get you back." I don't know Cassie personally, but it doesn't seem a coincidence that she saw us together and then the video made its rounds. Yes, Zack made that choice, but for it to come out a year later? That's bold.

On the other, I'm jealous. I can say that to myself, in the hustle and bustle of this coffee shop, tucked in a corner booth where people can barely see me. I've always felt something for Zack, call it a crush or catching feelings, but I've never acted on them. Like, it wasn't even in the realm of possibility.

Zack was right. I had a chance to tell him no, not to do the whole fake dating thing for my sister's wedding, but I didn't. It doesn't take a genius to figure out why.

Then there's the whole Zack taking care of me aspect. He took charge. Made me feel safe. He dressed me, for crying out loud. This thing happened to him—the video and my reaction—and he made me feel like a priority.

Once everything had calmed down and the power came back on, Zack left my apartment early Saturday morning. The only communication we've exchanged since then was him asking if I was going to the game, and I said I was. Willow's out of town, and Zack's family isn't coming—doesn't feel right not to have someone there for him.

If this is fake, why are you so upset?

The question that I keep coming back to. But now, the answer is easy: it's because I never wanted this to be fake.

Now, I'm sitting at this coffee shop, listening to the same track from the same potential opening artist, for probably the fifth time, trying to figure out what I'm going to do next.

My phone buzzes with a text from Willow.

Willow

> you are kidding me with this

> you two are adorable

I open what she sent, and it takes me to one of Zack's social media accounts. It's a picture of me in his jersey after the first home game, and I'm smiling over my shoulder. He must've taken it as I was turning back around. When I swipe, I see a picture of the two of us, the selfie we took after the game.

It's the caption that makes my jaw drop: **here's to one of the strongest women I know**, with a Cosmos blue heart emoji.

This is him making a statement on the video, without making a statement directly. This is the post telling everyone he's still with me—I'm still in the picture. But more importantly, this is Zack telling me he thinks I'm strong.

When I think about how I've struggled with my OCD, in various forms, I've never looked at myself as strong. I've always been embarrassed; wished my brain was different and did my best to hide it from everyone I could. It's hard to understand obsessive-compulsive disorder, especially with the way people have started using it as a term that describes someone who likes things organized. Compulsions are not fun—they're not something to romanticize. They're something that makes you feel out of control with dire consequences if you don't go along with it.

Obsessive-compulsive disorders have a lot of rules.

I let Zack in on one of my darkest corners—he saw it in action—and he's still here... telling me I'm strong. My cheeks pinch from an anxious smile, because this is such a disaster. Murky chaos at best.

It's hard not to compare Zack and Mitch to learning about this piece of me. Even after all this time, Mitch's reaction is a punch to the gut.

He once told me, "You're a lot of work" when I asked if we could make a coffee stop after a night of pacing. Believe me, he meant it. This was before we stopped sleeping over at each other's places. He'd blame it on work, needing to get up early or the commute, but it only happened after I woke up one night, frantic and checking my pulse.

Then he found his way to the better sister—the one who lives to be agreeable and doesn't wake up from a dead sleep wondering if she's alive, or if something terrible is going to happen if you don't immediately get out of bed.

Therapy taught me there's not "a better sister" storyline at play, and I believe my therapist. But it's still something I spent too much time thinking about, and where my brain still goes when it's really looking to hurt my feelings.

It's like I'm the ribbon on a tug-of-war rope, being pulled back and forth between what I should care about. Zack. The video. Zack taking care of me. What this means. What I do next.

This is a lot to take in. Immediately, I start to laugh, my favorite coping mechanism when I'm overwhelmed.

I take a long drink from my iced coffee, urging the caffeine to help me be productive. I need to make progress on the openers for Willow, then I can get into Cosmos mode.

One thing is certain: Zack and I need to talk.

THE COSMOS MADE IT look too easy and won their first Monday night game, 42-10. Even with a large lead, the stadium never relented, which is like a natural serotonin boost. I'm always after one of those, in addition to my daily meds.

I'm in the hallway, waiting for Zack to come out of the locker room. I spin a gold ring on my right hand as I switch my weight from one leg to the next. If you didn't know I was someone with crippling anxiety, you might think I was dancing.

Zack sees me, and his face is hard to read. I smile when I see him, because no matter what's going on, that's my natural reaction to seeing him. He practically skips over to me and wraps me up in a hug, his head on my shoulder and his arms around my waist.

He doesn't say anything as he sways us back and forth. His arms squeeze around me, and it's like every immediate worry and concern drifts away as I melt into him. It's like his frame is meant for me—I fit perfectly.

I feel like I never fit. This is a nice change of pace.

He finally pulls away, but puts my face in his hands and says, "I'm so glad you came." His eyes remind me of a perfect summer day, not a cloud in the sky.

My bones are made of goo and he might be holding me up at this point. Not sure what would happen if he just let go.

"I feel like we should talk. Are you up for that?" He moves his hands from my face, I'm still standing—which is good—and puts his hand out for me to take.

I barely feel ready, like I don't even know what I'm going to say, but I know we can't put this off any longer. Or I can't, at least.

"Yes, we should."

Chapter 27
Zack

EMILIE'S IN MY APARTMENT for the first time, and I've got to be honest, I thought it'd be with less clothes and heaviness.

Ever since Friday, I've done nothing but think about her. Wondering if she's safe, if she's pacing her hallway, checking her pulse. She has infiltrated my brain with no signs of leaving.

She sits on my navy-blue velvet couch, the vibrancy of her curls contrasting as she tips her head.

"You would have velvet furniture," she muses, running her hands on the sides of where she's sitting. "I love this color."

"I like color. And soft things," I say as I sit down across from her, wanting to give her space.

The silence is awkward for a few seconds, before I jump right in.

"The video. Not my finest moment," I say while rubbing my hands together, before cracking some of my knuckles. "I know when people have things leak like this, the first question is always how could they be so stupid? I'm not stupid but sometimes I'm reckless, but usually only when I'm at risk. We didn't record everything—like, being naked on film, not good—but I wasn't dumb enough to go all the way."

I've thought about what I was going to say, even tried practicing it a few times, because I feel like I get one chance to make it right.

"I don't like that it came out for my own personal reasons, obviously, but I hate that it made you feel bad."

Emilie nods. "I appreciate it. Really, I do. But it wasn't fair for me to take this thing that happened to you and make it about me. That was selfish."

Well, fuck. I didn't even think of it that way.

"Thank you."

"Are you doing okay?" She leans forward, taking me in.

"Yes. I mean, not ideal, but we both consented. I had to talk to Tripp about a statement from *When We Play*. Again, the timing with the youth event could've been better."

"Okay, if that changes. I'm happy to listen without judgment."

"Thank you. Seriously."

I pause for a few moments, making sure my thoughts are in order before continuing. "I googled a lot the last few days about OCD and intrusive thoughts because I want to understand it. I want to understand you. Even reading it hurt because I can't imagine you going through this regularly."

Emilie's cheeks redden. "That isn't part of me I try to share with too many people. I know it's a lot to take in or take on. The whole thing is complicated, and I've worked hard at coming to terms with it, just myself, and telling people about it is a whole other thing."

Basically, she feels like too much. This is something that takes up too much space.

"I can't tell you how to feel ,but it's not too much for me. You're never too much for me. You always seem to be just enough."

She stops, frozen, eyes searching for something specific.

"That's one of the kindest things anyone has ever said to me." Surprise is in the lines of her face.

"If you need more room, I'll make it." I look around my apartment. "There's lots of room here. Take as much as you need." I laugh at the heaviness.

Emilie scratches her arm, the red marks bright on her milky skin.

The weight is in the silence swirling around us, making it hard to breathe. It feels like my mind is stuck on one thing. The question I asked her and the one she never answered. The one I need an answer to.

She takes a breath but holds it in, like she wants to say something but doesn't.

Fuck. Here goes nothing.

"Emilie. I'm going to ask you again. If this," I point between the two of us, "is fake, then why were you so upset?"

She tilts her head, her lips pressed in a thin line, like she'll do anything to keep her mouth closed. Her eyes, intense and almost completely green instead of hazel, go from mine to the floor, and back to me again.

"I'm not sure." She says it like a question.

"Do you want me to guess?" I'm surprised how badly I want her to say yes.

"No. Not really," Emilie answers much too fast, immediately covering her eyes after.

I sigh, leaning back. "Why not?" I don't want to put my cards on the table, until I know this won't ruin what we have. No matter what, I can't lose her, even if we're just friends.

She takes a deep breath, one where I watch her stretch into it. The seconds between us are like a snowball that's being rolled down a hill, getting bigger and bigger—more substantial.

"Because I'm afraid you might be right." She stands, and I feel like she's looking for a place to pace in my apartment.

I walk over to her and she stops, her arms crossed and pushing her shoulders damn near her ears. When her eyes meet mine, it's like the air leaves my lungs. She's so fucking beautiful, no matter how unsure of herself she is.

I take one step and being this close to her, without touching, is torture. I raise one hand and lightly touch under her chin, her skin hot under my fingers, and tip her face up to mine.

"This is against the rules," she says, her voice quiet, as she looks around the room. "No touching if we're not in public." Her voice is breathy.

"It's your rule to break, EJ." I'm so close I can smell the vanilla from her lip balm. "I propose a new rule. Why don't we do what feels right?"

I catch my breath after offering my suggestion—the rule to basically have no rules.

"What feels right for you?" Her voice is quiet enough that a whisper would most likely be louder.

I look at her eyes, golden and like they're shining for me, and to her lips. It's unlike me to hold back, not go for what I want. Holding back is killing me.

"Right now, it feels like if I don't kiss you, I'll never fucking forgive myself." My voice comes out like I'm begging. I hate being in limbo. Do what you're going to do and deal with consequences, or don't—but make a decision. "But to be honest, that's how it always feels when I'm with you."

Her eyes sparkle at the confession. Me telling her how badly I want to kiss her. It's almost like she didn't think I felt what she does. I know why she's so jealous, and I'd be the same, if not worse, but one of us has to say it.

"Then do it." She bites her lip in the brief second between her giving me permission and my mouth landing on hers.

I kiss her the way I promised myself I would if I ever got the chance. Like she deserves. Like I've thought about her perfect fucking lips for months. I try to put all the pent-up feelings of wanting to do this for so long, this and so much fucking more, in this kiss.

Her lips press into mine—fucking finally—smooth like silk. When she smiles into me, I almost combust. It's like my skin is about to burst into flames and she's the gasoline. I'm not afraid of catching fire. Instead, I want to.

It's soft, urgent, needy, and electrifying all at once.

When she opens her mouth, just enough for me to brush my tongue with hers, she tastes like vanilla and citrus. My hands go into her hair, those curls—the ones I dream of. I lean into her, and she lets me. Her back arches, pushing her hips into mine, and she moans into my mouth.

My arms wrap around her lower back, I dip my knees, and then pick her up. At first, her legs are straight off the floor, until she wraps them around my waist. I walk her to the bar off the side of my kitchen and set her ass on it.

That perfect ass.

I kiss her with my hands on each side of her, keeping my dick far away from the bunched-up area of her jersey dress. I've never been turned on like this while wearing so many clothes. I don't trust my dick any closer to her.

I put my forehead to hers and when she looks at me, I can barely breathe.

"You can't look at me like that," I say, not breaking eye contact, because that look is about to be my new obsession.

"Or what?" she asks while grabbing a fistful of my shirt, pulling me as close to her as I could be.

I bite my lip, stifling my laugh at her attitude. "I've been waiting too long to kiss you, to have you like this, and I need to take my time. Frantically fucking you on this bar doesn't go along with that plan."

She laughs and throws her head back, her hand still gripping the fabric of my shirt.

"I want to take my time with you," I repeat, and she's not laughing anymore. I'm surprised by how serious I sound. I wrap a curl around my finger and pull, letting it bounce back.

Emilie doesn't say anything else before putting her arms on my shoulders, wrapping me up and putting her lips back mine. She trails her tongue along the seam of my lips, and I open for her. She moans again, and I know those are something I'll chase for as long as she'll let me. Maybe even longer than that.

It's like I'm starved for her. Every inch. Every sound. Every piece of her.

My mouth moves from her lips to her neck, turning her head with my hands in her curls, to kiss the soft spot behind her ear. She slowly tilts her head.

"That," she releases a quick breath, "feels so good."

I nip and nibble, and then I float my lips right in front of her skin. She's practically panting and almost hits my mouth with the heaving of her chest. I lightly blow before placing soft, intentional kisses.

Emilie turns my face by putting her hands through my hair, scratching my scalp with her nails, before lightly pulling them down the front of my neck. The whole time, her lips are locked on mine and I don't ever want to find the key.

This moment is a place I know I'll go to in my dreams. For fuck's sake, my brain even knows I'm being insufferably sweet, but this moment? It's everything.

We separate, and she wraps her arms back around me and I hug her, my hands splayed on her back.

She puts a hand on my chest and creates a little space between us. "You kissed me," Emilie says, wearing a smile that would stop me dead in my tracks.

"You kissed me back," I say.

"Did you think I wouldn't?"

"I didn't know for sure... but I fucking *dreamed* that you would."

Chapter 28
Emilie

New phone number who dis

it's Zack

I didn't want you to block me thinking I'm some creep

why the new number

you said it bothered you, the random texts and pictures

from people I used to date or whatever

and it's been out of control for a while tbh

you didn't have to do that

no, I did

<3

you're the first person I texted, consider yourself special

I'll be at your place in ten

My stomach flips and somersaults, and I realize I'm smiling at my phone like a completely unhinged human being. Call me the Joker from Batman. I set my phone down on my vanity, like it's hot and going to burn my fingers, and put my hands over my mouth. Even with the hands, I can see the ridiculous smile underneath.

It feels like my lips have been on fire ever since we kissed, or since I lived out one of my fantasies. A hot professional athlete picking me up, setting me on his bar, and kissing me silly? Okay, yes. I'm on board with this.

Zack kissed me.

I'd be lying if I said I hadn't said those words aloud, to myself in the mirror, to reiterate the point. It happened. In real life.

If my heart could sing, it would. I've had hookups where men have driven me wild, or have made me see stars, but I've never felt like this during a first kiss. Like it's what the universe had planned and has just been cackling at the two of us trying to figure it out. Like I want to do it forever. Like I want him kissing every single inch of me.

Now, Zack is picking me up to go to dinner with his family. This was planned before the kiss that changed my entire outlook on life, but it somehow feels like this is exactly how things were supposed to go.

Luckily, Willow needed to move a meeting we had scheduled. I know she'll take one look at me and know something isn't the same. The flush of breaking the rules crawls up my neck, showing on my reflection in the mirror.

I watch my fingers as they graze my lips and try to think back to the exact feeling, everywhere Zack kissed me—but it's like a fever dream.

Snapping out of it, I change into the outfit I picked out for dinner. His mom is cooking, and Zack said it's laid back, but that doesn't mean I didn't agonize over what to wear. I landed on a black and white striped boat-neck top with a black midi skirt.

There's a knock on my door as I smooth the skirt a final time and grab a quick look at my reflection.

I open the door to see Zack, propped against the frame. He's doing the door lean—I might pass out. Before I can utter a single word, sound, anything to confirm I'm still awake, he beats me to it.

"How do you do this? Look this good for a meal I said my mom was cooking." He pops off the door frame and walks toward me.

For a split second, I wonder if this will be awkward—seeing each other after an almost too-hot make out session slash first kiss slash jump into whatever this is. Before my brain has time to spiral, Zack answers my question.

With his hand on the side of my face and his thumb below my chin, he puts his lips on mine.

Zack is kissing me. Again. I can't help but smile into him. Part of me wondered if the other night was a fluke. This would argue it wasn't, that we aren't.

He tastes like sugar as I deepen the kiss, my tongue touching the seam of his lips. My rib cage feels like it's too small and my heart is going to crack it open. I can feel it in every inch of my body, no need to check my pulse.

I take my hand and put it at the hem of his forest green henley. Moving it between my fingers a few times before I reach for him beneath the shirt, my hands on his skin. He flexes at the touch, surprised, and the muscles push back against my fingers.

"If you keep doing that, we're going to miss dinner." He pulls back but I keep my hand under his shirt, laughing. "And I don't piss off my sister, when I can help it." He gives me a quick, chaste kiss.

"Baby, you ready?"

I don't know if anyone has ever called me that. *Baby.* I feel like it's something people say but don't actually like. In this moment, I know one thing to be true.

Zack can call me baby whenever he wants.

× × ×
○ × × ×
○○○
○

WE PULL INTO THE driveway, and Zack smiles as he says, "I love coming home."

It's a brick two-story house, with white paint and a wraparound porch—rocking chairs and all. The house sits back, farther from the road, purple flowers and greenery decorate the front.

A wave of nostalgia hits me. This reminds me of Michigan.

My childhood home now belongs to another family, with new kids, where they'll make new memories. That house also had a porch. I find myself aching for a home I can't go back to.

Zack reaches for my hand as he looks back. "You ready?"

I nod, and he swings open the door to his childhood home.

A wave of comfort hits me, the air slightly cooler than outside, with wafts of butter, parmesan cheese, and garlic. My mouth waters at whatever is being cooked for dinner. I don't have any dietary restrictions, and if Zack is excited to eat here, it must be good.

"Mom, we're here!" We take our shoes off at the door and then round the corner from the hallway into the kitchen.

Zack's mom squeals as soon as she sees us. She's wearing a classic white linen shirt with dark jeans as she stirs something over the stove.

"Zack! Emilie!" She comes over and hugs us both at the same time, her head in between ours.

"Let me see you," she says, stepping back and literally taking me in from top to bottom. "Ah, it's so good to *finally* meet you. Zack is always gabbing about you. Now I know why."

It's hard not to blush. *Zack is always gabbing about you.* Was that before or after the fake dating turned into whatever the hell this is? A speck of nervousness flutters in my chest.

Her eyes are blue, like the water you dream of when you're going on vacation. Her hair is almost the same color as Zack's; a dark blonde, one that people try to re-create at the salon but can never get right. She's stunning, just like I thought she'd be.

"I'm Mackenzie, you can call me Mack." She rests her hand on my shoulder before walking back to the stove, moving whatever's in the pan with a wooden spoon. "Grab a seat, dinner's in probably twenty. I made a pitcher of Aperol Spritz for dinner. I remember Zack telling us how that's your go-to, and I thought to myself, when's the last time I had one of those?"

I'm going to melt from the sweetness.

"Zack, check the pantry. Got something for you."

He yells, "Hell yeah!" from what I'm guessing is the pantry and walks out with a massive box of Pop Rocks.

"You're the best." He kisses his mom on the cheek before bringing his ginormous box of candy to the bar, setting it down.

I can't help but raise an eyebrow. "I feel like I'm missing something."

"We used to bribe Zack with Pop Rocks to go to football practice when he first started playing. If I'm remembering correctly, it might've been flag football. Then it just turned into something we kept doing—"

"We should've invested in that company. Bought some stock or some-thing." A man walks in from the outside. He must be Zack's dad.

"I'm Chris. It's great to finally meet you." He puts his hand out for a hand shake, which I take him up on. "Somehow, we're still buying our NFL-playing son his favorite candy in bulk—at least, whenever we see it."

"Thank you for having me for dinner."

"Oh, it's not a problem. We've been excited ever since it's been on the calendar," he says before going to stand behind his wife, wrapping his arms around her from behind. He kisses her cheek, and it's like I can hear her smiling from here.

I'm a firm believer that my parents don't love each other. They may have at one point, but it feels very past tense for as long as I can remember. They respected each other enough to maintain a marriage, but there was never kissing, affection, or walking in on them doing something inti-mate—thank god. Seeing Zack's parents like this has my cheeks aching from smiling. It's lovely.

For a second, I think about what it'd be like growing up in a home like this.

"Your favorite daughter is here!" someone calls as the door shuts. She walks into the kitchen and claps her hands when she sees me. "You came! You're real!" she squeals before hugging me.

"This is Riley. My sister. My *only* sister," Zack laughs, while popping an olive in his mouth from the carefully constructed charcuterie board sitting on the bar.

Riley is gorgeous. This family has the good genetics or something because wow— even Chris is what you'd call a daddy. The man is a silver fox and ridiculously hot. I wonder if he was blonde like Zack when he was younger?

After greeting the rest of the family, Riley sits next to me and pours us each an Aperol Spritz.

"Okay, I want to know everything. Tell me *all* your secrets." She bumps my shoulder and lifts her glass up to me.

"And that's my cue. I'm going to help Dad outside." Zack gives me a few seconds to object, but when I don't, he opens the glass door and walks to the patio. He looks back for the quickest of seconds, and the whole things feels oddly familiar.

Riley takes a sip of her drink, her golden-brown eyes looking at me over her short glass, and says, "You don't really have to tell me your secrets, unless you want to, but tell me about Michigan."

It's not that I have a difficult time meeting new people, but sometimes it's like I'm trying to figure out the vibe. What version of myself best fits? What shouldn't I do? Is there anything I should avoid or hold back?

But right now, in this kitchen, it feels like I can just be Emilie.

And it feels so good.

Chapter 29
Zck

"THOSE LOOK GREAT," I say as my dad puts seasoned steaks on the grill.

There's a hesitancy between us, a weighted silence. We were supposed to go to a golf simulator spot together a few days ago, but he bailed last minute. As in, I was already there, waiting for him, and he texted saying something came up.

The last time he did this, it was because he talked trash about one of my teammates while he was getting a beer with a friend, and he was afraid it was going to come out in the press.

It never did. No one was listening who cared enough. To be honest, few people knew who the long snapper was from the mediocre team in Florida. When he finally told me what was going on, you could see the weight lift with each word that came out of his mouth.

"Hey, ugh, sorry about the other day. I got wrapped up in something here and couldn't make the golf thing work," he says, like he's reading my mind, but his eyes don't leave the grill.

It feels like there's something. Something in the way, between us. We've always had an open relationship, able to talk about anything, and I know he'll come to me when he's ready. I don't want to push him because that's now how we operate.

"It's not a big deal, Dad. We can always reschedule," I assure him while sitting down in one of the patio chairs.

It's got the vibes of an early fall day—one of my favorite times of year. The air is still warm, but it was much cooler in the morning. Some of the leaves on the trees, and some that have already fallen off their branch, are changing from green to a burning red, kind of like Emilie's hair.

Our backyard, fenced in with enough space to teach me how to properly snap a ball, is meticulously landscaped. Not a surprise, considering my parents love doing yard work together—enough that they rarely asked Riley or me to help when we were younger. We had chores but never anything to do with the yard.

We spent a ton of time out here as a family—dinners on the patio in the summer, jumping in piles of leaves in the fall, and playing in the first heavy snow. The wave of nostalgia, and gratitude, hits me at the same time. I love those memories and being able to come back to this home.

I already told my parents if they ever want to sell the house, I'd buy it—no questions asked. I can't imagine not being able to make the drive and come back here.

"Are you making a career change we should know about?" my dad questions.

I don't get it, and when I don't answer he says, "You know, porn? Or the adult film industry? OnlyFans?"

The joke warms my chest. "No, not a career change. Hoping to keep playing football and not give the world access to my junk."

"Maybe don't agree to any sort of filming in the bedroom, yes?" My dad is more awkward about that line than he was when he gave Riley and me countless talks about sex.

I nod and reply, "Great advice. I'll be using that one."

He smiles at me before clapping me on the back. A few seconds later, he changes the subject. "Team looks solid so far. You feel good?"

My dad turns the steaks, the sizzle a satisfying sound, as we talk about football.

Riley is monopolizing Emilie, and I fucking love it. We're at the dining room table, almost ready to eat, and the two of them laugh and chat like they've been friends for years. My mom joins in every once in a while, and who knows what they're talking about.

"He didn't!" Emilie gasps, her hand flying to her mouth when she sees I'm in hearing distance.

"Riley. What are you doing?" I ask cautiously.

"Oh, nothing. Definitely not telling Emilie about the time we went trick-or-treating as Beauty and the Beast." She takes a drink and locks her eyes on mine.

I smile, shaking my head. It was Riley's idea to match, and she wanted to be the Beast, so I went as Belle. Riley may be younger than me, but she's always had a knack for getting me to do exactly what she wanted.

My sister nudges Emilie and says, "I'll send you pictures."

I shake my head and scoff, kind of laughing, mostly because I know it doesn't matter what I say. Riley and Emilie have probably already exchanged numbers *and* incriminating photos of me. Compared to some of the things that are out there, including the video where you can see 95% of my naked body, a picture of me dressed as a princess shouldn't even move the needle.

"Time to eat," my mom announces, setting a massive bowl of pasta on the table. "The pasta is fresh. Chris and I made it this morning, and it's just garlic, parmesan, a little salt and pepper."

My mouth is watering, and I'm already putting a pile of it on my plate.

"Fresh pasta. Yum! I learned how to do that at a cooking class this year," Emilie says, before grabbing some for her plate.

"I need the details. Chris and I love cooking together." Mom reaches over and rubs my dad's forearm, her sleeves rolled up a little.

"Oh my gosh, is that a tattoo?" Emilie asks, looking at my mom's wrist.

It is. My jersey number, 34, in a blocky font, with a small airplane. Jersey number for me and the airplane for Riley.

"Yes. We all have one. Riley asked for matching tattoos for her eighteenth birthday."

"Stop, I love that so much," Emilie says to the table. Then she turns to me with her brows raised. "Where's yours?" she asks, quietly enough for just the two of us.

"My ribs." I lift my arm, rubbing the place where the ink lives on my skin. I look to see Riley, not paying attention and I'm thankful. If Emilie and I had really been dating for almost eight weeks at this point, she wouldn't buy that Emilie hasn't seen me naked yet.

"Do you have any tattoos?" Riley asks.

Emilie swallows, and I can see her rubbing her hands together in her lap before she answers. "No. I want to get one though. My family had a drastically different view on them, and even though I'm a grown adult, I'm still afraid of what my parents would say."

Naturally. Her family stepping in and making her feel some type of way about something that doesn't impact them at all seems completely on brand.

My mom shakes her head. "We've always wanted Riley and Zack to be able to express themselves, however it worked for them."

"Like him spelling his name with a 'K,'" Emilie says, spinning pasta on her spoon.

"Just like that," my mom responds with a look of fondness, like she's pleased I told Emilie that story.

"Now, do I wish there were times where someone didn't express themselves so much? Like when the beginning of a sex tape drops?" My dad gives me a look and Riley starts to laugh, before my parents join in, and then Emilie and me.

I know it was stupid and a bit careless, but my parents supporting me, no matter what, means the world to me.

Her laugh runs out, and she looks at me, eyes bright but watery. I reach my hand over, squeezing Emilie's knee.

AFTER THE GOODBYES ARE said, phone numbers are exchanged between my mom and Emilie, and we both leave with containers full of leftover pasta, we're in the car.

While I'm turning the GPS on to avoid any accidents or traffic, I hear a sniffle.

I look over to see Emilie crying.

Panic runs over my body in thick, heavy waves. "What's the matter?" I ask, turning my body toward her, as much as my Jeep will allow.

She wipes her eyes with her fingers and replies, "I'm being stupid. Don't mind me."

Is she for real? Thinks she's going to get in my car, start to cry, and I'm just going to be like sure, whatever you say? Not a chance.

I don't say anything—letting the silence drag on, letting her know I'm not going to accept her previous answer.

"I had such a lovely time," she says, right into a sob.

"It doesn't sound like you did." I hand her a tissue from the center console. "EJ, what is this?"

Emilie takes a couple deep breaths, calming herself down.

"No, I really did. Your family is a dream come true. I feel like the universe is showing me what it's like to have one that truly loves you, flaws and all. I'll never have that. Fuck, I never had it when I was younger and needed it most." She takes a few seconds to gather herself before she continues. "I felt like myself with them. No mask needed, and it's so refreshing; like my bones feel lighter. I know every family has their issues but they just joked with you about your recent leaked video like it was nothing. I once got a B- in the fifth grade on a midterm, and my parents brought it up for years."

I take my fingers and tuck a stray curl behind her ear. I don't want to interrupt. I want her to keep going, get it all out.

She shakes her head. "Your family really loves you. That's all. I don't know what that's like."

Ouch.

"I know you're going to tell me that they love me. And they do. I feel like they love me the programmed amount, but nothing more. It's not surprising. I've never seen my parents hold hands, or kiss, like really kiss, you know?"

I frown before speaking, "That isn't what I was going to say. I was going to tell you that you deserve better than that. They might think they know what they're giving up, but they don't have a fucking clue. You're brilliant, brave, strong, and you love them even when they don't deserve it."

She cries harder, but it's silent as her shoulders shake with tears.

"EJ, look at me." I try to keep my voice gentle and level.

When her eyes finally look up to mine, there's some part of me that splinters and cracks. Her eyelids are rimmed with red, some of her mascara is smeared on the sides of her eyes, and her lip trembles.

I put my mouth on hers, doing anything to stop that trembling lip. The one that could damn near ruin me.

Her lips are soft and hesitant under mine. I can't tell if she's surprised or if she's holding back. But it doesn't matter. She tastes like Aperol and orange. When she kisses me back, it's like she falls into it. I could spend days holding onto her just like this.

This is much different than the first time we kissed in my apartment. That was deliciously frantic and like I'd never catch my breath again if I wasn't touching her, covering as much of her body with mine. It was scorching. Tense. Hot as hell.

This kiss means something else. I'm trying to tell her things I don't have the words for. It's comfort. Reassurance. An apology that shouldn't come from me but I do it anyway.

When we break the kiss, our foreheads press together, and it's just our breaths in the front seat of my Jeep. I twirl a curl of her hair around my finger.

"Do you really want a tattoo?" I ask, changing the subject but something I've been thinking about since dinner.

She laughs, wiping her eyes. "Yes. I don't even know what I'd want. I've almost gotten one a few times but never could see it all the way through. I feel like I have enough going on with my family, and I don't need something else that would just be problematic."

I'm surprised. Emilie always seems like she's got the upper hand, with everything, but maybe not her family. The differences between her family and mine couldn't be louder tonight.

"Thank you for everything. For bringing me here, introducing me to your family, " she says, tears still heavy on her thick black lashes. "For kissing me the way you do."

"Don't worry, we'll be back." I kiss her forehead.

I don't have it in me to tell her that I've never brought home a girlfriend as an adult man. How I've never let myself get close enough. How I've put up the silly, go-lucky, version of myself as the mask I wear.

How I've never put myself at risk, honestly.

But now? I'm wondering if I'd risk it all for her.

Chapter 30
Emilie

My brain is a mess. A tornado full of things I need to accomplish and things I shouldn't be thinking about. It's hard to keep things straight. Plus, I've had a string of a few rough nights with my OCD.

Not uncommon for a streak of anxious days and almost sleepless nights to stack on top of each other. Nothing like your brain working against you when you're already down and out.

That means I'm drinking an iced coffee bigger than my face and I'm convinced it won't be the last one I have today. My eyelids are heavy, like my lashes are weighing them down, and my muscles ache like I've been working out too much. But really, I've just been awake.

It's one of the first days where it feels like summer is truly on its way out. The wind blows, kissing my skin with the type of chill I love. Leaves are tinged with red and gold, most of them holding onto their branches—for now at least.

I'm walking from the coffee shop back to my apartment when my phone buzzes.

I like surprises so yes

same time, see you soon

and yes, we'll still get food

He does it again—answers a question before I have the chance to even ask.

When I've been pacing my hallway, unable to sleep, I almost called Zack this week. I know he'd come over, but I also know he's had a rough practice week. Part of me is afraid to rely on him.

My intrusive thoughts aren't going away.

I don't know what Zack's plan is.

His suggestion of 'let's do what feels right' changes this whole thing and I find I'm more reserved. Like I don't want to come on too strong, because now it's for real. Maybe it's always been real?

Reaching my apartment door, I yawn as I let myself in. I look at the time and have a few hours before Zack will pick me up. I place my iced coffee in the fridge, trying to keep the integrity as much as possible.

I fall onto the couch, grab a blanket, and set an alarm on my phone.

Time for a powernap.

A SOFT KNOCK WAKES me up. I shoot up off the couch, gasping, looking at the time on my phone.

"Emilie... are you in there?" Zack practically croons from outside the door.

I smooth my hair as best I can and open the door.

"Sorry, sorry, sorry. I fell asleep and my alarm didn't go off."

Zack laughs, coming in and closing the door behind him. "It's totally fine. There's no rush."

A tiny piece of the panic falls away with his reassurance.

"What do I wear? What's the vibe?"

Zack rubs his hands together, his forearms flexing, and I need a drink of water. Fuck, this man is so hot.

"Two surprises. Wear something comfortable. Nothing physically active."

Huh? That's not really a clue. I change into my favorite pair of black leggings, tank top, and a lilac quarter zip sweatshirt. This is comfortable.

"I want pants *that* color." He points to my quarter zip when I walk out of my bedroom.

He could wear the hell out of this color. No doubt about it.

"I'm so fucking excited! Let's go, baby." He reaches for my hand, and we're out the door.

"Where the hell are we?" I ask, as we stand outside what looks like a small warehouse. "Should I have told a friend I was going somewhere with you? This gives off a real murdery vibe." I raise my eyebrows, looking at the building and back to Zack, who is grinning bigger than ever.

"We're going shopping. Private shopping. Just you and me," he says, like it doesn't make me have even more questions.

I shake my head, clearly needing more information.

"You said you didn't have a dress for the wedding, right? Now's the time." He opens the door for me.

He has a way of remembering everything. It was about a week ago when we were having dinner with Willow and Tripp, when I made a single comment about still needing clothes for the destination wedding.

And he's right. The wedding is only a couple weeks away and this is a task I've procrastinated long enough.

We walk in, and it's just a basic entrance way with one woman sitting at a reception desk. There's no signage or anything indicating a brand or store.

"You must be Emilie." The woman stands and offers a handshake. "I'm Mia. Your stylist for the evening." She smiles. "I called Willow's stylist and she had some measurements for you, so we've got lots for you to choose from."

"Good to see you, Mia. Thanks for pulling this together for me," Zack says.

Wait. Personal shopping like a single stylist, a bunch of clothes, and me and Zack?

I did not see this coming.

Mia walks, we follow, and when she pulls open a massive industrial sliding door, I see racks of clothes split down the middle. I'm guessing one side is for me and one is for Zack.

"I have some of my assistants around so they can help coordinate and with whatever you need. Dressing rooms are in that back corner."

Zack looks at me, grinning ear-to-ear as Mia walks further in.

"Tell me you're surprised!"

"Yes. I would've never guessed this." I take in all the racks and still can't quite believe it.

"This is usually open for brand influencers, models, celebrities—whoever has a connection. I rented it out and had stuff brought in for you and me."

What the fuck? I can't get over how thoughtful this is.

"If we're going to this beach wedding, we gotta look fly."

I shake my head, putting my hand to my forehead. "Don't say fly," I joke.

"So fly. Like a damn stylish bird." He doubles down. "Let's shop."

Mia immediately swirls me away and is asking me about colors, fabrics, overall vibes of the wedding, and anything I want to stay away from. She takes me through racks of clothes, grabbing items and putting them up to me, but taking them away before I get a good grasp on it. One of the assistants follows like there's a string connecting their hip to Mia's. They work together, effortlessly exchanging dresses, some to keep and some to put back, without a word.

After forty minutes of building out my own rack—everything I want to try on—I'm ushered into a dressing room unlike anything I've ever seen. There's a massive mirror, which is basically the entire wall, with a touch functionality to change the type of light. In the corner is an accent chair, next to a full sofa.

There's a refreshment station in the opposite corner with a high-top table that boasts quite the spread: water, seltzer, champagne, juice, and a few canned cocktails.

"I feel like you're a champagne girl," Mia says as one of the assistants is reaching for a flute and the bottle.

"I want champagne!" Zack yells from somewhere before walking in. "My room is right next door," he points.

When each of us has a glass of bubbly, Zack offers up a toast. "Let's get this poppin'!"

I shake my head, clinking his glass with mine. "That's better than when you told me *you put the champ in champagne* so I'll take it."

"We're going to go through a few other racks in case you don't find what you're looking for. While we're pulling back up options, press this button if you need anything. We're going to be at the front of the warehouse so we won't be able to hear if you just call out," Mia explains, pointing out the button on the wall.

I can't imagine not finding something in what's already in this room. There has to be at least twenty dresses and a few two-piece sets.

I take a sip of the champagne, the fizz promising.

"Want to show each other what we try on?" Zack asks. "Even if you don't like it."

"Let's do it," I agree.

I'VE PUT ON TEN dresses, and so far, they've all been duds. I mean, they're fine, but they don't speak to me in the way that makes me think it's *the one*. I'm on my second glass of champagne and starting to get winded.

Why is it that trying on clothes does that to you? Makes it feel like you're doing strenuous activity?

"Oooh, wait until you see these shorts, EJ. You're going to lose it!" Zack yells from his dressing room.

I step into the next dress. Already, I'm obsessed with the color—almost like a dusty lavender with a touch of blue with it. When I put my arms in and start to pull it up, I already have a great feeling. I zip up the side effortlessly, like it's about to fit perfectly.

I look into the mirror, set to natural light since we're going to be on the beach.

Yes. We're on to something here.

I spin to see the back, and already know I'll be buying this, whether I wear it to the wedding or not. This is so coming home with me.

The fabric is a light and flowy chiffon, the type that lifts a bit when you spin. It's a maxi dress and I stand on my tip toes to confirm my suspicion—this will be perfect with the right heel.

Thick straps sit on my shoulders before trailing down the front, creating a dramatically deep V—my cleavage looks solid, even without any type of bra, meaning it will look way better when I'm wearing one. The bottom is classic, the type of skirt that moves and sashays with each step you take.

The same V is mirrored on the back, creating a mostly open, and deeply low, back. I smirk into the mirror and almost squeal. I love this dress so much.

I can't wait to show Zack. My mouth feels like sandpaper, making it hard to swallow. Reaching for the flute of champagne, I take a sip, trying to push down the nerves. Why wouldn't I be nervous to show the first dress I sincerely like to my very fashion forward fake, but sort of not fake, boyfriend?

Being someone with high anxiety, I prefer clear situations and relationships. Naturally, I'd find myself in something complicated like whatever Zack and I are doing. I'm going to overthink, no matter what, but right now it feels like there's too much to overthink.

I shake my hands, trying to release the tension, and stop the impending clamminess that comes with sweaty, anxious palms. Tipping my head from left to right, I stretch my neck and shoulders, trying to create space between my chin and shoulders.

I walk the short distance to the area where Zack and I have been showing whatever we're trying on.

"I'm serious. These shorts are going to turn into my whole personality in Mexico. I can't wait—" Zack stops as soon as he sees me, his mouth dropping open and eyes taking me in from the top of my head to where the dress sweeps the floor.

His eyes on me feel like an itch you finally get to scratch. I do my best not to melt in a puddle because that's my first response when he looks at me like this.

"That dress...," he says while putting his hands on his hips. "Are you for real right now? You beachy goddess." He reaches for a hand, which I give, and he spins me around.

I let out a laugh as he continues, "Great dancing dress. Nice and fluffy when you're moving." He's gone from mouth open to a solid smile, and it hits me in the stomach, stealing my breath.

The dress is a little long, and I trip but fall right into Zack's chest, like I'm on the set of a romcom movie. The one where the clumsy nobody falls into the arms of the handsome athlete. It's humbling but also like a dream come true.

"It's fucking gorgeous. Please get this one." His voice is little as he leans forward, still holding me up.

I get myself upright with no assistance and take a couple steps back.

"You're right on the shorts." I need a topic shift—less me and more of anyone else. Zack is wearing blush pink shorts and a black shirt. I don't know if I've seen another person pull off pink like this man can. Plus, it's that short inseam that no one can get enough of.

We smile at each other before walking back to our respective rooms. When I'm in front of the mirror, I put my hands on my cheeks, feeling the warmth of my skin. I turn the fan setting up, needing more air.

I grab the zipper and pull. It only gets an inch down before it gets caught. *Be gentle, Emilie, you want to wear this later, don't ruin the zipper,* I scold myself while pulling the zipper back up and trying again.

Stuck.

I think I need someone to pull the fabric as I zip. With the placement of it, I'm not able to get an angle or do it with two hands.

"Zack, can you help me with this zipper?" I call out.

He comes in a few seconds later.

"It's stuck, I think if I pull the fabric, you can unzip it—but remember I want to buy this. Don't ruin it with your man hands."

He turns, facing my hip with the zipper, and spreads his legs before putting his hands on the inside of the fabric, his fingers touching my ribcage. His other hand goes to the zipper, and my hands pull the fabric together—a bit awkward, but I think it will work.

Zack looks at me. "Are you ready?"

His voice pricks my skin. It's delicious and a tiny bit uncomfortable. I want more. More of his eyes on me, his voice like this, his fingers on my skin.

Why do I feel like we're not talking about zippers anymore?

Chapter 31
Zack

IT'S NOT LOST ON me that I'm practically touching Emilie's tits as we try to unzip this dress. The one that short circuited my brain. The purplish-blue color, light and like it was made for her skin, and the plunging front where I was begging to see more of her.

In my dreams, it will keep going and going, until it's her, bare for me.

Fucking hell.

"Ready," she confirms.

Emilie bunches the fabric, and I pull the zipper down and toward me.

"I don't have man hands. These are hands of a champion," I say, still focused on the zipper, moving like a knife through butter.

Just when I think we're in the clear, the zipper snags one more time.

"Hands of a champion, huh?" Her eyes lock on mine, her voice teasing on the edges of her words.

I take my fingers that are not on the zipper and hook them to the inside of the fabric, needing more leverage. What I didn't consider is the spark from touching her somewhere new. Closer to her waist than her ribs this time.

It's also not helping that she's not wearing a bra, which I realize as the fabric no longer held together by the faulty zipper gapes open at the top.

My dick is painfully aware of how much she's not wearing a bra, and if I just pulled the fabric back a touch more, I'd see what I've been dreaming of.

Working together, I'm able to get the zipper past whatever it was caught on. I stand there, my hand still touching her, afraid to breathe, to change the moment. When Emilie doesn't move or say anything, I take a chance and follow our new rule.

The new rule is doing what feels right.

I take the hand that's on her side, below her ribs, and slowly draw it up her body, feeling her reaction underneath me. I can't tell if she's actually leaning into the touch or if I'm imagining the best-case scenario—her wanting this as much as I do.

"What feels right for you?" she asks, like she's part reading my mind and part taunting me.

"You. All of you. All the time." My fingers that crawled up her ribs are going back down.

"Well, we don't want to break the rules, do we?" She catches my eyes in the mirror, and she offers this devilish grin that's so fucking sexy. She's tempting me. It's a dare, one I'm happy to take her up on.

I step behind her, keeping her back to my front, and her eyes flash as the tip of my erection touches her ass.

"I must feel good," she says, almost laughing, leaning back into me for real this time, not questioning it at all. This lean is everything. Every stolen glance. Every piece of tension.

Her hands stay at her sides, and the strap on the zipper side is almost falling off her shoulder. In the mirror, I see her glance at the strap and back to me.

I hook a finger under each of the straps and look at her one more time before doing what I think she wants. When she nods, giving me the green light, I slowly pull the straps down.

The fabric falls away from her skin, and my eyes trail the small of her back until a black lacy thong shows. I stop for a second, but Emilie pushes my hands down until the dress falls to the floor.

My hands touch the side of her hips and then up her sides, pausing at her ribs. Her heartbeat is quick under my touch, which damn near matches mine. I peel my eyes from her ass and watch her in the mirror. In just a pair of panties, she reaches an arm up around and hooks it around my neck, scratching the nape.

Without a second thought, my hands find her tits, the ones she's put on display for me. I press a kiss to the side of her neck, and she turns, giving me more room. More area to cover.

I lick and kiss my way down to the spot where her neck and shoulder meet. I lightly bite, even though I want to fucking devour her. No matter how bad I want her, I know we're in a fucking dressing room with other people in the building.

"That *does* feel right," Emilie moans.

With that compliment, I feel her nipples in my hands, rolling the pink buds. I don't quit kissing her, but look forward, and find her watching me through the mirror. Her eyes are wide, wild, and taking in every one of my movements. Her chest heaves as I squeeze her breasts, and when I shift back to her nipples, she closes her eyes.

Fuck.

"You're actually killing me, you know that?" I turn and say into her ear, and then I'm kissing the soft spot behind it.

"*You're* the one making me needy. I want those hands," she swallows and sucks in a breath, "everywhere."

"Watch me through the mirror and maybe I will." I draw soft circles on her sides, by her waist. My fingers are slow, teasing, and drawing out what we both crave.

Her eyes lock on mine, and I lazily move my hands down the front of her, until they're at the top of her panties. Emilie's breathing picks up, and her whole body moves with each breath she reaches for.

It's intoxicating—seeing her respond this way to my touch.

I reach one arm up and across her body, grasping one of her breasts, and Emilie moans. Those sounds she makes, they're unlike anything I've ever heard. It's like my body wants to get them from her and then find a way to hoard them, keep them all to myself. I don't want to share them. Fuck, I don't want her making that noise for anyone else.

My other hand is still touching the lace of her panties, running my fingers along the place where the fabric meets her skin.

She watches me as I press my hand flat to her stomach and push it down, into her panties. Her head falls forward, eyes focused, and she bites her lip, pushing it into her teeth.

It's hard to keep the pace slow. I'm torturing both of us but I have a feeling Emilie likes to be teased. The way she keeps following my lead, not rushing me. Not rushing us.

Fuck it, I can't take it. I want to rush.

I go to put my fingers on her clit, but right before I can touch her, there's a knock on the door.

"Are you two good in there? Do you need anything?" Mia's cheerful voice kills the vibe.

We both freeze. I slowly remove my hands from Emilie and swallow. "Yeah, we're good. Just had a zipper situation. We'll be out front in a few minutes," I call out.

"You got it," she responds.

Emilie turns toward me, her tits still out, and she presses them to my chest when she wraps her arms around my neck.

Right before her lips find mine, she says, "A zipper situation, huh?"

"It wasn't a lie." My voice is like gravel, and I need something to drink.

Emilie puts her lips on mine for a kiss that puts the period at the end of whatever just happened.

Carefully, she picks the dress up, looks at me and says, "Looks like you need a minute."

I look down and my erection is there, teasing me about falling short.

"That would be correct."

Chapter 32
Emilie

AFTER I'M BACK IN my own clothes and Zack is no longer pitching a pink tent, we're at the front of the warehouse, each with our own "keeper rack" of things we'd like to purchase.

I love the dress—a one hundred percent yes—but the price on the sticker almost had me falling over. It's hard to splurge on luxury items even when I know I can afford it. Getting the dress means probably putting everything back and not touching another clothing purchase for a month.

I'm looking at my keeper rack and rifling through the price tags when Zack says, "This is on me. Don't worry about it."

"No. You're not buying me clothes."

"Why not?" he shrugs. "This was my date idea, and I tempted you with all these beautiful clothes. Let me pay."

Anxiety fills my gut. Guilt creeps into my cheeks. I feel bad for telling Zack no, but I'll inherently feel terrible if I let him buy me what's on the rack.

"I am a legit millionaire. Don't want to brag," he's being sarcastic and trying to make me feel better, "but my contract extension last year *was* public." He puts his hands in his pockets and closes the space between us.

I press my lips down hard enough on my teeth that I'm afraid I'll taste copper.

"You're already going to travel internationally for the wedding. It's a lot to ask."

Zack rolls his eyes. "You mean taking a long weekend trip with you? With beautiful weather? The beach? All-inclusive? That's *definitely* not a lot to ask."

I shake my head slowly, trying to find the words to help him understand. Zack is always so light, agreeable. He can make a joke out of anything, but I need him to know what this means to me.

"I have a thing about money, and I'll spare you the details for another day. I'll let you do this for me today, but this can't be something you do all the time, ok?"

"Not to interrupt, but if there's something wrong with the zipper on this," Mia touches the dress, "we'll get it fixed but it's actually no cost. All I ask is that you tag the designer on any social media posts from the wedding," she offers, her smile sweet.

Wow. The offer washes over me and I'm immediately thankful. "That's really kind of you. I'd be happy to do that."

"What about me? Any deals for me?" Zack asks.

She scoffs, "Mr. Millionaire? I think you'll pay full price today." She winks at him, and I can't help but laugh and shake my head.

✕○✕✕✕

"Truffle fries are always the answer," Zack says, dipping a fry in aioli and popping it in his mouth. "Plus, they taste better because you paid for them."

We're at one of our favorite burger spots in the city. It's a hole in the wall, under the radar, and that's how we like it. So much so I won't let Zack post a selfie of us here. I don't want to ruin this place.

I take a bite of my bacon brie cheeseburger, with granny apple slices and pickles, just as Zack's phone rings.

"It's my mom. Give me just a second." He stands from the booth, answers it, and walks outside, right in front of the restaurant.

I try my best not to hog all of the French fries while he's on the phone, which requires serious restraint on my part.

Instead, I think about the dressing room. I mean, let's be real, I'm never going to forget what happened tonight. The date. Zack. Us fooling around, or almost, when we weren't alone. That's not my typical date behavior.

I've never been one to want someone so bad that you just let yourself give in, even if it's only a little, when others may be around. But maybe it's that I've never wanted someone as much as I want Zack.

The typical weirdness of being intimate with someone feels different between the two of us. In the situations where I'd typically be terrified to show parts of my body or wonder if this or that is the right thing to do, I'm thinking about how much I want more of him, of us. There's no room for doubt or hyper-fixation.

Now, will I overthink the hell out of all of this when I'm back in my own apartment? Yes. But that's nothing new. I feel like there's more space for me to enjoy the small moments, like my mind has the room to do so.

I lean back into the booth, close my eyes, and check in—just like my therapist taught me. I feel pretty damn good. I've never done a shopping date, let alone something like tonight. Zack put in some effort, thinking about how I needed a dress for the wedding, and finding a way to be involved.

Zack slides back in the booth, his forehead scrunched.

"Is everything alright?" I ask.

He takes a long drink of water, still not meeting my eyes. His phone buzzes, he checks it, and then puts it in his pocket before responding.

"Things are... weird?" he answers, his eyes finding mine.

"What do you mean?"

He shakes his head and says, "My mom called because she doesn't know where my dad is. She thought maybe he was with me. I couldn't tell if that's because he told her that or if she was just trying to figure things out."

My stomach pinches as I take in Zack, what he's saying, how he says it. I try to keep my words to myself and give him the room to keep going.

"I texted him and the message didn't go through, like his phone is off or it's on airplane mode." He starts boxing up his leftover food in the takeout box. "This isn't like him. Definitely out of the norm."

Now, if this were my parents, it would be the norm for one to not know where the other was or what they were doing. Their lives are barely connected at this point. From what I saw, even in the one family dinner with the Andersen's, they're close—which makes this situation very different.

"That's scary," I say, reaching over and grabbing his hand for a few seconds. "What can I do?"

Zack takes a deep breath and sighs out, his lips blowing out with the air. "Give me five minutes to call my sister. And then let's go to the second part of my surprise." His voice is far away.

"Wait, I thought this was the second part?" I look down at the half of my burger that will either be a perfect snack for late tonight or lunch tomorrow.

Zack rolls his eyes and says, "EJ, this is a cheeseburger. Not a surprise." He puts his hand on his chest, and I'm thinking about how it would feel to touch him there—my hands, his chest, and his muscles.

"I'm better than that." He takes his phone out of his pocket and gives me a side-eye. He's got the phone to his ear and is out the door before I can ask another question.

Obviously, I know he's better than that.

Chapter 33
Zack

"W HY ARE WE PARKED outside of a place called Pulse and Needle?" Emilie asks, reading the neon sign.

I look at the sign then back to her again, wanting her to figure it out.

"Wait. Your surprise is tattoos? Is this a tattoo shop?" She leans forward, hands on her knees in the front seat of my Jeep.

I clap my hands, borderline too loud for the inside of a vehicle, but I can't help it. I'm so damn excited.

"I saw your face when you asked my parents about theirs. If you don't want to get one, you don't have to. You have an appointment, but it's completely up to you."

Her mouth hangs open, and I don't know if that's a good thing or not. All I know is how bad I need a distraction from whatever the fuck is going on with my family. I called my dad, it went straight to voicemail. I got a hold of my sister, and she's pretending not to panic but I know her too well to fall for that shit.

Bottom line is that my dad is a grown man. Maybe he got held up at work or he's out with a friend and his phone is dead. It's only been a few hours. Now is not the time to panic or jump to conclusions.

I give myself the same talk I gave to my mom and sister twenty minutes ago.

Emilie unbuckles her seatbelt and says, "Yes. Let's do it."

A wave of excitement hits me, taking the edge off the worry that's been like a weighted vest.

After getting checked in and Emilie deciding on what she wants, it's clear she's about to jump out of her skin with excitement. It's like she's buzzing—she fidgets and talks ridiculously fast, and the smile won't leave her face.

"You don't have to stay with me. If you want to check in with your family," she offers, her cheeks pink.

I check my phone—still no messages or calls from anyone. "Are you sure?" I act like I'm contemplating her suggestion.

"One hundred percent. I'm good here."

By the look of it, she's *fucking great* here. In the tank top she wore under her quarter zip, she's grinning as the tattoo artist places the stencil on her skin.

"Let me know if you need me, ok?"

I leave Emilie behind, to do something she's always wanted to do. Not because I'm going to call my family, but because I'm getting a tattoo of my own.

And it's not something I'm ready to share. With anyone.

"You're like the human version of a glowstick," I say to Emilie as she walks into our private waiting area. There's something electric about the way she moves.

She quickly moves her feet when she sees me. "I did it!" she squeals, pride dripping from her words.

Emilie shows me her arm, the delicate spot right before the crook of her elbow, where a small daisy tattoo is inked.

"I've always wanted a daisy." The words tumble out through a grin that reaches each corner of her eyes. "In mythology, they're used to symbolize new beginnings. I want to try and remember that when I have a horrible night, or OCD episode, I can always start over and move forward."

She turns her arm, showing me all of it, and her joy is contagious. Anxiety runs through my blood, sprinting and trying to touch all it can. Emilie is the perfect thing to give me a break from the nagging of it.

"It's perfect. Good call, EJ." I kiss her on the forehead and pull her shoulder into me. After we take a picture at the tattoo shop, one I can post on my socials later—or print and put on my god damn fridge because I'm becoming all the way wrapped up in Emilie—we're about to get in the car when she stops me.

"Tonight was the type of night I dreamt about as a teenager. Hot athlete boyfriend, taking me shopping, getting cheeseburgers, and ending up at a tattoo shop." She laughs as she steps in to me, putting her hand on my chest. "But this was way better than I could've imagined. Thank you for doing this for me."

I press my lips together in a thin line, trying to find the words. Yes, I did this for her, but it's not as selfless as all that she's making it out to be.

"You're welcome, but you do get this was as much for me as it was for you? I knew you wanted to get a tattoo and needed to shop for a dress, but I wanted to be there. Be a part of it."

Emile puts her mouth on mine in a kiss that makes me forget we're in public. She walks me back to the door of my Jeep, the handle hitting my back. Emilie throws her arms around me, running her hands through my hair, lightly scratching before setting them around my neck.

My arms find her lower back and I squeeze her into me. I nip her bottom lip, and she runs her tongue along mine. I bend my knees and pick her up so we're almost level. Our noses touch, and she laughs into the kiss.

Her hazel eyes shimmer in the light from the street, specifically the neon sign. Every time she looks at me like this, it's like she's tying a string to me, one only she and I can feel.

"Prepare yourself, I'm going to say something really cheesy." Her voice is almost a whisper through her smile. "I'm convinced I could kiss you forever." She kisses me again for emphasis.

I laugh, feeling the shake of my ribs against her.

"Ready for the extra cheese?" I tilt my head, pressing my forehead to hers. "I'm convinced forever wouldn't even be enough."

"We're the worst," Emilie says before putting her smirking lips on mine.

Chapter 34
Emilie

WHAT AM I DOING inviting Zack back to my place when it's this late? I'm not really sure, but I know I want to soak up as much of him as I can on his night off. His practice tomorrow isn't until ten am and I don't meet with Willow until eleven—feels like we need to take advantage of the late morning commitment.

"I can't believe I got a tattoo!" I say, looking at the clear wrap covering the daisy I've almost gotten done a handful of times.

Zack walks over, hands on my arm, leaning down and inspects it. "Looks so good."

"Have you heard from your family? Any news?" I ask. I don't want to keep bringing it up but I can tell he's worried, like his smile is only hitting a seven when it's usually an easy nine.

He takes a breath, slow and deep. "No. But I don't want to think about it. Makes me all itchy and like I should be doing something but, like, I don't know what it is."

"Sounds like you need something to take your mind off it," I muse, stepping in closer, taking a shot in my apartment, my space. "Last time, you took care of me. It's my turn."

He says nothing, but his eyes are glued to mine. I offer him my hand, which he takes, and I slowly walk to my bedroom.

I press one of four buttons near the light switch. Music fills the room, and soft lighting turns on. This is one of the ridiculous high-tech pieces of Willow's apartment that I use—preset playlists and lights to match.

When I was setting it up, I thought how unnecessary it was, but I secretly love it.

I lightly touch his shoulders, pushing him down so he's sitting on the edge of the bed.

Zack looks up at me, his eyes intense and deeply blue, like a sapphire. He bites his lip as I stand in between his legs. His hands grip my hips until they reach under my quarter zip, and then under my tank top. I shiver as his fingers start raking up my upper body, skin on skin. Putting my head back, I look at the ceiling as I breathe into his touch. He lightly scratches down, and my body thrums with want.

I put my hands through his hair, pulling harder than I've done before, and put one knee on the side of each of his hips. I straddle him and grab the bottom of my quarter zip and tank top, pulling them up and over.

"You're really good at this distraction thing," Zack murmurs, fixated on my black bralette, which plunges low.

His lips find the place right below my breasts, and he slowly kisses. With a hand in his hair, I pull him closer, needing more. His arms move from touching the top of my ass to the tiny bralette straps. He hooks the straps and pulls them down.

I arch my back, pushing my tits into him. He immediately puts a nipple in his mouth, frantic, like he can't get enough. I sigh out a heavy breath and tip my head back. His fingers grasp my other, rolling the bud back and forth, pinching.

"Harder," I ask.

Zack smiles into my skin, I can feel it. Then he bites with his teeth, playful, but the pressure is exactly what I was hoping for. His fingers flick the nipple not in his mouth before squeezing more than he was.

He switches his mouth and fingers, and each time he nips, sucks, or flicks his tongue, I know I'm about to be soaking wet, and he's still completely clothed.

"I wanted these perfect tits in my mouth earlier in the dressing room."

"How bad?" I say between sighs and a groan.

He lets out a frenzied laugh before tipping his chin up. "Fucking bad. Like, walked around thinking of crocheting and baseball and anything that wasn't remotely hot, longer than was appropriate, to take care of my *situation*." His eyes look down toward his crotch, where I can feel his erection again.

Fuck. I've thought of him. What he'd feel like. In my hand, in my mouth.

I put my hands on the front of his shoulders and push him back on the bed. Grinding on top of him, with fabric still separating us, I purr, "Seems like we have another situation." The words coming out of my mouth surprise me—I'm rarely this forward or confident.

"You give me many situations," he laughs, his hands digging into my hips.

My hands find the top of his shorts, my fingers toying with the band. I stand up and pull them down to see him straining, *and I mean straining*, against his navy-blue briefs. I touch him, stroking through the fabric, and he moans at the sensation.

It's official. Zack Andersen moaning is one of the best sounds I've ever heard. Goosebumps pop up on my arms and neck.

"Should we talk about this?" he asks.

I lean back, keeping my hands to myself. "I'm doing what feels right. Is that okay?"

"Fuck yes. I don't want you to ever stop." His hands run up my outer thighs over my leggings. "I haven't been with anyone since the charity event this summer. I get tested monthly and there's nothing for you to worry about."

I didn't think he had been, but the thought of him committing to our fake dating—or whatever the hell we're doing now—makes something inside me sing.

"My last partner was in July and I'm all good for you, too." Within seconds, I have my hands inside his briefs and pulling them down.

I've not seen a ton of men naked, but the ones I have did a terrible job of preparing me for this. I don't know what I was expecting, but he's much bigger than that. I look at my hand to try and make a comparison.

"Are you okay?" Zack asks as I'm taking him in.

"I mean, maybe? I don't even know if I can fit that in my mouth." I rub my lips with the back of my hand.

"First, you can't say shit like that. I'm going to come before you even fucking touch me. And second, you don't have to do anything you're not comfortable with."

I smirk at him calling me out and then say, "No, I want to."

I place a kiss on the head of his dick, a bead of precum already formed at the top, now on my lips. Looking up, I see Zack watching me, which makes me want to burst into flames.

My hands slowly stroke him, up and down, until I put the tip in my mouth, swirling my tongue around the swollen head. I run my tongue from the head to the base and then pepper him with slow kisses.

Zack moans and shivers—it makes me want to give him everything.

I put him in my mouth, as much as I can take, and moan at the fullness.

"Fuck," he sucks in a breath, "that's so hot."

I look up for a second to see him still watching me, but his hands gripping my comforter has me trying to take more of him.

I suck him and use my hands at the base, where my mouth can't reach. Zack lets out a breath through his teeth, and I can feel his muscles contracting.

His breathing is ragged as I change up the pressure of my mouth and my hands. I move my head to give him different angles and try to take more of him.

I gag but have no intentions of stopping.

"You're going to—" Zack tries to take a breath "—make me come." He picks his head and shoulders up from the bed and then throws them back.

I smile, kissing the tip of his cock and say, "That's the point."

Trying to mimic what I was doing before, his dick is more sensitive in my mouth, and I feel him writhing beneath me. He moves his hips, getting the angle and pressure just right. I wrap my hands tighter around the base of his thick shaft and stroke quickly as I suck the top, matching the pace.

His hands find my hair, and he pulls enough to let me know he's there. "EJ, I'm going to —" Zack gasps.

I hear his warning, but it just spurs me on. The power I feel, being able to make him feel this good, to talk to me like that. I'm a woman obsessed. I want him to finish in my mouth.

Which is exactly what happens. Zack contracts with his climax, his hands pressing my head just where he wants it, and he spills down my throat.

I swallow and shift off my heels to face him, and his mouth grabs mine before I can even think about what's next. He kisses me like I'm a life force, like he needs me to keep going. It's intense, rough, and I love it. The feeling of being needed is so underrated.

He rolls us over, so I'm on the bottom and he hovers on top of me. He bites down my throat and all the way down the front of me. He only stops when he reaches the top of my leggings.

And then his phone rings.

His head falls forward on me while it rings in the kitchen.

"Should you get that?" I ask.

"I really don't want to."

When the phone finishes ringing, he looks back at me, smiling and devilish. He runs his hands up the front of my thighs until his fingers touch the band.

But his phone starts ringing again, this time a different tone.

"This has to be a fucking joke," he says, closing his eyes. "That's my sister. I should answer it. Don't move." Zack stands up, pulls his shorts back up, and closes the bedroom door.

I do what I'm told but his time away quickly turns into minutes, and keep dragging, until I'm no longer itching to be touched. I look at the clock to see that almost twenty minutes have passed. I don't want to interrupt, so I sit quietly on my bed.

A few moments later, Zack slowly opens my bedroom door, but he doesn't look like the same man I was with before the phone call.

Immediately, I snap to attention. "What's wrong?"

"My dad is fine. My sister is not. She and my mom are freaking out. Apparently, my dad said he had a work thing but came home almost black-out drunk." He sits on the bed, running his hands through his messy hair before rubbing his face. "I don't know what's going on with him, and my sister and mom want me to have the answers."

"Have you talked to your dad?"

"No, apparently he came home and immediately passed out. Acted like it was no big deal."

Concern etches in the lines of his face, in his forehead, around his eyes. It looks like he might start to cry. The man is tapped out.

"I'm so tired," Zack whispers. "Mentally. I don't have the answers."

I sit next to him, lean my head on his shoulder, and say, "I have an idea. Let's get ready for bed. Take a hot shower and we'll get some sleep. Sometimes issues like this need a little space."

"I can sleep here tonight?" he asks, his eyes hopeful.

I put my hands on the side of his face and give him a sweet kiss. "Of course."

After getting him everything he'd need in the master suite, I grab a quick shower in the guest bathroom. I think we both need a little space; Zack for thinking through whatever is going on with his family, and I need to not distract him.

Plus, I don't know if I'd be able to keep my hands to myself.

Chapter 35
Zack

"I WAS BANKING ON getting drinks or something, not hot yoga," Riley whines as we walk out of the studio. "How is it that the hot water still felt cold after that? Brutal." She piles on how much she didn't have a good time.

"Hot yoga is better for the fact that game day is tomorrow afternoon. Plus, I've had some shoulder knots I've been working on," I explain.

Tomorrow is the last game before our bye week, or my vacation slash wedding with Emilie. It's also been hard to get time with Riley due to her work schedule.

She takes her hair out of the ponytail and shakes her head. "Fine, but maybe I won't try so hard to align my flight schedule with your away games." She rolls her eyes and shoves me but wears a smile.

We walk into Riley's favorite smoothie spot—the one with an acai bowl that I swear could cure all hangovers—and grab a booth. She places our order, which I know will be a mix of anything and everything that sounds good, and we'll end up sharing.

I've always been particular about sharing food. The thing about having a younger sibling is you need to play the long game. Riley was always going to be there, asking for things off my plate, so sharing food with her is the compromise.

She slides into the booth, her cheeks still red from the forty-minute yoga session, or maybe the shower after.

"What's the deal? Did you talk to Dad yet or what?" she asks, downing an entire glass of water.

I shake my head. "I've tried, but he hasn't had much to say. He told me the guys were blowing off steam and it just got late. His phone died. The same thing he told you."

Riley rolls her eyes, crosses her arms, and leans back in the booth. "It feels like bullshit. Right?"

My dad has always been our hero. He's never done anything to make us wonder if he was ever into anything he needed out of. I agree with Riley though, this doesn't add up.

"Definitely. I think something's going on, but I don't know what. I don't know how to get him to open up."

My sister and I re-hash the whole him yelling at me thing while we were at dinner, all over a random person giving me her number that I wasn't going to use, and our order is dropped off: smoothie bowls, a smoothie, fresh pressed juice, and homemade granola bars.

"When's the last time you guys golfed?" Riley asks. "Or did something like that?"

My brain tries to remember, but I know it's been a while.

"Couldn't tell you. He's bailed the last few times." I take a bite of an acai bowl with flakes of coconut, chia seeds, and honey on it. It's tart and sweet at the same time—the coolness perfect for after a yoga session like we just did.

The worry hits my sister's face and it's like a sucker punch, taking my breath away. I wish I had the answers but I don't.

"Listen. I flat out asked him if he was sick; he said he wasn't. I think the plan is to keep supporting him like we've always done—make ourselves available, and he'll tell us when he's ready."

She finishes the fresh kiwi papaya juice and nods in understanding. "You're right. I know, I just wish there was more we could do."

I don't say anything because I feel like I've said it all.

"Give me the dirt on this wedding." She switches the topic and I'm grateful.

"It's next week. Emilie's little sister and her longtime college boyfriend. They seem okay, but her parents are not my favorite people."

Riley's eyes go wide. "So you're okay with the little sister marrying the ex? Her parents are that bad?"

"Without a doubt. It's like she's a shell of herself when we're with them. She has it figured out: what she can or cannot do, what she should talk about, how to divert conversations she knows will only bother them. They water her down, and I hate it."

I take a bite of a peanut butter honey and oat granola bar, fresh enough that the peanut butter leaves traces on my fingertips.

"Fuck that. How awful." Riley takes a drink of a smoothie. "I'm still amazed you brought someone like her home. Quite the show coming from the guy who doesn't ever date."

It's not lost on me. I've thought a lot about this since I brought Emilie to my childhood home. How easy it was for her to melt in with my family, like we've been together for much longer. My brain keeps thinking of holidays and how it'd be to have her with us there.

It's also wildly clear that we haven't talked about what happens after the wedding.

"Mom and Dad loved her. I loved her. I feel like you already love her or are really close." She pinches her fingers together, demonstrating the closeness with a small gap between her fingers. My sister looks at me with a knowing glare.

I lean back in the booth. "Just say what you want to say."

"I think you could love her. You've been happier than any time you were with any of the jersey chasers I remember you'd entertain on a nightly basis. I mean, you flat out got a new phone number because you knew it'd make her more comfortable. Shut down the warehouse to shop with her. There's no way I'm telling you something you don't already know." Riley flips her hair off her shoulder.

I take a deep breath, looking at my smirking sister.

I don't say anything.

Because I think she's right.

THE UPSTATE COSMOS ARE first in our division as we stole a game we should've lost—according to Vegas—on the road. We won today, 33-31, and nothing feels better going into a bye week. Tripp was out of his mind, snagging passes that were over or underthrown by our quarterback—the Cosmos version of superman.

I'm on the team plane, about to take off when Emilie sends a photo. It's a picture of her luggage, ready to go for when we leave in a few days.

Me

damn, already packed, huh?

seems like you're excited for the wedding

EJ

I'm excited for the trip

particularly my travel buddy

it's going to be fun.

are you coming over when you get home?

My cheeks hurt because I'm smiling like an unhinged idiot in my seat, both from her wanting to travel with me, and asking if I'm coming over. Our interrupted night after shopping and tattoos is haunting me, but I'm also so tired after the game.

> as much as I'd love to

> i'm fucking beat and you deserve better than that ;)

well if you want to sleep in my bed, invitation is there

> seriously?

yes but you need to decide so I can put your name on the afterhours list with a code to get in the building

> I'm in

And I am. I'm so in. For all of it.

Chapter 36
Emilie

"How did you know sour gummy worms are my favorite?" I ask as Zack pulls out all the snacks he grabbed for the flight, including my go-to candy choice. To be honest, any sour candy will do but I do have an affinity to gummy worms.

"I have my ways," he smirks.

I open my backpack. "That reminds me, I have something for you." I pull out a three pack of Pop Rocks. "I saw these the other day and thought of you."

His mouth hangs open in excitement. "You're the best." He kisses me quickly on the lips.

My phone buzzes.

Mom

> seems like poor timing with the wedding

Next, she sends a link to an article. It's basically a few pictures of Zack and me outside of Pulse and Needle. Us in the car before, us inside—blurry and zoomed in—and us kissing after the tattoos. It's not the first time I've seen it.

> hope you'll be able to cover up whatever you put on your body forever

> it's your sister's wedding for crying out loud. You couldn't wait a couple weeks?

I roll my eyes and show the text exchange to Zack.

He scoffs. "It's not like you're in the wedding. Do you think your sister will even care?"

"I don't think she will. And I did bring stuff to cover it up, just in case."

Zack holds my hand, drawing circles on my palm. "Don't worry about her."

Me

We're about to board in a few minutes

I'll chat with Eliza when I get there

There's no way to have this conversation with her right now. I knew she'd see those pictures eventually, but I just hoped it would be after the wedding. I close my eyes and realize how annoyed I am but I'm not spiraling. When I got the tattoo, which I still love, it came to me: no matter how much I do to please my parents, they've never relented or had it be enough. I can't do enough for them to look at my choices as my own, instead of something that impacts them.

I thought my mom calling it out would make me panic, anxious. But I'm not really any of those things. I'm fucking proud of myself.

"Hey, ugh, hate to bother you, but can we get a photo?" a dad and his son ask Zack. They're both wearing Cosmo T-shirts, and the kid looks like he's going to scream in excitement.

Zack, like the guy he is, jumps up. "Absolutely! Do you want me to sign your shirt or anything, little man?"

I hand Zack a Sharpie I keep in my bag, Willow tends to need them when we're out in public too, and I grab the dad's phone to take pictures of the interaction. Zack doesn't rush them, even when a few people stand on the edge of our small bubble, also wanting a photo.

I take pictures with fans of all ages and types. Zack gives out high fives and takes quality photos, always hitting a couple different poses, and the whole thing makes me ache. How kind he is. How happy he makes me.

Zack is currently talking to a nine-year-old girl about how she joined her youth football team and wants to be a long snapper, just like him. When she knows his position, I swear he's choking back tears.

"You seem to be a very lucky woman. You can tell a lot by how someone treats strangers," an older woman, maybe the little girl's mom, says quietly in my ear.

The comment catches me off guard, only because I was just thinking it. It's like she read my mind.

I smile at the woman, and then at Zack. "Believe me, I know."

AFTER A FOUR HOUR flight, and a thirty minute drive from the airport, we pull up to the resort. I'd looked it up online and knew it was going to be ridiculously nice, and expensive—Mitch and Eliza wouldn't have it any other way. Even with the preferred room rate, I was twitching thinking about the cost to stay for the wedding—sweating when I was booking it earlier this year.

"It's fucking beautiful here," Zack says in awe, giving me his hand and helping me out of the car.

It really is. The pictures online didn't do this place any sort of justice. Plus, it's 82 degrees and sunny—perfect beach weather.

We reach the front desk to check in, and Zack steps in at the last minute.

"I'm Zack Andersen, I called a few days ago about the room for me and my girlfriend." My heart feels like it's beating loud enough that the entire lobby can hear it when he calls me that.

"Yes, yes. The upgrade. We're all set; let me pull it up for you."

I grab his arm and turn him toward me. "What do they mean upgrade?"

"Well, I called to see what other rooms they had, just in case there was something amazing, you know? There was and I paid the difference. I almost paid for the whole thing but I didn't think you'd like that very much."

Well, fuck. That seems like a respectful compromise.

"Actually, the upgrade helped us out, Miss Hayes. We have a basketball team staying and we were short a few of the standard rooms. So, it's like you're doing the resort a favor." The woman behind the desk smiles and shrugs her shoulders.

"What am I going to do with you?" I ask, my hands on my hips.

"Well, I hope you'll enjoy yourself in our big ass room." He leans in, pressing a kiss to the place where my cheek and ear meet, and whispers, "I can also think of some other things you could do with me."

My cheeks are all the way red right now. I can feel the warmth spread down my body.

WE OPEN THE DOOR to our room and see our luggage, and a welcome basket from

Eliza and Mitch, waiting for us. Sunlight pours in from a wall of windows, which lead out to a private balcony. I'm only a few steps in and realize this is much more than a single room.

"This is like an apartment," I say, walking into the living area and falling into a massive chair, which feels like a gentle hug.

"We love an upgrade!" Zack calls from the kitchen. "How about some champagne?"

"Do you even need to ask?" I answer, and it's punctuated with the pop of the champagne cork.

I meet Zack in the kitchen, admiring how all the appliances are brand new, stainless steel, and the cabinets are open and modern. He hands me a flute and gestures to the balcony. He slides the door, which just looks like a massive window, and steps outside.

I take a moment and close my eyes, feeling the wind whip through my curls, probably making them wild and unmanageable. It smells like sea water and something sweet, like a blooming flower. Waves crash and it's one of my favorite sounds in the whole world.

After taking in the moment, I open my eyes and gasp. "Is that a hot tub?"

"You know it is," he says while stepping next to me.

He offers his glass up, like he's going to give a toast.

"Cheers, baby. I can't wait for the next few days with you." Zack smirks at me.

I take a sip of the champagne, which tastes like it was made for a balcony in Mexico. "This balcony feels like its own little world. I can barely tell anyone else is here, like it doesn't even feel part of the resort."

"Believe me, I have *plans* for this balcony. You'll see."

His words rake down my body, giving me goosebumps and quickening my pulse. Zack presses his mouth to mine, and we share a champagne flavored kiss. He pulls away quicker than I'd hoped.

"What's on our itinerary for today?" he asks, looking out toward the ocean.

I walk back to the welcome basket, which includes a full schedule of the wedding festivities. I scan for what's on the list for today.

"Looks like a welcome dinner and cocktails tonight, 7 PM."

Zack looks at me, rubbing his hands together. "You know what that means? We have time to go to the beach. I'm going to show you how to throw a football."

"Bring it on, Andersen."

Chapter 37
Zack

"Quit looking at me like that," I scold. Emilie is wearing a red dress, with a red lip because she's trying to give me a heart attack. Or get me to say *fuck it* to the welcome dinner and take her back to our room the way I've been dying to. We're walking to the event, not even inside, and I'm already contemplating how to make a quick exit.

"Like what?" she asks, innocently sarcastic.

I lean and whisper into her curls, "Like you want me to devour you."

She stops, turns me to face her, and puts a single hand on her chest before she murmurs, "Maybe I do?" Her eyes are like daggers, and her mouth is just as sharp.

Fuck.

"You and that smart fucking mouth," I growl, touching my nose to hers, not kissing her only because I don't want to wear red lipstick at dinner tonight.

She has the audacity to look at my dick, which may or may not be twitching to life, and laugh. Emilie grabs my hand and we both giggle as we walk into the dinner spot.

We're a few steps in when we're approached with mezcal margaritas. I take one swipe of the salty rim with my tongue before taking a drink, the smoky liquor a perfect balance with fresh lime, not losing eye contact with Emilie until we're interrupted.

"Zack fucking Andersen is at my wedding," Mitch cheers, reaching for a handshake. "I told you he was coming," he turns and says to a few guys behind him.

"Happy to be here. Congrats, man." I shake his hand and can see his whole face light up. "Do you all know Emilie?" I place my hand on her lower back.

"Yes, we all have met," she says but there's nothing hidden. She hugs one of the guys and says hi to the rest. I was guessing they'd probably met when she and Mitch dated, but you never know.

After I've introduced myself to Mitch's groomsmen, Eliza walks over. Even *I* can tell her smile is strained. She immediately goes to hug Emilie.

"Eliza, this place is gorgeous. What a venue," I say, offering her a side hug, which she surprisingly takes me up on.

She stuns in a white dress, tight to her body, her hair pinned back away from her face.

"Thank you! We're excited," she replies, but like she's told the same thing to fifty other people. Maybe she has?

"Looks like your team has had a great season so far. All good?" Eliza asks and Emilie's eyes are raised enough to almost touch her eyebrows.

I cough back being caught off guard and answer, "For sure. The team is having a great year. Glad to have the bye week though."

"Since when do you watch sports?" Emilie asks Eliza, loud enough for me to hear but not everyone.

Eliza crosses her arms and shifts her weight to one leg. "Ever since you apparently date professional athletes. I'm trying to be supportive." She says it in a way that's a bit forced, but I think she means well.

"Don't want this to be a surprise, but I sort of got a tattoo, and Mom was already texting me about covering it up." Emilie shows Eliza the dainty daisy on the inside of her arm.

"I figured as much. I saw the same article. You absolutely do not have to cover that up." Eliza looks at it, a touch of awe in her face. I can tell Emilie's caught off guard again, her face scrunched in places. "Did it hurt?" Eliza asks.

Emilie shakes her head and says, "No, not really. I think I was so excited that it might have but you know, adrenaline and everything."

Eliza smiles at Emile and then taps Mitch on the shoulder.

"We should mingle with the other guests." Eliza loops her arm with Mitch's, the first time I've seen her be physical with him since she walked up.

The newlyweds to be, and the groomsmen, leave Emilie and me behind.

"Wow, Eliza showing interest in others. Maybe we do all mature with time," Emilie jokes.

I look around the room and see food being brought out and set at tables along the perimeter of the room.

Just as we're about to grab a plate and check out the spread, someone taps on a microphone.

"I'm Ethan, Eliza's dad, and I want to say thank you to everyone for making the trip. The food is being set up now, feel free to grab some and as many drinks as you'd like. Remember, it's an all-inclusive resort."

That's it. There's no speech about how happy he is to have everyone together or what it's going to be like for one of his daughters to be married. It's cold and to the point.

It's sad.

I've heard my family talk more about a piece of chocolate cake at a random dinner than this man did about his little girl's own wedding. Stealing a look at Emilie, she's already looking around the room, seeming completely unphased. Why would she be? This is what she's used to. It's probably been like this her whole life.

She deserves better.

Hell, Eliza deserves more than whatever the hell that was.

"You good?" Emilie asks.

I take her in; the crimson curls, cheeks glowing from a few hours out in the sun where she learned to throw a decent spiral pass. I put my finger under her chin and put a kiss to her mouth, tasting the smokiness of the mezcal.

"All good. Let's get some food and how about we try to catch the sunset on the beach?"

"Sounds perfect."

WE'RE WALKING TOWARD THE ocean as the sun is about to go down. There's baskets full of blankets and pillows before you hit the sand. I grab a blanket as Emilie takes her heels off. We walk closer to the water and find a spot, put the blanket down, and I sit first.

"I always forget how cold it can get by the ocean at night." She rubs her shoulders with her hands.

I spread my legs. "Sit here, lean back on me."

Emilie gets comfortable, and I wrap my arms around her.

"You're warm," she says, content and quiet.

"I think you mean hot. I'm hot," I joke.

She snickers and leans harder into me. "Yes, you are hot."

All jokes aside, we sit and soak in the serenity. It's the rhythm of the waves crashing into the beach, the smell of the sand and salt. The sun dipping down, transforming the sky into blues, pinks, and oranges.

I take a deep breath, my chest pushing into Emilie's back, and it's comfortable.

"Can I ask you a question?" Emilie starts.

"Always."

"Riley said you'd never brought someone home, as an adult. Is that true?"

I'm sure Riley did tell her that, plus whatever random thought crossed her brain and fell out of her mouth. Out of everything she could've asked, this is tame.

"That's true. I mean, I've been on lots of dates, but never with the same person. It wasn't really a thought to bring any of them home," I tell her the truth.

"But your fake girlfriend was?"

I take a few seconds to try and get my thoughts together.

"Emilie, whatever we are, whatever this is," I shake her shoulders for good measure, "Isn't fake. I don't know if it ever was."

She peels her back from my front and turns to face me. She's quickly on her knees, sitting back on her heels, her red dress splayed out in front of her.

"Say it again."

"This isn't fake." I lean forward and capture her mouth with a searing kiss. It lingers and presses. My tongue reaches for hers, and then touches the seam of her lips.

"You mean it?" Emilie looks dazed and almost like she's dreaming.

I tilt my head and search her eyes. "Does it feel like I don't?"

She plays with her fingers in her lap. "It feels like you do but part of me wonders if it's because I want you. So badly. Like I want this to be true."

"It is true. Remember, we broke your rules. We made it true. This is what feels right."

"Shouldn't we talk more about this?" She points between the two of us.

"What do you want to talk about?" I want to give her the space but don't know what she's looking for.

"I don't know yet," she laughs.

"I'm not going anywhere, EJ. I'm right here. When you're ready to talk, we'll talk. There's no time limit." I kiss her one more time to make my point and say, "You're the type of woman who's worth the wait."

Emilie smiles at the end of the kiss before turning back to watch the sunset. She falls into me, more relaxed.

The sky is like pastel wisps and smoke with only about half of the sun left. It's breathtaking, the kind of thing I'll take a beach vacation for any day.

Emilie asked why I'd never brought anyone home. Part of me wanted to tell her, because she's the first person who felt like home to me.

There's always tomorrow.

Chapter 38
Emilie

I practically float back to the room on realizations and the most beautiful sunset I've ever seen.

Because this isn't fake.

It's rare in life, where you get exactly what you want, and it's even better than you dreamt it would be. I thought this fake dating thing would be fun, but it's turned into so much more. It's uncovered feelings that I've probably always had but has shown me what Zack means to me.

"What now?" I ask when we get situated in the room. I kick my shoes off, mostly wondering if I should put my pajamas on or maybe we'll get in the hot tub on the balcony. I look down at my hands focusing on my nail color like it's not the same black they've been for years.

Zack unbuttons the top button of his dress shirt, hitting me with an evil smirk.

"I told you. I have plans for that balcony." He looks toward the glass door and back again.

"What kind of plans?"

He unbuttons his sleeves, rolls them up, and I'm trying not to drool. And then he says, "Go out there and let's find out."

His words brush my skin in a way that make me want to beg for him. I do as I'm told because I like that he's taking control. The balcony is facing the ocean, but we're not getting hit with the wind. It's perfect.

Zack trails me and closes the door, almost all of the way, but leaves it open just a crack.

"What now?"

He comes up behind me, bites my ear lobe and growls, "Put your hands on the railing."

"What if someone sees?" I ask.

"No one can see us; another reason I asked for the upgrade."

I look around and confirm I can't see any other signs of rooms around us.

He puts his hands on my hips, lightly pushing my back forward with his thumbs—he really wants me to lean.

Oh. Okay.

I'm almost bent over a full ninety degrees, when he dips down, touching behind my calves with his fingers, scratching them up the length of my legs. It's painfully slow and I'm trying not to fidget. He's bringing the hem of my dress up with his fingers. When he reaches my hips, he has it hanging forward.

Soon my ass is bare to him and he finds out one of my secrets.

"You're not wearing any panties," he says.

I turn my head, looking over my shoulder, and say, "No. I'm not. Surprise."

"You're a fucking dream come true," Zack says, and if I wasn't already wet, that would probably do it.

Zack starts by peppering kissing from the sensitive spot behind my knee all the way up to the back of my thighs.

He stops, right in front of my entrance, and lightly blows on it.

Fuck.

"Is this okay?" he asks.

"As long as you don't stop." My words tumble out onto one another.

He takes a finger and swipes, checking my wetness.

"It's a good thing you weren't wearing panties. We'd have to ring them out."

Zack kisses me, around all the areas besides the ones where I want his mouth. He grips the backs of my thighs and doesn't touch me anywhere else.

I shift my hips, clearly impatient.

"You've been so patient. So good. I shouldn't make you wait any longer, should I?" He starts to insert a finger and stops.

"No, you shouldn't," I whisper breathlessly.

And he doesn't. He inserts one finger, pumping in and out of me, and then he adds another. I groan, and he picks up the pace. They move easily with the wetness, and I find myself leaning further forward, wanting more from him.

"You're taking these fingers so well. You're so wet for me."

Zack then puts his tongue where his fingers were and kisses me, before using his tongue. I whimper and when his fingers reach forward, finding my clit, I almost cry out but then remember I'm out on the balcony.

"Can you keep quiet, like a good girl?" Zack asks, pulling his mouth from me for a second too long.

"Uh huh," I answer, my breath ragged and eager.

"That's my girl." And he's back to using his mouth and his tongue on me.

"Fuck, that feels so good." I do my best to keep my voice a whisper.

Zack smacks my ass with one hand, the other still working me, and I have to press my lips down to keep my sounds muffled. It's not lost on me that I'm outside, in a place with other people, no matter if I can see them or not.

I keep pressing my hips further into him, rolling into his touch, finding the right angle, needing more pressure. Zack turns his face and it's hitting me just right. I'm gripping the railing so tight my hands are starting to cramp.

It hurts but I fucking love it. Need it.

My orgasm builds, each touch from Zack's tongue, lips, fingers, bringing me closer. It's frustratingly delicious and I'm about to reach the place I've dreamt about.

"My girl," Zack moans into me with his mouth, his fingers still filling me.

The vibrations from his words is what puts me over the edge. My center throbs and finally explodes with the release I've needed. My legs shake as I come all over his mouth, his fingers, and he doesn't stop. The shocks keep coming, one after another, each one hitting harder than the one before.

I try to let go of the railing when Zack says, "Don't let go. Not yet."

He stands up, gripping my hips and rubbing his erection into me. I hear him grab his belt buckle and undo it—I'm practically drooling, craving him every way I can take him.

Bang! Bang! Bang!

We freeze when someone knocks aggressively on the door.

"We're all set. We don't need anything tonight, " Zack calls out, hopefully shooing whatever the resort is trying to bring us.

"It's Mitch."

What the fuck?

"Not a good time. Can you come back a little later?" Zack asks, almost laughing.

"No, not really. It's Eliza. She needs Emilie. Now."

Something inside me runs cold. I can't remember the last time Eliza has ever asked me for something, needed me.

Zack senses our time is up, puts his belt back on, and pulls my dress down. He grabs my hips and helps me stand, my arms practically mush at this point.

"I'll be out in a second," I yell out to Mitch.

Zack gives me a quick kiss. "Don't rush. Do whatever you have to do."

Part of me melts in that moment, for just a second, until I'm out the door, following Mitch to their room.

Chapter 39
Emilie

"SHE LOCKED HERSELF IN the bathroom. I can hear her crying but she won't open up. She's been asking for you." Mitch is trying to explain what's going on but I still don't get it.

"She asked for me, by name? Or did she ask for someone?" I look at him as we're practically jogging.

"I tried asking if she wanted any of her bridesmaids or friends here, and she basically screamed to get you and only you."

My heart hurts. I don't know what's wrong, but I feel like it must be bad for her to call for me like that.

I try to get a good look at Mitch. In the moonlight, he looks sober—put together—and like he's on a mission.

"Did you do something you want to own up to?" I ask.

Mitch stops. "No. Absolutely not. You might think I'm scum but believe it or not, I love her. I want to marry her. I didn't do anything." He's pleading, his hand on his heart as his voice cracks.

"I believe you."

And I do. I can't recall a time when Mitch was this emotional.

We're walking inside their Villa—this is not a room and makes our upgrade look puny. It's like the top floor of an apartment, with multiple rooms, sitting areas, and a private swim out pool.

"She's in there." He gestures to the closed door in the hallway. "I'm going out on the balcony. Give the two of you some space." Mitch walks with his head down and arms crossed.

Fuck. I actually feel bad for him.

I take a deep breath, make sure my hair isn't wild from the light jog or the balcony activities a few minutes ago, and knock lightly on the door.

"It's me. Emilie," I say in a soft voice.

Eliza rustles on the other side, getting up and coming to the door. She swings it open, and my heart cracks right in two. Her eyes are puffy and swollen from crying but are blown out with fear. Black streaks paint her cheeks, and her lips look raw—maybe from biting them? She doesn't say a word but pulls me in and closes the door behind us.

I don't say anything. Instead, I grab a washcloth and wet it with warm water. I sit her down on the floor, kneeling to start cleaning her up. The second the wet washcloth touches her skin, silent tears start to fall. When the makeup is gone, I'm the first one to speak.

"What's the matter?" I grab both of her hands with mine, squeezing hard.

She squeezes back.

"You can tell me. I'll help you as much as I can."

"I keep thinking of these horrible things. These situations. Hypotheticals. Things that could happen. I can't get myself to stop, and it feels like it's killing me." She pulls a hand away to touch her chest. "My heart was racing so fast that I passed out in here. It was just for a second, and I was already going to sit down. But it's like my mind won't quit showing me nightmares, but I'm awake."

Well, fuck. Poor Eliza.

"What else do you feel?"

She rubs her chest, the skin flushed and red. "Like I can't breathe. Like my lungs are made of cement and can't move. They're heavy. Something is wrong with me. I'm sick or something. I'm dying. I'm going to die before I can get married." The panic gets stronger with each word.

I pull her into me and wrap my arms around her as tight as I can. She's having a panic attack.

"Eliza, listen to me. You're not dying. It feels like you're dying, but you're not. You're breathing. Your heart is beating." She cries into me, almost hyperventilating. "Breathe in, slowly. It's hard but you have to try."

I give her a few seconds to get her breathing under control.

"You're having a panic attack. I get them too, and they do make you feel like you're dying. But your brain is tricking you." She goes almost slack around me. I sit back so I can see her face.

"Put your hand on your heart." I place Eliza's hand on her chest. "Feel that? Heart beating. Blood pumping. You're not dying. Now, try to slow your breathing; you'll feel your heartbeat change."

My little sister is almost gripping her chest but she does what I say. The panic drips off a little with each breath. I can see her coming back to herself.

"Do you want to tell me what you're seeing? Or will that make this worse?"

"No, I want to tell someone. I didn't know how to tell Mitch." She takes a breath. "It's like the plane is crashing and I'm on it. A plane crashing into the resort. A tsunami wave hitting us, my family and friends, watching people drown, not being able to save them. And then it's things like, what would it be like to touch my curling iron? Wrap my fingers around it?" Her eyes move to the floor.

My heart hurts for her. I'm not a professional but I think I know exactly what this is.

"Did something happen to set this off?"

She wipes the back of her eyes with her hands, "The wedding has been stressful. But I expected it. I don't know what it is, but Mom and Dad are just treating me like... I'm not enough. Like if I don't follow exactly what they think I should do, it's wrong. They're treating me like I'm..."

"Me." I finish her sentence.

Eliza doesn't correct me but does keep going.

"And some of my friends, if you can call them that, aren't any better. They talk bad about Mitch. They have nothing good to say ever. And the amount of questions they've asked about you, or Zack, or how you know Willow. Their motives couldn't be more apparent."

"Do you want to marry Mitch?"

"Yes. No questions asked."

"Then do it. That's what this is all about. Marry Mitch and try to do it your way, but know that at the end of the day, that's what counts. As far as your friends, sometimes you have to let people go, no matter how long they've been around. Then you'll have room for people who care."

"What about Mom and Dad?"

I let out a loud laugh. It bounces off the walls and the closed door. Throwing a hand over my mouth, I keep laughing but it's not nearly as offensive.

"I'm sorry. I don't have any advice, except learning about yourself and setting boundaries. I'm still working on it, and I see a therapist specifically for Mom and Dad."

Eliza laughs at me, and it's nice to see her do that, even if the tears are still fresh on her face.

"As far as what you're seeing, the thoughts? You need to see a doctor. It sounds like intrusive thoughts, a type of OCD, which I have. It's scary, but learning how to cope is a game changer."

Eliza and I sit on the floor in the bathroom, and I tell her about my thoughts; about all the wild things that have run through my brain, brought me to my knees on occasion. I tell her about some of the things

I do that help. I even tell her about the night with Zack, what happened, how he took care of me.

"You know, when he first came up to Mitch and me at that event, I thought you guys were lying. Like, not actually dating. But I was wrong."

She's not the only one.

I keep thinking about how we're in this gray area. We want each other but it's still kind of tainted with the fake premise we started with. I want something new and fresh. Something that makes Zack mine.

I look at the time and see that hours have gone by. I get Eliza in her pajamas and go get Mitch from the balcony. I give him the thirty-second version, just so he can help her in the short term.

I hug him and say, "Thank you for taking care of her."

And he hugs me back.

Chapter 40
Zack

I WAKE UP TO Emilie draped across my chest. I didn't wake up when she came in last night. Mitch came back to let me know that she and Eliza were together. I appreciated the update.

She stirs and looks at me, then at the clock.

"Ugh, I'm almost late," she says, her head falling back on my chest.

"For?"

Emilie rolls on her back, stretching her arms above her head and replies, "Spa day with Eliza. Maybe some of the bridesmaids."

"Is she okay? You don't have to share any of the details."

"She will be okay."

Emilie rolls back to my chest, locking her eyes on mine. "Hey, I want to formally do this. For real. Like make it official."

My smile is wide. I can't get over this woman.

"Whatever you want. What do you want me to do?"

"I'm going to be tied up with Eliza today, up until the rehearsal dinner. Meet me at the beach at four. Where we watched the sunset."

"And?"

"Tell me you want me. Want this. For real. No faking it." She gives me a quick kiss.

"You got it. See you then," I say as Emilie hops out of bed, turning on the shower.

I don't need the starting point, or the clear transition, but she does. It's not much to ask considering how much she's already given me.

I'm getting ready, and my dad sends me a text.

Dad

> everything is fine but we need to talk

> when you're home

> have fun at the wedding

Me

> sounds good. Looking forward to it

And I am. Looks like I'm going to finally get some insight into what's been going on. There's a few seconds where nervousness runs up my spine but is quickly replaced with some relief. I don't know what he's going to say, but knowing is better than not knowing.

I turn the iron off; my light blue shirt is free of wrinkles and is ready for me. I put it on and button it up, thinking about Emilie and smiling to myself. I kind of like this whole "if you want me, come tell me" thing. I've been thinking about what I'll say all day.

It's like I can't get the words right, but I'm hoping to have some clarity when I see her. All I know is that she's the only woman I've brought home, and I don't care how wild this next part sounds, but I'd be happy if she was the only one. She fits into my life in a way I didn't think women could.

When people would say that someone feels like a piece they were missing, I used to roll my eyes and laugh to myself, but now? I get it. It's like she brightens up the best version of myself. Being around her makes my mood better, no matter what.

Maybe I've been playing it safe by dating around, hooking up with whoever is interested. Maybe, deep down, I knew I'd never be serious with anyone like that. It's like my mind wanted to keep the energy and space for someone like her. I don't want to play it safe anymore, I want to break the rules.

Emilie is the adventure I want to take.

I'm out the door and practically running to the beach. It's close to four, and I don't want to be late.

I walk by a group of guys, some of them ridiculously tall. When I see the logo for the Jersey Jaguars, it makes sense. These must be the NBA players the front desk was telling us about when we checked in.

I try to walk by them, because professional athlete or not, I've got somewhere to be and they're moving too slow for me.

When I think I'm in the clear, I hear someone yell, "Zack! Zack Andersen."

As much as I want to bolt to the beach, pretend I didn't hear them, or that I'm someone else, I can't. I'm not that guy, even though I wish I was in the moment.

I turn around and see one of the guys walking toward me, the group walking in the other direction.

"Hey, man." I shake his hand. "I have somewhere to be but if you want to find me later—"

"You're Zack Andersen? Football player from New York? Cosmos?"

"Yes. That's me and not trying to be a dick, but literally late for something—"

The guy looks at the ground and back up to me, shaking his head. The look on his face makes me stop.

"Are you good?" I ask.

"I'm not sure how to answer that."

"Well, if you figure it out, I'll be right over there." I go to take another step.

"I did figure it out." He grabs my arm before I can go any further; his blue eyes are burning into mine. "I'm Brooks."

"Okay, good to meet you. Let's do this later." I'm itching to get to the beach.

"Wait, you don't get it. I'm your brother."

What the fuck did he just say?

Chapter 41
Emilie

My dress, pink like the color of Zack's favorite shorts, trails behind me as I walk to the beach. I tried this one on and quickly changed out of it before Zack could see me, so it'd be a surprise on the trip. I even got ready with Eliza and her bridesmaids so I wouldn't risk running into him in our room.

The sun beats down on me as I walk out to our spot from the other night. The beach isn't very busy, and I'm thankful for that. Closing my eyes, I put my hand on my chest, feeling for a heartbeat I know is racing. With excitement. With a dash of nervous energy.

A smile has been living on my face almost the entire day. From what felt like a silent resolution with Mitch last night to thinking of Zack and I on the balcony. It's almost like I'm about to get everything I want.

I feel lucky.

I check my phone and it's five minutes until four. Trying to stay off the beach until it was almost time was much harder than I thought it'd be. It's like Christmas morning when you wake up at five in the morning to see if Santa came or not.

The spa day was perfect for Eliza and me. It let everyone chill out, spend time with themselves and their thoughts, while being with others. It gave me the space to think about what I wanted to say to Zack.

Surprisingly, the words have been difficult to nail down.

When I'm with him, I don't worry about being too much—he never wants me to tone myself down. He likes to match my energy or help lift me up closer to his when I'm lower than usual. Zack encourages me to be honest—say how I'm feeling or what I want. He looks at me like I'm something worth keeping.

He makes me feel like I'm worth keeping.

It's like I've held out for someone like him, my whole life. He's someone I could love, day in and day out. And I feel like he'd let me.

I put my head in my hands, thinking about love—what that means, how it fits in my life, as the waves crash on the beach. How it seems like so much work until you meet someone and you enrich each other's lives.

I'm not saying I love him.

But I'm not saying I don't either.

While I'm waiting for Zack to find me, the minutes stretch and feel too long. I watch as people from the wedding start heading toward where we're having the rehearsal.

Checking the time, I see he's fifteen minutes late—no texts or calls from him.

Where is he?

Chapter 42
Zack

"WHAT DID YOU JUST say?" I ask the random person standing in front of me, who I've never met in my entire life, claiming to be my brother.

"I know it sounds bizarre, and us running into each other like this is a complete coincidence. But you're my brother. My half-brother."

He's speaking English but it feels like these words don't belong together.

"I think you've got your lines crossed. I don't have a brother. I have a sister—"

"Riley. Yeah. I know. Chris told me."

Chris. My dad.

I put my hands on my hips and stare at him. Now, this is information someone could get from a Google search, but why? What's the angle?

"This isn't bullshit. I'm telling you the truth. I'll tell you everything." He waves as he takes a couple steps forward.

My brain can't compute what's happening. The gaps can't be filled in.

When he realizes I'm not following, he stops. "Let me guess. Your dad just got a hold of you about needing to talk when you're back home, right?"

How the fuck does he know that?

"If you're fucking with me—" I say, rubbing my hands together.

"Why would I do that? I'm not fucking with you. Come on."

I look to the beach and then back at this guy. Brooks. I take him in, and it's hard to not notice the similarities. My stomach turns into a pit, a mile deep, because all I can think about is my dad and how he's been acting.

He's not sick but he does have a secret he's been keeping.

"I'm Brooks Pittman. I play for the New Jersey Jaguars."

"Did you follow me here?"

He wipes sweat from his forehead with the back of his hand. "What? No. Fuck no. It's the opening week for the NBA, and they're trying to tap into some international markets. Our first two games are in Mexico. I didn't know you were here until I legit saw you walking around five minutes ago."

I follow enough about the NBA to know he's telling the truth about the markets.

Brooks continues. "Listen, I know this is shocking, and I fucking get it. I didn't sign up for any of this either."

The waves crashing on the beach remind me of Emilie, waiting for me. If anyone would understand, it's her. I'll listen to whatever Brooks has to say, and then I'll find her. Fuck, I'll bring him with me if I think I'll need it.

I pull my phone out to text her but it slips out of my clammy hands, face down paired with a terrible cracking sound, on the paved walkway. Shards of glass sparkle in the sunlight—a bad fucking sign for me. I hesitantly pick it up, praying to anyone who will listen that the glass was already there and not from my phone. When I turn it over, it's nothing but a black screen with a corner completely missing, showing me the inside of my phone, something you shouldn't ever see.

"This isn't fucking ideal," I groan, shaking it out enough to put it in my pocket.

Brooks watches me and tries to help. "You can use mine."

I don't know Emilie's phone number. Fuck.

We walk in silence together and find a café. I don't know if I'm making the right call, my stomach thick with knots and doubt. We slip into a booth, almost hidden and tucked away from the rest.

I refuse to talk first.

Brooks takes a long drink from his glass of water. "I grew up with a single mom. She never dated and never talked about my dad, no matter how many times I asked. I thought maybe she didn't know? That I was the product of a one-night-stand or some shit. A few months ago, I was helping clean out her house to move her into a new one. Contract money, you know?"

I do know. It's the first thing I tried to do for my family when I had enough.

"I was cleaning the attic and found a box. It had a few pictures of her and this man. I didn't think it was anything until I read some of the letters that were in there." He clears his throat before looking up at me, his fingers playing with the straw wrapper. "They were in envelopes, not sealed, but with a stamp and an address. Like, she was going to send them but never did. I read a few of them, and it was her telling Chris about me." Brooks gets his phone out, looking for something. After a few seconds, he places it down in front of me.

No fucking way.

It's my dad but from another lifetime—at least twenty years ago—with a woman. My eyes fill with tears, out of surprise or maybe fear for what this means.

"I told my mom I found the box. She came clean. Told me that he was my dad, and he didn't know I existed. Apparently, they met when he was on the outs with his wife before he was married. When they met up, he told her he worked things out, and that he couldn't see her anymore."

I wipe my eyes with the back of my hand.

"It was easy to find him, considering he still lives in the same house."

He shows me his phone, a picture of an envelope with my address on it.

"You're my brother," I say mostly to myself.

"I called him, we set up a time to meet, and at first he was so upset. Like pissed off. Angry. It doesn't matter that I had a great life and did well for myself. I don't hold it against the guy for not knowing, but I would like to know him now. He sort of panicked. We were supposed to meet up when he came to one of your away games, but he bailed last minute."

The night we went to dinner comes roaring back. He was anxious in the hotel lobby because he thought Brooks was going to show up.

Fuck.

"Do you believe me?" he asks, his voice smaller than before.

"Yeah. I do. I just, my brain. It can't focus on one thing and—"

"I'll cut to the chase. I'm not going to tell anyone. Not the press. Not anyone else. I'm an only child. I do want to know him now, if that's an option."

"How old are you?" I ask, trying to put a timeline together.

"Just turned twenty-five."

That means he was born between Riley and me. *Fuck.* I was born before my parents were married, but I wonder if my mom knew my dad met someone else. I mean, the timeline isn't a secret. My blood runs cold but my heartbeat beats hard and fast.

"That makes you my younger brother."

"I guess so," Brooks replies, focusing on the condensation of the glass.

I don't know how long we sit there in silence. I think about my dad the last few months, the erratic behavior. How this must be killing him. If he truly didn't know, this would be devastating to hear.

My brain runs from one thought to the next.

"Well, it's good to meet you... I think." I reach for a handshake. "I don't know what the rules are for something like this."

"It's good to meet you. I promise I didn't know you were going to be here but I couldn't let you walk by."

"So, what now?"

"I'd like to meet up, not at a random resort on my way to shootaround, but for dinner. A drink? I'd also like to meet Riley. I don't need to infiltrate your family or anything like that. I just want to know a little bit about where I came from."

This all seems reasonable. I don't know if this is how I'd be if the tables were turned.

I crack my knuckles. "That seems reasonable. But to be completely honest, my brain is kind of like scrambled eggs at this point. It's like I hear you but I'm trying to process."

He laughs at my choice of words and puts his hands up. "I get it. I've had lots of time to think about this. Take as much time as you need." He grabs his phone. "I'd offer to exchange numbers but yours is kind of busted. Do you want to give me yours?"

Such an easy question but the answer feels so much more complicated. Before the silence stretches into being completely unbearable, I reach for the phone and put in my number.

I'M STILL SITTING IN this booth, an hour later. Brooks left, needing to get to practice, and I've been staring at the wall. It's like putting together a puzzle but you only have some of the pieces.

I need to get to Emilie.

I have to call my dad.

I need a phone but the café is technically closed, there's no one working. I run to the resort lobby, which is closer than my room, to use theirs.

When I reach the front desk, I'm sweating and breathing heavily. Yes, I'm a professional athlete, but running in dress pants and a button up shirt, in Mexico, is different. I awkwardly ask if I can use their phone. They set the phone on the ledge, turning it toward me.

I walk to the side of the reception desk; luckily, there's no one needing anything right now. I dial his number and my heartbeat feels too fast. It rings and suddenly I'm lightheaded and my chest is tight. I try to get further away from the desk, and when I think the corded telephone is going to pull tight, I've found a perfect spot in the corner.

My dad answers after a few rings. "Zack, is that you? I think this is the resort you're staying at—"

"Yes, it's me. I'm not physically hurt or anything."

A sigh fills the other line.

"Dad, is it true?" It's the only thing that I can think to ask.

"Is what true?" he asks on the other line, his voice hesitant.

"Brooks. Is it true?" It feels odd saying his name.

My dad takes a deep breath and sighs it out, the silence stretching thousands of miles between us.

"Yes."

My stomach drops, and I rest my head on the cold tile of the wall.

"Did you really not know?"

"No!" he practically yells on the other line. "Things would've been much different if I had known. I'd never have just left him without a dad—" His voice crackles with emotion, and there's a lump in my throat to match.

"I told Mack last week. I needed to tell her before I told you and Riley."

I can't believe how small his voice sounds—like pebbles where boulders used to be.

"How is Mom?" I ask the question I've been nervous to spend too long thinking about.

"Incredible. Like she always is. She's pissed I kept this secret to myself for so long. When I didn't need to." He pauses, and I sit in the wave of relief that's hit my body. "After you were born, there were a few months where we broke up. We co-parented, but we weren't together. I went out with the guys one night and met someone, which Mack knew about, and I think you get the rest."

This isn't the first time I'm hearing this. They've mentioned it in passing but when they brought it up, it always felt much smaller than this. I looked at my parents and thought they'd meant a fight, or a few days, or a week. Their love always felt so big that it couldn't be much more than that.

I guess love like that can make it through something like this.

My stomach clenches as I think about Emilie being on the beach, alone, waiting for me.

"Dad, I love you, but I have to go. My phone is trashed so you won't be able to get a hold of me, but let's have dinner when I'm back."

"I love you too," he says in a way that hits the inside of my rib cage.

I hang up the phone, thank the front desk worker for letting me use it, and then I start running.

Chapter 43
Emilie

ZACK DIDN'T COME TO the beach. He left me standing there, like a hopeless idiot. He didn't text. He didn't call. Fuck, for all I know, he's on a plane back to New York.

Would he do that? Leave without saying anything? No, I don't think so. But maybe I don't know him at all.

I thought we were on the same page, but maybe I was wrong? Maybe I scared him away with my whole "tell me you want me." Was I too needy? Is this the thing that was too much for him?

I don't know.

I really thought he'd come.

The doubt drips in anxiety with a dash of stress. I know it's going to do nothing but roll downhill, until it's impossible to hold in. My hands clench until the muscles in my forearm ache.

There's no room for any air in my lungs. I can't catch a breath. I'm emotionally exhausted from the high of waiting for him on the beach and the low of realizing he wasn't coming.

I thought I'd get a chance to tell him how much he means to me. No matter how we started, I know what I want—maybe it was something I always knew. I want him, and only him.

Now, I'm pouting at my sister's rehearsal dinner. Thank god I'm not in the wedding—I'm just there for moral support. They practice walking down the aisle, getting the spacing right, and I try to stay in the moment.

Maybe if I focus on something good.

First, Eliza looks better today than she did yesterday. Our spa day was relaxing and quiet—some of her friends came and everyone was on their best behavior. I may or may not have cornered all of them and told them to get their shit together before the day started.

Second, the weather is gorgeous today. The sun is golden in the way you dream about. Warm air, touched with sea salt and sand, circles around me but there's a light breeze to keep it from being uncomfortable. It's going to be just as nice tomorrow for the actual wedding.

Third, my parents couldn't be any less interested in me or what I'm doing. There's no mask for me to wear, no eggshells to walk on.

Lastly, Mitch looks at Eliza like she's the sun and his whole world.

Seeing him look at her this way is healing and heartbreaking at the same time. I've held on to a lot of anger for the two of them ending up together. Honestly, I wasn't right for Mitch, and while I would've went about this a much different way if I was in their shoes, it's not worth being angry about anymore.

They clearly love each other.

A tear falls down my cheek. I quickly wipe it away, trying to figure out if it's out of frustration, sadness, anger, or something I can't even name. All I know is that it hurts, and I don't know how something could surprise me like this.

I never thought Zack wouldn't show up. It's the surprise that stings the most.

Eliza and Mitch walk back to the beginning of the aisle and do the ceremony practice again.

I check my phone—still nothing from Zack. I sit quietly, trying not to panic.

THE EMPTY CHAIR NEXT to mine is taunting me. It's Zack's place at our small rehearsal dinner. His absence is clear and people keep asking me where he is—the best I could come up with is that he's not feeling well and is back in our room.

I wish that were true.

I still haven't heard from him. It's been hours at this point. I wrestle with worry and anger. Is everything okay? And how the fuck could he do this to me?

Dinner is about to be served, and Mitch's parents both give a speech. They talk about love, partnership, and the magic of having someone next to you, no matter what.

Love is about not giving up on each other.

One of them said this line, and it keeps rattling in my brain, echoing in my bones.

The staff is starting to deliver dinner plates when I think I'm going to crack myself open with pity, concern, anger, or sadness. Pick an emotion and I bet you I'm feeling it.

I put my head in my hands for a few seconds, trying to get my shit together. I feel somebody sit down, and I have no capacity. No energy left besides what's being used to keep myself somewhat together.

"EJ. I'm so sorry I'm late."

My head snaps up to see Zack, cheeks pink and face sweaty. I can't say anything because my mouth hangs open—I close my eyes for a few seconds and open them to make sure I'm not dreaming.

"Where were you?" I ask, my voice cracking with anger and sadness.

Zack takes a deep breath, running his hands through his messy hair. "You wouldn't believe me if I told you. It's a long story, and I'll tell you every detail but first, let me tell you what I was going to say on the beach."

"Why didn't you call? Text? You fucking just left me out there, and then I was panicking that something was wrong. That something happened to you." I put a finger in his chest.

Zack slowly reaches into his pocket and pulls out his phone, the screen smashed, and a piece of glass falls off it as he places it on the table.

"I dropped my phone, and then I didn't know your phone number. I only know three numbers: my mom, dad, and Riley," he rambles, and his words are quick and chaotic. "I need to memorize yours; well, I guess that depends on how this next part goes." He rubs his neck and looks at me.

The way his eyes find mine, it's like they're begging me to listen.

"I would've called you. I swear," he pleads and leans forward, his hands on his legs. "I want the chance to memorize your phone number."

I believe him.

I take a deep breath, cross my arms, and sit back in my chair. "Go on. Tell me," I say, unsure how to feel. I was so caught up in wondering what happened to Zack that I didn't think about what would happen if he just showed up.

"Emilie James, I don't think there's a day that's gone by since I've met you that I didn't want you. Even if I tried to hide it, or convince myself you were too good for me, or that you'd never be interested… there's no denying it, I've always wanted you."

His voice is firm but quick, like he's grateful to get this off his chest. With each word, his shoulders relax and he leans closer.

"And when you showed that you might want me, the way I wanted you—when you broke your rules—that's when I knew I was a goner. I'm long gone for you."

It's like I'm wearing a shell made of ice and each word that comes out of his mouth chips away, little by little.

"I promise, I will tell you everything about today. I won't leave out a single thing. One, because you deserve it, and two, because I need you. When I look at challenges or things that I must get through, you're someone I want by my side. In more ways than one..."

Zack starts unbuttoning his shirt.

"What the hell are you doing?" I put my hand on his, already cruising through the buttons on the middle of his shirt.

He has the audacity to smile and say, "Relax, I'll put it right back on."

Zack finishes the buttons and then takes off half his shirt.

"I don't get it. What's happening?"

And then he lifts up his arm, showing me the side of his ribcage. Right there, literally on his side, are the letters EJ.

He has my initials tattooed on him.

"When? How?" I can't string together a sentence and it feels like my eyes might fall out of my head.

"When we were at Pulse and Needle. We talked about doing what felt right. This felt right." He points to his tattoo. "And this," he points between the two of us, "has always felt right."

Zack puts his arm back in his sleeve, and I can't help but throw my arms around him. His hands hold my lower back, pressing me to him. I pull back far enough that I can see those blue eyes, piercing and intense, like ocean waves crashing on the beach.

"I know I hurt you, leaving you on the beach, and I'm sorry. Like, it hurts me thinking of you out there." His voice cracks with honesty and the weight of the moment. "I promise to make it up to you."

I put a finger to his lips. "How could I not want you?" I ask and then my lips are on his, replacing my finger. The kiss is honest and an unexpected turn of events from standing alone on the beach to being with a man who has my nickname inked on his skin.

He wraps his arm around me and lifts me up, all while kissing me.

"Zack Andersen, I'll break whatever rules necessary, do whatever it takes, if it means I get to keep you."

Zack holds me to him, his nose almost touching mine and says, "You've always had me, EJ."

His mouth covers mine, and we soak in the moment—one full of honesty and heart, true and aligned.

"What do we do now?" I ask.

"Well, it looks like we eat dinner. And then we go back to the room, and I tell you everything that happened in the last few hours."

I catch his eyes and there's something behind them. "Are you okay?"

"I'm much better now."

He holds onto me, tight, like I'm something valuable. A treasure. Something he doesn't want to lose.

"It's nice you could join us," my mom's voice cuts through the bliss, like a knife to butter. "Emilie said you weren't feeling well."

It takes everything I have not to roll my eyes.

"Ah, sorry about that. I'm, ugh, feeling better now. Looking forward to the wedding tomorrow," Zack says, syrupy sweet.

"We hope you'll leave your shirt on for the entire ceremony."

I cover a laugh and lock eyes with Eliza at the table next to us. She looks at Zack, and back to me again, offering a small smile.

"That's something I definitely can do," Zack replies, wiping his forehead with the back of his hand.

She looks me up and down, to the dress I was so excited to wear. My mom clicks her tongue and says, "Pink is a bold choice for you."

No one says anything and the silence feels sharp.

"What? I'm just saying. There are so many other colors for your skin tone." She brushes a finger down my arm.

I'm about to say something when a hand touches my shoulder.

"Mom, stop it. Please. Give it a rest." Eliza's voice is strong and clear.

"Eliza—"

"No, not today. You always are giving Emilie such a hard time." She stands next to me, putting her hand in mine. "And when it's not her, it's me, or dad, or anyone in your orbit." Eliza's voice has a wave of confidence, one I'm proud of.

"I'm getting married tomorrow. Do you think you can at least hold off until *after* the wedding?"

"I guess I just won't say anything," my mom snaps, crossing her arms and immediately going on the defense.

"That's the thing, Mom. If you can't say anything nice, you shouldn't say anything at all. I think it's *you* who taught us that."

My parents can't believe Eliza. Fuck, I can't believe her. They turn and practically run back to their seats.

My heart swells, and I'm afraid to breathe. Tears make my vision blurry as Eliza squeezes my hand hard, in a way that I know she's with me—on my team. I look over at her—chest quickly rising and falling—and a tear falls down my cheek. I wipe it with the hand that isn't grasped by Eliza.

Mitch stands by his soon to be bride, and the irony of the moment isn't lost on me. I never thought it would be Eliza, with the man of my parent's dreams, who would be putting them in their place.

"Thank you." My voice comes out all gravely and full of cracks. Zack puts his hand on my lower back, just letting me know he's there.

"You're welcome, EJ."

Chapter 44
Zack

I should be exhausted, considering Emilie and I stayed up until almost four in the morning talking about Brooks, my family, and Eliza standing up to her mom, but I'm not. Well, maybe I'm emotionally tired after going through all the family stuff, but whatever toll it took, Emilie's affection made up for it.

When we weren't talking, we were kissing. I'm so gone for this woman; I don't know if I'll ever get enough of her. She's like an ocean I'd happily drown in.

The last day has been something I never could've planned for, with unanswered questions and uncertainty for the future. How are my parents? How will Riley take it? Will Brooks be part of our lives in some way?

There's no answers for me to find today. These questions, and the ones I haven't even thought of, will be waiting for me back in New York.

Now, we're on the dance floor at the wedding reception. Emilie is wearing that fucking dress from our shopping date, dusty purple and flowy. Mitch and Eliza, all newly married and adorable, haven't left each other's side since the "you may kiss the bride."

Emilie's parents behaved today, and by that, I mean they didn't really say much. But they didn't say anything inappropriate or make anyone feel bad, so I think that's a win.

The ceremony was beautiful, the weather was on point, and the vibes were immaculate. I've not thought a lot about marriage or where I'd want to get married, but right now, it's hard to beat the beach.

Time with Emilie is hard to beat.

Her arms are wrapped around my neck, her head on my chest, and I pull her close to me as we dance to a slow song. My fingers dance along her lower back and the top of her ass, like we're the only people in the room.

Fuck, I wish that were true.

"What are you thinking about?" Emilie asks, lifting her head off my chest.

I laugh and look at the ceiling, at the fabric and twinkly lights above us, before putting my eyes on hers. "I was thinking about how this dress looks fucking perfect but I can't wait until we're alone and I tear it off you."

"What if I say you can only use your teeth."

I find her earlobe, nipping it before whispering, "Game on."

And then she grabs the back of my neck and puts a crushing kiss to my mouth.

WE SPEED WALK BACK to the room—no complaints here. When I swing the door open, letting Emilie inside first, she turns and stops a few steps ahead. The door shuts behind me as she lifts her arms up slowly with a mischievous grin.

"You can use your hands now if you promise to use your teeth later." Her voice is devilish and greedy.

My dick comes to life at the sound of her voice telling me what to do.

"Careful what you ask for," I growl while my hands find the dress zipper along her side. My hands reach over the fabric, touching her bare skin. With a single motion, I rip the zipper and then use another to pull the fabric apart.

Emilie moans in response, and her arms stay where they are. I grab the skirt of the dress, bunching the fabric, before lifting it up and over her arms.

I'm frozen. Taking her in, from head to toe. Her tits are bare, her nipples perfectly pink, and her skin a beautiful contrast to the gray lacy thong.

"What's wrong?" she asks timidly, looking down at herself and then back to me.

The question catches me off guard. "Nothing is wrong. What are you talking about? I'm just trying to let my brain catch up." I take in all the smooth skin on display in front of me. The curves of her hips and ass are making me fucking salivate.

There's too much space between us so I step in closer and she throws her arm around my neck, our lips crashing. I lift her up and she wraps her legs around my waist, like she can read my mind. When she feels my erection against her, she groans into my mouth.

That groan.

The most perfect fucking sound.

My hands grip her ass, the skin soft and tantalizing, and my tongue sweeps across the seam of her lips—it's like she's the breath I've been dying to take.

I walk her to the bedroom, her fingers tangled in my hair. I bite her lip and she pulls my hair in response.

"You told me to use my teeth," I tease into our kiss.

I'm at the side of the king size bed when I toss her onto the mattress. Her hands immediately feel up her body, stopping at her perfect tits. When she rolls her nipples in her own fingers, I'm about to come unglued.

I hover my body over hers, my knees pressing into the bed on each side of her thighs. I replace her hands with mine, before my mouth gets to work. Emilie cries out when I flick her nipple with my tongue while squeezing the other with my fingers.

Her back arches off the bed, and her hips try to meet mine when I go from sucking to light biting, changing the pace and the pressure.

Fuck, this is a dream.

Emilie pushes me back and bunches my shirt in her hands.

"Too many clothes," she whines and then helps with the buttons. I toss my shirt to the floor, and Emilie uses her fingernails to rake down the front of me, her fingers touching my core.

She sits up as I lean back, and she has her hands on my belt. It's a joint effort when we get my pants unzipped and she puts her hands on the inside of my briefs' waistband. She teases me, making sure to lick her lips the second my eyes catch hers. My pants are down and it's just my dick straining against my briefs.

"Off," she pleads with her voice husky and full of breath.

"Only if you touch yourself," I barter.

And what does my girl do? She lays back and slowly puts her fingers over the charcoal lace of her panties. Emilie bites her lip and closes her eyes while she rubs over the fabric.

"Tell me how wet you are for me, baby," I urge, putting my hands on my hips, because I'm about to start stroking my cock or touching her, and I don't want to rush this. We've waited long enough.

Emilie pulls her knees up, bending them and giving me more of a view. Her finger dips into herself, under the fabric, and my mouth is watering. Electricity sparks and sizzles on my skin, trying to be patient.

She moans as she inserts another finger.

"Come feel for yourself," she baits me without opening her eyes or moving her fingers.

I take my mouth and blow close to her center before biting the top of her panties and pulling them down to her knees, my mouth so close to her clit. She's still touching herself and seeing her fingers buried inside make me lose it.

I hold myself up but use my tongue with her fingers. She tastes sweet and I'll never get enough of this.

"Fucking soaked for me." My voice is low and rocky.

Emilie tries to hum a response but her back bucks off the bed when I use my tongue on her clit.

One of my hands runs up her thigh, and I use the other to remove her hand and slowly insert a single finger. Pulling it out, painfully slow for the both of us, I change the position of my mouth and pick up the pace of my tongue.

"More," she begs.

I insert two fingers this time but still refuse to match the pace of my tongue.

Emilie cries out, "Zack! I'm close," and hearing her say my name like that has ruined me for everyone else.

Chapter 45
Emilie

My body is like a firecracker, the fuse about to detonate. Every touch of Zack's hands, mouth, tongue, lips has this ache in my low belly screaming. It grows with each second, with every swipe of his tongue, every kiss to the inside of my thigh.

He pulls back from my pussy, and I sit up, like there's a thread connecting us. Like I need him back.

Zack takes a foil packet from the side table, slides his briefs down, his dick springing out. Seeing him hard for me has my orgasm just within reach. He opens the condom and covers himself.

I lie back, running my hands up my body and into my hair—my body responding to my own touch.

"This is okay?" Zack says while holding himself up, his dick so close to my entrance.

"Yes!" I try not to yell but I'm about to unravel.

He nudges my entrance before swiping my pussy with the tip of his cock. My back arches, and I throw my head back to the bed.

He drops a kiss to my mouth, all feverish and demanding, and then slowly pushes inside me. I appreciate the caution as I breathe through taking him, all of him.

Zack moves inside me, but I know he's holding back, his arms holding his weight up. My hands reach up and grab for his ass, digging my nails in, and he turns his head, going a touch faster.

Feeling him respond this way to my touch is fucking hot. Like, I could combust without him even touching me.

"I need you," I beg, pulling his neck down to me and kissing him. I lightly pull his hair, and his deep blue eyes find mine—deep blue, like the ocean waves crashing outside our room.

His mouth finds my neck, and he bites, possibly leaving a mark but I don't care. I want him to devour me.

"You're so tight, baby," he says, still going too slowly, the orgasm within my reach but not close enough.

I scratch my hands down his chest and respond, "I want all of it. You don't have to be careful with me." I take my nipples in my own fingers, pinching and pushing closer and closer to the edge.

He lets me have all of him and I gasp but grab his hips and move with him. He's pushing me to my limit, and I still can't get enough of him—I don't think I ever will. Zack reaches one hand into my curls and tugs, like I did to him, and I fucking love it.

"Just like that. Pull on it, baby."

He pushes into me, letting some of his weight land on me, and he's going harder, faster. I bite my lip and am steps away from my climax with each pump inside me.

"EJ, fuck. I'm going to come. Your pussy is so tight," he moans through broken words and seeing him be this close to his own orgasm is all it takes.

His words are a spark to kindling, and my whole body is burning from the inside out. I reach for him, and he pounds into me, each one pulling a cry from me. I cover my mouth to muffle my sounds, and Zack's hand removes it, pinning it above me.

I tremble and shake for him, coming all over his cock. He falls into me with his own finish, and I feel him sensitive and satisfied inside me.

My breathing is ragged and loud, looking for the air to come back to my lungs. Zack holds himself up and kisses me. It's soft and genuine—full and telling. His lips are telling me secrets.

Honestly, this kiss is like the ending of a sentence, but the start of the story.

Chapter 46
Zack

"Are you nervous?" Emilie asks, putting her hand on my forearm, rubbing her fingers back and forth.

I look from the door of my childhood home and back to her before telling the truth. "I'm overwhelmed and nothing's even happened yet." I wipe my clammy hands on the front of my jeans.

"A lot has happened. Give yourself some credit."

I guess she's right. My body feels like it's tied in a million little knots. I even went to hot yoga this morning, trying to lose some of this tension. My body feels like it's been flexing, holding tight to something, for days.

We got back from Mexico a few days ago. Emilie offered to skip dinner and let me come alone. There's no way. I feel like I need her. She squeezes my hand and it soothes the heart that's currently rattling around my chest.

I walk in and the air feels crackly and thick. I can't imagine the words that have been said in the last few weeks—if these walls could talk. We round the corner and see my parents sitting at the kitchen island, drinking coffee and chatting.

When Mom and Dad see us, they stand. My dad's face is pale and he rubs his hands together, clearly nervous, while my mom runs up and wraps me in a hug. I can feel her smiling as she squeezes me, swaying us back and forth. She rubs circles on my back, and it sort of feels like I'm just a kid who needs his mom.

She pulls back and asks, "Are you okay?"

I'm caught off guard by her immediate need to comfort me when I feel like it should be the other way around.

"Yes. But are you?" My mom glances at my dad with nothing but love and adoration. I swear to god her eyes are practically sparkling.

"Of course I am. I'll answer whatever questions you have for me, but let's let you and your dad talk, ok?"

I look over at my dad, the strongest man I know, and I swear his lip is trembling.

"Emilie and I are going to finish dessert and have a drink. Take your time." She rubs the side of my arm and looks to her husband, not a line of concern on her face.

My dad and I walk outside to the patio, the late October air crisp and the promise of winter hangs in the clouds. We sit down and the chairs are warm from the outdoor fireplace.

"I didn't mean for this to happen. I just, it was so long ago. Your mom and I weren't together, and if I would've known, I would've done something. You know that—"

"Dad. Breathe. I know." I reach over and put my hand on his knee squeezing. He dips his head in his hands and taps a foot with anxious energy.

"I just feel like part of me has been ripped out. He didn't have a dad. I left him without a dad." His eyes are full of tears, and I swallow past the lump in my throat.

"You didn't know. You didn't do it on purpose. There's nothing we can do about that now. We can only go forward."

My dad picks his head up, and the way he looks at me hits my core—like it's running through my ribs and chest. I don't say anything but instead think about life—the big picture. It can seem like you're doing everything right and then something like this comes along, jerking you back to what ifs. The thing about the past is that it can swallow you whole, if you let it.

I'm proud to be part of this family. I know if my dad would've found out about Brooks earlier, he would've done anything he could to make it right. I know I'm lucky and not everyone has these kinds of people to call home.

This isn't about being perfect or keeping score. Family is all about how you handle the difficult times, how you show up for people when they need you.

I take a big breath, trying to compose myself. "The thing I'm pissed about is how you kept this to yourself. You didn't need to carry this alone."

"I love you, Zack. I want to do what's right for Brooks, and for us, and I'm an open book from here on out."

We stand together and he wraps me in a hug I know he's needed. I squeeze him as tight as I can and say, "Dad, I love you. I'm proud to be your son."

My dad and I talk on the patio for a long time. The sun sets and the moon takes its place as we warm our hands with the outdoor fire. I can see Emilie and my mom sitting at the island, talking and hanging out, and a warmth spreads from the inside.

"Listen, everyone is much more patient than me, but I'm starving. Can we have dinner?" Riley calls, standing in the kitchen with the patio door open, shaking as the cold air comes inside.

My dad jumps up, walking toward the house. "Honey, when did you get here?"

"Thirty minutes ago, I didn't want to interrupt."

We just talked about Riley and how she took the Brooks news. She was so happy my dad wasn't ill or part of an illegal gambling ring that she actually cried tears of relief. She's planning to meet Brooks, one-on-one, when he's back in New Jersey. The NBA season just started, and he's got a string of away games.

We walk inside, the warm air welcomed. I didn't realize how cold I was outside until now. I sit in the barstool next to Emilie and give her a kiss.

"Your lips are freezing!" she shrieks, putting her warm hands on my cheeks, which must feel like icicles to her.

Next she runs her hands through my hair, something that I've come to love and crave, and asks, "How are things up there?" She taps my temple.

I look around the kitchen, to my sister and parents getting everything out for dinner, just like they always do. To be honest, I was afraid this would break us, crack our dynamic in some way, but I don't think that's the case.

"Thankful. Good. Relieved," I answer.

"And what about here?" She puts her hand on my chest, right above my heart.

I put a finger under her chin, tilt her mouth up, and press a kiss to her lips.

"The best it's ever been."

Chapter 47
Emilie

"I THOUGHT WE WERE going to dinner?" I ask as Zack parks outside my favorite bakery. He says nothing but gives me one of those devilish smirks, one that makes me want to take us back home and throw him into the bedroom. I stretch my neck, pushing the attraction down as Zack opens the door for me and offers a hand.

I stand and take in New York City in peak fall. Soon, the leaves will be clinging to the trees for as long as they can, and then the snow will come. I take a deep breath and it's almost like the air is telling me I'm right—it's also saying it's time to find my winter coat.

Zack walks me to the door, and I look in to see lights on and some of my favorite bakers moving around the space. They close at 3 PM so there's no reason anyone should be here four hours later than that.

"What's going on?" I ask, looking up into the eyes of the man who has stolen my heart. The man who worships my body and makes me feel like I'm worthy of his affection and time.

"It's our real first date." His face lights up as he gestures to the building. "I'm taking you on the one I told myself I would if I ever got the chance."

The memory hits me. Zack telling my parents, Eliza, and Mitch about our first date at the family dinner I brought him to. The one we never went on but I still think about. The one that took my breath away.

"We're making croissants?" I squeal, looking inside to someone waving at me.

"Yes, my girl. Croissants and coffee. They'll make us something for dinner since we can't eat these croissants tonight."

My heart melts with each thoughtful word. I go on my tiptoes to kiss him, and I can't pull myself close enough.

"You're so sweet to me. Thank you," I say in between kisses.

"I know it might be unconventional to do something like this on a first date, but I don't care." He looks around before finding my eyes, and my stomach drops.

"Emilie James, I love you. All of you. All the time." He holds my hands with his. "I've been trying to find the right time to say it, but all I know is I can't go another second without telling you."

I feel a smile reaching my eyes, my cheeks pinch.

"My dream first date with the love of my life," he says before placing a sweet kiss on my mouth.

"I love you. To the moon. To the stars. To wherever life takes us. I'm yours, Zack."

He presses his forehead to mine, and we soak in each other's confession before my teeth start to chatter.

Zack opens the door and the warmth of the bakery wraps around me, comforting and soothing. But even that isn't a match for the way Zack's love makes me feel.

Epilogue
Emilie

ONE YEAR LATER

"It's a trick play!" someone screams in the suite and everyone has their noses practically touching the glass as they jump up and down in excitement.

Zack doesn't throw a touchdown, but he does snap the ball to the punter who picks up a few yards with his legs before throwing it to a Cosmos player. First down! The drive stays alive, and Willow hugs me as we watch Tripp run back out to the field.

When Zack and Tripp pass each other, running on and off the field, they take the time to do their ridiculous handshake, which ends with them acting like they're taking a selfie. I'm sure Tripp is rolling his eyes behind his helmet, but this has Zack written all over it.

"This is wild!" Brooks cheers, standing next to me, eyes wide and cheeks warm with a smile. He claps loudly and goes along with a Cosmos chant Riley starts in the suite.

"I can't believe I'm at a Cosmos game, in a suite, and fucking Brooks Pittman is here," Mitch says, eyes wide as he looks up to the 6'5 NBA player. Eliza pats his chest and shakes her head as she takes a swig of her white wine.

The Cosmos are on their revenge tour, or that's what Zack calls it. Last season, the team fell short in the division round and didn't make it to the Super Bowl. Right now, they have the best record in the league with only one loss, which is saying something for October football.

There's a ton to cheer for but mostly my heart swells at the full suite. We have the full Andersen family: Brooks, Riley, and even Zack's parents. Seeing them together makes my heart squeeze in the best way. While things may have been uncertain and rocky in the beginning, it's been a dream watching Zack get to know his half-brother. It's amazing they're within driving distance of one another—it's wild how life works out sometimes.

The Andersen family is the kind of accepting you'd hope for in your own. Unfortunately, my parents don't have that same view. And you know what? That's okay. Eliza and I see each other once a week and are working on building a relationship that isn't tarnished or influenced by my parents. We still do family dinner every other month or so, but it's not the same. Conversation is surface level when my parents participate, but mostly, they watch the four of us interact.

For now, I still don't understand what it is about me that makes my parents want to pick everything I do apart, but I do know it has nothing to do with me. That's something they need to work on. Maybe they will? Maybe they won't.

Eliza slides in next to me as Mitch starts talking basketball with Brooks. She doesn't say anything but offers me a smile before reaching for my hand and squeezing it.

"Thanks for coming, El," I say, squeezing back.

"Anytime, EJ."

One play later, the Cosmos score a touchdown and they're up by twenty-eight points. The second quarter is running out while the opposing team tries to get into field goal range. I drink my Aperol Spritz as the Cosmos defense goes to work for the last two minutes.

The half runs out without the other team scoring—a solid defensive stand. I go to the snack section and load up a bowl with truffle fries.

Willow brings me a fresh drink just as I finish the spritz in my hand. She doesn't say anything but smiles like she knows a secret. I tilt my head to look at her, but she doesn't do anything besides smile at me, before falling back into conversation with Keegan and Eliza.

A few minutes later, I'm eating the last of my fries when someone comes into the suite and everyone is looking toward the doorway.

Curious, I look over and I do a double take.

Zack. In his uniform, head to toe, minus the helmet.

I stand so fast I almost spill the drink next to me. "Are you okay? Are you hurt?" I try to find the reason he'd be up here and not in the locker room with his teammates.

He smiles at me in a way that makes my body freeze. I swear my heart stops in my chest and I have to feel to make sure it's still beating.

"I'm not hurt but I'm not okay either."

"Okay, what's wrong?" I ask, searching his face for a clue.

"Well, it's just that..." He rubs his jaw with a pause. "You're not my wife."

I keep listening for the rest. I don't even think I heard him right. Someone in the suite lets out a low whistle.

"What did you say to me?"

Zack gets down on one knee and shows me a ring. "I said, what's wrong is that you're not my wife." He hits each letter of each word so there's no way I'm missing the message.

Everyone around me oohs and ahhs or gasps in surprise. I look around the room waiting for someone to tell me this is a joke. Or a dream.

"EJ, I've learned a lot about family in the last year and it's never been clearer to me. You're my family. You're who I want to plan forever with, and I can't wait any longer."

I kneel down and put my hands in my lap in front of him.

"Tell me you'll marry me."

I shake my head, his blue eyes locking on mine. Zack is the most thoughtful and caring person I've had the privilege of knowing. He loves big, and I fucking love being on the receiving end of it.

He waits for my answer as I soak in one of the easiest questions I've ever been asked.

"Of course I'll marry you." The room erupts with clapping, pops of champagne, and cheering. Zack places the ring on my finger, a gorgeous emerald cut diamond on a platinum band.

I reach forward and kiss him. He stands, pulling us both up, and spins me around the suite, our lips never leaving one another.

He sets me down and kisses me on the cheek, pointing to the jumbotron.

There we are.

And then it hits me, it's not just the suite cheering but it's the entire stadium. It's faces of strangers wearing massive smiles, all for Zack and me.

He puts an arm around my lower back, dips me, and puts a kiss on my mouth that I couldn't forget if I wanted to. He kisses me like I'm going to be his forever. I can practically feel the ground shaking with people clapping and yelling, kind of like it feels when there's a Cosmos touchdown.

"EJ, I can't wait to be your husband," he says, a grin pulling from ear-to-ear.

The fake version of me and Zack feels like it was lifetimes away. I don't know if either of us can pinpoint when it was real? Maybe it always was.

I can't help but think about rules and what we do to try to keep ourselves on track, or keep our hearts protected. But, sometimes, the rules are meant to be broken.

THE END

Character art by Mary Gannon, @mkgannon.art

Acknowledgments

Another book and another chance to spill my guts on the page? You've got it.

Being an indie author is one of the most difficult and rewarding things I've ever done. I'm so thankful to be able to finish another book and craft love stories where different versions of myself, and so many others, are represented. I've found such power in sharing my own lived in experiences on the page. To all the readers who see themselves in the page, and reach out to tell me, you're the real MVP's and make me want to keep going.

First, I'd like to acknowledge the power of sports—something I've played and watched my entire life. I love the way it brings people together and the emotions it charges. Everyone is good enough to cheer on any team they'd like, without knowing every single rule or any all the innocuous facts NO MATTER WHAT SOME LOSERS MAY SAY. To the people who make others feel inferior, or like they have to defend themselves to be a fan of anything, you're the worst and I acknowledge that, formally, at the end of a sports romance book written by a woman.

I had the best alpha and beta readers for Emilie and Zack. All my love to Adah, Lillian, Amber, Tricia, Rose, Angela, Madison, Brinna, Kendra, and Stephanie.

Rachel and Grace, for making the time to read my work and help make it the best it can be. I HIT THE LITERAL JACKPOT.

Author friends like Carly, Ambar, Cleo, Rachel, Grace, Courtney for letting me whine about how bad the book is, just to squeal about how much I love it, and help get me through this wild process. I'm so thankful for the space you give me.

Keona, thanks for always helping me with content and PA things! You help keep my brain somewhat on track.

Stephanie, one of the best hype girls on the planet, I don't know what I did to deserve you. You make me feel like I can do this no matter how much of a bitch imposter syndrome tries to be.

To all my friends and colleagues who continue to ask me 'what's next?' while cheering me on... THANK YOU.

To my dad, for embracing a daughter who wanted to know everything about all the sports, from as early as I can remember, thank you. The way you encouraged me to be a fan is something I'll cherish forever. LOVE YOU.

Roberto, my sweet husband, who once surprised me with tickets to a football game for a team he despised and loved the idea of playing a college football game at our wedding reception, I love you.

Lastly, to the readers who pick up any of my books, you'll never know what it means to me. Thank you for all the messages, tags, comments, and excitement for my work—you're the best.

RACHEL LABERGE is the author of YOUR RULE TO BREAK, book two in The Play Caller series. When she's not reading or writing, she's probably thinking about donuts, sour candy, or looking for her next hyperfixation. She lives in Michigan with her husband (Roberto), her two Frenchies (Rafa and Ruby), and cat (Riley). You can connect with her on Instagram, TikTok, and Threads **@rachellabergeauthor** (no 'R' name required).

Want to be first in line for updates and bonus content? Sign up for Rachel's newsletter at rachellaberge.com.